TWO-FACE

TWO-FACE

ERNEST DUDLEY

WILDSIDE PRESS

For Mother with love.

Published by Wildside Press LLC.
www.wildsidebooks.com

1

Huddled in her seat in the Zurich-Paris plane, she remembered only all the most awful air disasters she had ever read about.

Desperately she tried to fight down her panicky thoughts. Told herself again and again: "for every aeroplane that crashes, thousands don't." But she wasn't comforted or reassured. The actual physical sensations she was experiencing were no more alarming than if she were floating in a boat down some placid stream. The other passengers, too, were either calmly indifferent or plainly thrilled at being hurtled through space.

But try as hard as she might, it was no good. She was incapable of shaking off her blind, unreasonable terror.

When she first received Henri Tallier's letter, telling her he had made all arrangements for her to fly to Paris immediately, the prospect had merely filled her with vague apprehension.

But as the time for her departure approached, that vague apprehension became intensified into something horrid at the pit of her stomach. Then, as the great air-liner bore her up, and she glimpsed the swiftly and sickeningly receding earth, fear engulfed her in overwhelming waves.

Once, when the machine slipped suddenly in an air-pocket, she gave a scream. The man sitting in front of her turned round. His smile of amusement faded, however, when he saw the terror in her eyes.

"Don't worry! You're as safe as houses!"

He spoke in French, but his accent was obviously English. She tried to force a wan smile to her stiff lips. But it was a pitiful failure.

The man explained to her in careful French what it was caused the plane to slip.

"It's nothing really," he said. "No more than a bump on a road—and you know how that feels when you're travelling fast in a car! Like a young mountain!"

As she tried to gain courage from his casual tone, she wanted to tell him he needn't speak French. That she herself was half-English, spoke his own language quite well. But the words remained a whisper somewhere at the back of her dry throat. When he returned to his newspaper terror paralysed her once more.

For the remainder of the journey she sat as one awaiting inevitable doom, fingernails cutting into her moist palms, praying for the nightmare to end.

And after an eternity the mighty steel bird was zooming away on its final stage of the journey. At last it was circling over Le Bourget, airport for Paris.

She stumbled out of the cabin on to the wooden steps and cautiously descended to the tarmac. Her head ached abominably, her ears buzzed with the throb-throb of the engines, and she felt sick.

But so enormous was her relief at feeling solid ground beneath her feet that these discomforts were forgotten. She had arrived. She was safe—safe! As the Englishman had said: "Safe as houses!"

She tried to grasp that fact as she stood staring dazedly about her, tightly clutching a shabby handbag with both hands.

She could not believe that the frightful adventure was over. That Paris was but half an hour's car drive away.

She really *had* flown all the way from Zurich, had come through the ordeal without either crashing to destruction or dying of fright. With this realization there came a hot, prickly sensation at the back of her eyes. She groped for a handkerchief in the depths of her bag.

"I mustn't, I mustn't! I *won't* cry!" she told herself and choked back the tears. She longed to cry. Not only now the strain of the journey was over—but because she knew it really wouldn't have mattered much if she *had* died.

All the time the thought of death had terrified her, a part of her would have welcomed it as a blessed release. Release from the grief which she felt would never leave her as long as she lived.

Behind her was Zurich and her dreams.

Zurich, where she had lived since childhood. Had known years of serene, rich happiness. Until… And now in a tiny churchyard atop a little hill, where the Springtime song of the birds was a gentle hymn, lay her mother, the earth fresh on her grave.

That morning she had breathed the air of her beloved city for the last time. Henceforth it would be only a city of memories. Such memories which only the one, recent and cruelly bitter, could ever mar.

Now Paris faced her, strange and frightening, and she was alone. With a future that held little for her to dream about. Conjecture about it, yes, and that but half-heartedly. Her dreams though, they would search backwards, she felt. Always.

Here the job old Henri Tallier had offered her was waiting. Work that was to help her continue the job of living. Though she knew of no reason why she should go on doing so.

That was all Paris could give her.

"Remember Henri, cherie…" Those had been her mother's last words. "He will see that all is well with you, for my memory's sake." And had smiled a tender little smile as she whispered half to herself, "Dear fat Henri, so kind and loving—and so dull he was…"

Because there was no one else, she had turned for help to the man who had loved her mother long ago. His reply had been characteristically kind and understanding. He had not offered her charity. Come and work in my shop, he had said—his shop, the great multiple store in the centre of Paris.

As she stood there indecisively amid the bustle of disembarking passengers, the babel of half a dozen foreign tongues, hearing but not understanding the crisp utterances of the stewards and airport officials, and the raucous voices of two cheeky newsboys, a steward touched her arm.

"You are going by bus, Mademoiselle?"

She saw that he had placed her luggage beside her.

"Bus?"

"Company's bus takes all passengers on to the Place Lafayette, Paris," he explained. "But—er—perhaps you are being met by car?" smiling as he glanced at her clothes as if to say: "Though I'd think that most unlikely."

His expression changed when she said:

"Yes, I am expecting a car to meet me." And he picked up her two dilapidated suitcases with a flourish.

"If you will please follow me, Mademoiselle, we will find your car."

With a murmured word of thanks, she collected her thoughts, gave a furtive dab at her eyes with her handkerchief, made an effort to brace her slim shoulders, and followed.

Her head still continued to whirl, however. The feeling of being completely and hopelessly lost enveloped her like a great cloak. She kept up with the steward blindly, without knowing which way she was going.

She had half hoped and expected that Tallier himself would be there to meet her. But then she knew that would be impossible, he would be too busy. He had not mentioned that in his letter, either. Had simply said that she would be met by a car, that she would be guided through the Customs. Everything would be perfectly easy and she had nothing to worry about.

Arrived at the barrier, she was searching her bag for her passport, when a Frenchman behind her said to someone:

"Have you read this about Henri Tallier?"

At the mention of the name she turned sharply.

"Monsieur Tallier…?" she queried involuntarily.

The man pushed his head round the newspaper he was reading. He stared at her. Overcome with confusion, she stammered:

"I am so sorry! I wasn't thinking—the name was in my thoughts—I—I—"

"Do *you* know him?" he asked, and there was a curious note in his voice. She saw his companion was also staring at her. Other people, too, had stopped and were giving her wondering glances.

She blushed hotly. Dropped her handbag, started to pick it up, then decided to answer the question which had been shot at her.

"Well—yes, you see—I—I—"

His next words stopped her.

"Do you know what's happened?"

"Happened?"

The man thrust the newspaper before her, pointing at the page with a thick finger.

"Read," he said quietly.

The letters leapt up at her in a great black headline:

HENRI TALLIER FOUND DEAD
REVOLVER BY HIS SIDE
SUICIDE?

Then the words started to go away from her horribly quickly. They suddenly formed into a circle and spun round faster, faster. She heard a voice as if from far away cry out something.

Someone caught her as the whole world turned turtle and went black.

2

She opened her eyes to meet someone else's looking down at her. They're a funny slate-grey, she thought drowsily, closing hers again.

"That's it, take it easy," a voice said.

There was something vaguely familiar about it. She felt too tired to remember, though, and lay quiet and still.

"Drink this."

Gratefully, she sipped a glass of water held to her lips. It was very cold. It cleared the mists away from her brain. But the hammer beating at the back of her head still went on mercilessly.

She gave a little moan. Tried to lift her head. An arm slipped very gently under her, helped her sit upright.

"How's that, now?"

She remembered now. The carefully pronounced French, with an obviously English accent. She opened her eyes, smiled wanly at the Englishman who had spoken to her in the airliner. He grinned at her, while she answered in English, slowly and distinctly:

"Thank you, that is much better."

"Oho, speak English, eh?"

"My father was an Englishman—I like to speak his language!"

He noticed her voice had a curious huskiness in it.

"I see. And was your father's French as bad as mine?"

"I am sorry, I did not mean to make you think that. But I knew you were English all right."

"Well, we won't bother about that now. And we'll speak your father's language. Still feeling a bit shaky?"

"It is only my head. It bangs a little."

"Keep quiet, and the bang will soon go."

He handed her the glass again and she drank. "That'll help the headache on its way."

She looked about her.

They were in a small waiting-room, and she had been placed on a long padded seat, with a rolled-up overcoat supporting her head. There was nobody else in the room. It was very peaceful after the noise before... Before...

Suddenly she remembered.

He took the glass from her. Comforted her with quiet strength. Calmed the turmoil of her brain, jangled thoughts from out of which the black headlines that had shrieked at her stood and danced their tragic dance.

She bowed her head in her hands and cried silently. Her anguish seemed to tear at the very roots of her heart. It shocked him with its intensity. Surprised him, too. He had not expected such grief from this slim, childishly young-looking girl. There was a hauntingly queer maturity about her grief which touched him deeply.

"This won't do, you know. Listen. Listen to me."

He sat and faced her. Watched the tears trickle through her fingers, and spoke to her very gently.

In a moment or two she ceased to weep and looked up at him. He pushed a lock of her mouse-coloured hair from off her face while she sat, her hands clasped tightly together, like a little child.

"You've got to pull yourself together," he said. "I don't know what poor Tallier meant to you—but you can't alter things by tears. You must be brave. He'd want you to be that—wouldn't he?"

She shook her head slowly.

"I don't know. I don't know. You see..." And she began to tell her story.

Right from the beginning. Hunched up there in that room whose silence only the faint hum of the arriving and departing airliners penetrated. Interrupted only by the appearance of a doctor, who saw she was recovered, and hurried off, she talked. Skilfully her listener prompted her.

Her name was Mitsi Linden, she said.

She told him how her father married her French mother after a whirlwind wooing. How he had deserted his wife soon after she was born. How this broken marriage had ultimately resulted in a wonderful bond of friendship and love between her and her mother. How, though they had to pinch and scrape to live, they were deeply content. They made no friends, for they were both shy and frightened of the world. But living for each other they had been terribly happy. They had drifted round France, then Italy, living in cheap pensions on the little money her mother had, then finally Switzerland and Zurich, a shabby, peaceful little villa outside the town.

Soon after her twentieth birthday that happiness ended with tragic suddenness. A short illness, and then...her mother's dying wish she should get into touch with Tallier. He had been a loving, devoted admirer of hers, long ago, when her mother was a student in Paris.

That was all, the rest he knew.

"So there's no one who can help you, now?"

"Nobody in the world…"

"Hmmm. It's bad."

He smiled at her, and stood up.

She watched him push his hands deep into his pockets and walk the length of the room and back. A wave of gratitude swept over her. She wanted to tell him how grateful she was to him for his kindness to her.

Somehow, she found it difficult to find words which would not sound trite and unreal. He is not an easy person to thank, she decided. He gave the impression he had done what he had as a matter of course. There was no fuss, no unnecessary words, or actions. Just a quiet method of dealing with everything.

No situation, she felt, would ever find him at a loss. There was a breadth about his entire personality, as well as the width of his shoulders. A roughness and a hardness which his present quietness seemed to emphasize.

Instinctively she was appraising him, his strength and his gentleness. He is rarely gentle, she told herself. Nor does he go out of his way to be charming, or nice. The set of his large, well-shaped head on his strong neck suggested a keen brain, but that of a man who disdained any subtleties.

She realized even the culminating tragedy of the last hour had not completely blotted out her inquisitive-ness. She plucked up courage and voice to ask his name.

"Sorry!" he apologized at once. "Here I've been cross-examining you from every angle, and you don't know the first thing about me! I'm Larry Curtis—I write for the *Courier*—a London newspaper—"

Her eyes darkened.

"I hate newspapers," she shuddered, remembering those dreadful headlines again.

"I know—well, forget all about 'em, or that I'm anything to do with them."

He stood looking down at her.

"You've got to be sensible. Got to try and forget all that's happened—not look back at all. I know that'll be enormously difficult. But I want you to try hard. See?"

She nodded dumbly.

He sat down and faced her.

"Now, I feel a bit responsible for you, and I want to help you. Maybe I can, too."

Her eyes were fixed on his face. In them such an expression of hope attempting to combat her tragic circumstances and her dark, utterly hopeless future. It moved him. Her helplessness seemed to reach out to him. Though she herself made no attempt to grab his sympathy.

Because she was so forlorn, because her dark eyes, big in her pale, tear-stained face, were so stricken. Because absolutely nothing about her was anything but a living picture of shabby human pathos, he knew he had to help her.

"I have two friends who live in Paris," he said. "They're brother and sister. Kindest, most understanding people in the world. Come along with me, and let them decide what's the best thing to be done about you. Does that sound rather as if you're a little stray dog?"

He smiled at her.

She shook her head seriously.

"That is what I feel like. Lost. But I cannot come with you. It would be impossible. You are a busy man, you cannot be worried by my troubles. Your friends, too. How can I ask them to bother about an utter stranger?"

"You aren't worrying me, you won't bother them. So put that right out of your head. Julia and Leo—my friends—will take care of you until you feel more able to take care of yourself. Glad to do it, and they'll think up something for you to do, find a job for you, so you won't be destitute in a Parisian gutter—which, so I'm told, is a most unpleasant place!"

She started to say something, but he stopped her.

"Why, you can't do anything else, but follow my suggestion! Don't you see? There was nobody here to meet you—I enquired about that…"

"You mean…?"

"Poor Tallier had too much on his mind the last day or two. He'd forgotten all about you. His own world crashed. He was ruined. If anybody else knew about your coming to Paris, well, they forgot, too. All this business has been a bolt from the blue—not only for you, but for everybody else, Henri Tallier as well."

He rose. Her eyes remained riveted to his face. Her fingers were intertwined convulsively in her lap. He saw her lower lip begin to tremble.

"Mitsi Linden!"

Her name came sharply, and the hard note in his voice stopped the tears that were about to come. She gulped, and blew her nose.

"Another thing—you'll find it difficult to leave Le Bourget without answering a lot of questions. There are several people outside there who are very anxious to learn why you fainted just now. I had quite a job to keep them away from you. Understand?"

"I could not bear to talk to anybody. It would be horrible. Oh, M'sieu—Mr. Curtis, what shall I do…?"

"Cut the 'Mr. Curtis', anyway. I'm Larry to my friends, and we're friends. Secondly, put your hat on—unless your head's still aching, and we'll go and have tea with Julia and Leo. You'd like some tea, wouldn't you? And an aspirin?"

She smiled. There was that in her smile which affected him profoundly. So full of courage and new hope it was.

"Yes," she said, "I would like a little tea—*and* some aspirin."

She stood up shakily. He took her arm, and she looked straight into his eyes with a queer frankness.

"Oh, thank you! I can never repay you. Never, never..." she whispered tremulously.

He tried to laugh, but a sudden tightness in his throat prevented him.

"I'm glad you think so well of me!" he said lightly.

Ten minutes later found them in a car, and on the road to Paris.

A silence fell between them. She was busy with her thoughts. Thoughts which went round and round in her head, and which she found impossible to sort out. They started with the Frenchman's stare when he had pushed his newspaper aside to answer her question about Tallier. Then those words leaping out at her in huge black letters suddenly dwindling to nothingness and oblivion.

Then the hammering at the back of her head. Larry's face when she had first regained consciousness, his voice, the import of his words. And, last of all, wonderment about where she was going, the two friends of his whom she was about to meet.

Everything seemed possessed of a curious dream-like quality. As if everything that had happened to her in the last hour had not really happened at all. She was only dreaming it. Presently she would wake up, and find herself back in Zurich.

"Or perhaps I'm dead," she thought once. "Perhaps the aeroplane *did* crash, after all!..."

She gave a quick, panic-stricken glance at the man beside her. No! He was here, with her, protecting her, there was nothing to be afraid of. She was alive. She wasn't dreaming. All the things had happened, and she was in this car with this wonderfully kind Englishman—going to have tea with two friends of his. Tea and aspirins, which would take away the hammering in her head.

Larry said nothing, the smoke curled up from his cigarette as he sat back wondering, too.

Paris, and the future drew nearer.

3

"She is a quaint little thing!" said Julia Green, as she fitted a cigarette into a long ivory holder and put it between her red lips. She was gracefully tall, and dark and attractive.

It was after dinner.

Larry, Leo and Julia were lounging comfortably in deep arm-chairs in the delightfully furnished sitting-room of the Greens' flat. Julia had just come in from the visitor's bedroom where she had tucked Mitsi in bed and given her a sleeping-draught.

Larry was smoking a pipe, and his eyes were closed. Leo also smoked a pipe, a heavy curved affair which hung from his teeth against the short, pointed beard which he affected. He had a pad perched on his knee, and was sketching on it, stopping every few minutes to survey his handiwork with a critical eye.

Julia looked at the two men, neither of whom made any reply to her remark. Smiling affectionately in the direction of Larry, she picked up a magazine and idly turned the pages.

There was a little silence.

Suddenly Leo, without looking up from his pencil, said:

"I think she has an amazingly interesting face—the bone structure's grand."

"Oh, do you think so?" his sister asked.

"Don't you?"

"Yes… I think I see what you mean…in a way."

"Which means you don't see anything of the sort, my dear!"

Leo made a sucking noise in his pipe. He turned to Larry.

"D'you see, old man?"

"Oh, don't wake the poor darling up, he's having such a lovely nap!" Julia cried.

Larry opened his eyes and grinned.

"Liar! I was thinking," he said. "What did you say, Leo?"

"I said this Linden kid has an amazingly interesting face. I also said the bone structure was all right, too, but you wouldn't know anything about that!"

"Uhuh! painter-of-pretty-pictures!" the other jibed. "I know plenty about bone structure. But, no, I can't say the child's a ravishing beauty!"

"She's very sweet and very pathetic," put in Julia.

"I might have known," muttered her brother. "You're a pair of undiscerning fools!"

"Charming brother of mine!"

"Bah!" ejaculated Leo, and made irritable strokes on his drawing-pad.

Larry laughed good-humouredly. He knew Leo Green's moods, his irritation with people who failed to see eye to eye with him about painting. Not that he was a highbrow, but his ideas were extremely original, and rather difficult to grasp at first acquaintance. But he was a brilliantly clever artist, and a good-hearted chap all right.

"I hope she sleeps well," he said to Julia.

"Like a top, she will!"

"You've been a darling to her. I'm awfully grateful to you and Leo for rising to the occasion so superbly. Bless you both!"

"Silly!" she laughed.

There was a hidden tenderness, though, in her laughter, but it escaped him. And she felt the thin stab of pain in her heart, as she always did when she realized that to him she was no more than a good friend, a grand person to drop in and see now and then.

"Poor kid! She's had a hell of a time…"

"She's been lucky to have had you to play ministering angel. And that's a thing I've never known you do before, Larry. Feel friendly towards a young woman, like you've done about her. You used to say women made you sick!"

He made a little grimace at her.

"Well, you're the only woman I know whose company I can bear for five minutes. And that still holds good—because our visitor from Switzerland isn't a woman. She's just a kid, and a darned pathetic one at that. What else could I have done? Tough, hard-boiled newspaperman as you would have me seem, I'm not so flint-hearted I could leave a baby alone and helpless like she was."

"You're nice, Larry."

Something like a sigh of relief escaped her. For one heart-chilling moment the suspicion had entered her mind that the girl, unattractive and drably forlorn as she was, had in some way made an appeal to him. His words had reassured her, and she was thankful.

At that moment the telephone rang. She crossed to the jangling instrument in the corner of the room.

"Hullo?… Yes… All right, I'll hold on." She turned to Larry. "Call from London. For you?"

"That'll be the paper. I left word they could probably get me here if I wasn't back tonight."

He got up and stood by her. She spoke again into the mouthpiece.

"Hullo? Yes. Yes, this is Julia Green speaking. I can hear you perfectly well. Who is it?... Yes, he is here—will you hold on?..."

She handed the phone to him. "Bob Raymond himself would like a word with you," she smiled.

"Bob! Good heavens, what the deuce does he want?"

"He'll probably tell you, my pet, if you'll take hold of this little toy."

"Hullo, Bob. What's on your mind? Sure I'll help you, if I can. I'm listening. Bad luck, darned bad luck. Yes, I know. All very difficult. Well, yes, I do know her. I'll see what I can do. And I'll try and think of someone else if she can't make it. I'll phone you to-morrow as soon as I know anything. Yes... G'bye, Bob, don't worry! It'll all come right in the wash!"

He replaced the receiver.

"So sorry for all that," he said, coming back to his chair.

"All sounds most odd!" Julia murmured.

Leo looked up from his sketching.

"There's been a lot of talking going on," he growled. "What's it all about?"

"Bob Raymond's in the soup. You know he's opening his own night-club next week—going to be the brightest spot in London, and all that..."

"Horrible!" groaned Leo.

"Well, he'd got Rosy Gordon—"

"The new American singer?" put in Julia.

Larry nodded.

"Revolting!" moaned her brother, and returned to his work.

"She was to have appeared at Bob's club, but she's got pneumonia, or mumps, or run off with some millionaire, or something! Anyway, she won't be there!"

"Bad luck."

"Yes, it'll ruin his opening night. She was the big attraction."

"What'll he do?"

"That's what he's called me about. Wants me to talk to Mirielle, the Bright Girl of Paris. Try and get her to appear at his club."

"But she'd want the earth!"

"Rosy Gordon was to get that! Money's no object with Bob. Got plenty of cash behind him. He wants the biggest drawing-card possible, and he'll pay for it! But I'm pretty sure Mirielle won't be any use. She's under contract here, sure as anything. There's no one else I can think of."

"What a nuisance the tall, dark and handsome Bob Raymond is!"

"You've met him, haven't you?"

"*And* heard all about him, too! Champion breaker of women's hearts!"

"He's a gay young lad! I don't mind him, he's amusing."

"And so terribly attractive!"

"A poisonous reptile!" muttered Leo, without taking his eye from his pencil.

Julia and Larry laughed. Larry's grin turned into a yawn.

"Well, I'm hitting the hay! Sorry to be unsociable, and all that! But I'm tired."

"Yes, of course, dear. You go on along—you can worry about young Raymond's pretty lady in the morning…"

4

But Larry's first thought when he awoke at half-past eight next day was not for any pretty lady, or Bob Raymond's troubles.

He awoke thinking of Mitsi, and for a moment wondered if she had invaded his dreams. But he couldn't remember dreaming at all, about anybody, he'd slept so soundly.

"Brat's getting on my mind, or something," he said to himself, as he made his way to the bathroom. The idea annoyed him a little, he didn't like having things on his mind.

He turned on the taps, found his shaving things, and started to think about how he could help Bob Raymond out of his mess. He felt sure Mirielle wouldn't agree to leave Paris.

On his way back to his bedroom, he heard voices in Leo's studio. Leo's and Mitsi's voices. He opened the studio door and poked his head round it.

"'Morning, early birds!"

"Good morning, Mister Lazybones!" she laughed at him.

Leo said: "There's no breakfast for you, the child's bolted the lot! And serve you right, you should get up at a respectable hour!"

"How are you feeling?" he asked her.

"Most well, thank you."

"Is this hideous man with the beard amusing you?"

"Yes, very much." And she laughed again.

He left them, glad to know that she was feeling better and happier. She would be all right in a day or two. Then they would think of something she could do. Find her a decent job of work, and all that.

Larry's fears about Mirielle were realized at midday, when he called upon the revue star. London could not offer her more than Paris, she said. And in any case she was under contract to stay with her show till it closed. She was very charming, but quite definite.

He cudgelled his brains on his way back to the Greens' flat. It must be someone sensational, someone who would draw all London to Bob's club, like a great magnet attracting pins. Who was there? He could think of no star like that who would be obtainable at such impossibly short notice.

He was not in too good a humour when he arrived, he hated being beaten by anything. And it looked as if the Bob Raymond mess was going to beat him.

No one was in the sitting-room. But there was the murmur of Julia's, Leo's and Mitsi's voices coming from the studio.

As he went in, Julia was saying: "Leo, it's simply marvellous! Amazing!"

He opened his mouth to speak, but said nothing, just stood staring at the figure who stood facing him. Stared as if he could not believe what he saw.

The figure was Mitsi.

She stood on the model's daïs, and about her was draped some clinging material. It revealed every line of her figure, while it cunningly enhanced the soft and alluring curves of her slim, enchantingly graceful body.

Her head was thrown back and turned to one side so that her profile and the curve of her slender neck were clear cut against the light. He caught his breath at the pure beauty of it.

Julia's and her brother's backs were turned to him. Leo worked carefully at the huge canvas which stood beside the girl. His sister watched in an attitude of tense absorption the strong, decisive movements of his brush.

Mitsi's eyes were closed, and none of them heard him enter.

He found his voice, and went towards them. "May I see?"

Julia swept round to greet him, and Mitsi uttered a little cry, turning her head to him as she did so.

Leo muttered: "Of course, you would have to come in and upset her! Don't take any notice of him, Mitsi, my girl, and turn your head again!"

Larry stood beside Julia.

"Isn't it wonderful?" she breathed.

He nodded, astonished. Surprised as he was by the living picture of the girl who confronted him, the picture on the canvas completely took his breath away.

Leo had performed a miracle.

He had painted Mitsi as she was, posed on the daïs. But he had done more than that. More than emphasized the beauty and the seductive symmetry of her with skilfully applied colours, shadows and highlights.

He had transformed her face.

Simply by changing the colour of her hair from nondescript mouse colour to pale, shimmering gold, he had given her a new face. Brought out the contour of her cheeks to fascinating perfection by slanting her eyebrows slightly, by careful shading. Her mouth was warm and soft. Her eyes deep, mysterious pools.

Yet, despite his brilliant effect, Leo had remained absolutely faithful in essentials to his model. Had simply stripped off her dowdy, disfiguring clothes. Given her face a golden halo of hair, subtly added a new beauty to her features.

The resemblance remained, definite and unmistakable. It *was* Mitsi who gazed at Larry from the canvas.

Mitsi Linden re-created.

"It's—it's terrific!"

"You like it, eh Larry?" asked Leo. "Mmmhhhmmm!" he breathed slowly through his nostrils. "What about the bone-structure, now?"

"The bone-structure impresses me beyond words!"

"Little girl into glamorous lady!" murmured Julia. She spoke very softly and almost to herself—but Larry caught her remark. Repeated the last two words.

"Glamorous lady!"

And suddenly, inspiration burst upon him. Born of those two words, of the magnificent painting before him. He pushed his hands through his hair with a gesture of suppressed excitement. Stared at the picture, at its original, and back again.

"For Pete's sake, Julia, you've said a mouthful! Why not?... Why not?"

"Why not what?"

Ignoring her question, he said quickly to Leo:

"Forgive me, old man, but I must interrupt!" and turned to Mitsi.

"You sing, don't you? You do! You *must* do!"

She stared at him in bewilderment.

"Sing? I—I—"

"You DO! You've got to, I say!"

"A little, yes. Mother used to give me lessons. But—"

"What are you talking about?" demanded Julia.

But he didn't hear her.

"Splendid! Splendid!" Turning to Julia and gripping her shoulder: "Quickly, the piano!" Swinging her round to where a baby grand stood in a corner of the studio.

"Larry—!"

"Yes, yes, I know! I'm crazy, but never mind! An idea's hit me!"

She gazed at him at a loss for words, and he pushed her towards the grand.

"The *piano*, my *dear!*" He plumped her firmly down, lifted the lid, raised her hands to the keyboard. "Play!"

"Play what?"

"Anything! Anything! Just a moment!" To Mitsi: "What do you know?"

"Know—?"

"What can you sing?"

"N-n-now—?"

"This very minute! Come here!"

She looked from him to Leo, working oblivious to the excitement, at his easel.

"Oh, don't worry about him!" Larry cried impatiently. With a swift movement he crossed to the daïs, lifted her in his arms and carried her to the piano, and sat her on it.

"Now, I'm serious! Sing any song you know—in French, in English, Greek, Armenian, Portuguese—*anything!*"

His dynamic force communicated itself to the two women. Awakened an answering thrill in them.

Mitsi hesitated, looked at Julia and at him, eyes wide with wonder, a puzzled frown on her brow.

"B-but why must I sing?" she stammered.

"Sing!"

"Larry, you're being very cruel," objected Julia. "The child doesn't want to sing—"

"Shut up!" He watched the girl, an expression of combined appeal and command on his face.

Her lips twitched with laughter that was hysterical. He stopped her with a word.

"Mitsi!" Then very quietly: "This is serious!"

She gulped.

"I know—'*J'Attendrai*'. I can't think of anything else—"

"That's fine! Julia—play!"

Mitsi moistened her lips, gripped the edge of the piano and took a deep breath. Opened her mouth, wavered on the first notes, then began the famous song. She sang in French, a little haltingly at first, then she gained confidence, relaxed and her voice came more easily.

Leo turned from his canvas to listen. Larry stood perfectly still staring out of the window.

Her voice was unexpectedly deep. Its throatiness had a peculiar warmth about it. With each word its appeal became more and more pronounced.

After a moment Larry stopped looking out of the window to gaze at her. Her eyes were closed, her head tilted back. She sang softly, almost whispered the words—her accent giving them a quaintness which added to the undoubted charm of her voice.

There was a little silence when the song was over. Julia looked at her with a half-smile of pleasure. Then Leo broke the tension with:

"Bravo! Bravo, Mitsi! That was charming!"

Larry stepped to her, took her hand as she turned to him with a tremulous smile.

"Lovely, lovely!"

And: "Very, very nice!" from Julia.

Mitsi blushed and laughed shyly. She began to say something, but he raised his hand.

"Not a word from anyone for a minute, while I explain all this! Now then—Bob Raymond is in a bad jam. Wants a star for his night-club almost immediately. Can't find one. I'm trying to help him, but so far— N.G.!"

He glanced at Mitsi with a smile.

"So far," he added.

"But I don't see what this—" began Julia.

"Quiet, my dear, and you shall! I can't get Mirielle. In fact, there's no one in Paris, or anywhere, who'd draw the crowds into Tony's club the way he wants 'em! No one who's gettable at such short notice. No one... except Mitsi!"

"Larry! You are crazy!" cried Julia.

Mitsi stared at him incredulously. Leo snorted at the impossibility of the idea.

"I've been crazy before!" said Larry.

His voice was modulated, but his eyes gleamed. Julia glanced at him, and sighed. She knew him. Knew he was determined to see this fantastic idea through.

"But I've got away with it!" he continued. "I'll do the same this time, or blow up!"

He shook his finger at Julia. The words tumbled out forcefully, concisely. Why, he demanded, shouldn't Mitsi—transformed in the glorious creature depicted on Leo's canvas—why *shouldn't* she star at the night-club? She can sing as well as any other cabaret favourite—better than most! With her foreign accent, her appealingly husky voice, cloaked in colourful mystery, she'd be a sensation!

He'd see her launched on the public on such a mighty wave of newspaper publicity that'd put her over with a wallop.

He stopped talking and laughed out loud.

Julia was looking at him with mixed admiration and incredulity. She said:

"Of course, this just suits your sense of humour!"

He waved the remark away.

"I tell you it's great! There's a job—and not such a bad one at that!—waiting for the girl to step right into! Am I right?"

Julia smiled, excited, and her shining eyes told him that he'd convinced her. He turned to her brother.

"I think it's the maddest idea I've ever heard of... But it's not half bad!"

"That's fine!" He turned to Mitsi. "Well—and what d'you think?... Not that it matters, really, because all you've got to do is—trust me."

She stood, her dark eyes full of wonder. But the amazing confidence of the man, his extraordinary power to convince her, to make her believe that whatever he said was right, seemed to sweep over her in electric waves.

"I—I cannot think... It is all so quick. You talk so quick. I feel helpless, as if I am wax to be moulded by you, and by—Fate..."

His expression softened. For a fleeting second they seemed to be quite alone.

"You trust me?" he said with infinite gentleness.

She nodded.

Julia banged down the piano-lid.

"Well—and what next, you resourceful fellow?" she asked.

"You've got to fix her up! Have her hair altered, have clothes made! She's got to look like Leo's picture overnight! We're in a hurry! You know how to do all those things, Julia! I leave her in your hands. Spend what you like, money doesn't matter. But make her look a million dollars! I'm going to phone Raymond."

"I think this is going to be fun!" exclaimed Julia, with a quick smile at Mitsi.

Mitsi gave a little laugh.

She watched Larry cross to the door, pausing to slap Leo on the shoulder. Her eyes never left him as he moved. At the door she found his look. Across the room they gazed at each other. She braced her shoulders, while her blood tingled in her veins. Her heartbeats quickened with the thrill of the adventure into which he was leading her.

"I'll tell Bob I've found the most sensational woman on the earth!" he said. "A star who'll pack his club to suffocation!"

With a quick grin he was gone. Julia was saying to her:

"We'll make you look all of that, Mitsi my pet. Now then, Leo—you must help, too..."

She took her hand, and they crossed to look at her brother's picture again, Julia rattling off a list of names of hairdressers, beauty specialists, and dress-experts.

5

Leaving Mitsi in Julia's capable hands, Larry hopped over to London the following day. He was to go ahead with preparations for Mitsi's arrival in London. With Bob Raymond's club due to open in a week's time it meant fast work, and plenty of it.

But it was a job after Larry's own heart, and he threw himself into it with zest.

While Julia went to work with equally expert enthusiasm.

With her brother's picture as a basis, and Larry's: "Make her look a million dollars!" echoing like a challenge in her ears, she shot dazed, dizzy and dragooned Mitsi from beauty-parlours to hairdressers, from hat-shops to dress-shops, and back to beautifiers and hair experts again.

Brought up quietly and unsensationally as she had been there were times when the excitement, the hectic rush, was almost too much for Mitsi.

At first she was inclined to be rebellious. When she longed for the quiet serenity that was no more—and it seemed would never be again.

But Julia's sympathy, tact and encouragement quickly got her on her toes, enthusiastic, thrilled. Particularly on the second afternoon of the mad round of beauticians. When she stared at herself in a mirror, and saw not her own face, but that which Leo had put on canvas.

Julia's hired army of beauty experts had done her proud.

This delicate, heart-shaped face, the beautifully modelled features—framed in its new blonde setting. Could it be hers? And this aureole of shimmering, pale gold glory that had been dull, indeterminately mouse-coloured hair?

She leant closer forward to examine the smooth, fine skin which glowed. Gazed deeper into her own eyes, violet pools fringed by dark lashes. Touched her soft, red lips—and noted, almost with a sense of shock, her slender, tapering fingers with the long, pointed nails, whose colour matched her mouth. So different from the badly cut nails and unkempt hands of yesterday.

With pleasurable satisfaction she smoothed a thinly pencilled and slanting eyebrow. Remembered the pain she had suffered under the swiftly plucking tweezers.

Julia herself hardly recognized this golden, transformed young creature who sat beside her in a taxi en *route* to a shoe shop.

"Will it not all cost so much money?" sighed Mitsi, remembering the shops they had already visited.

"But you have got to be a success Mitsi! Then you will be able to repay Larry for all this. You have the chance of fame, of making money, the chance such as few girls get nowadays. You are going to *live!* Meet all sorts of famous and interesting people. And you are going to charm them with your new beauty, your attractive voice and foreign accent. You must get assurance and confidence. Never let yourself be afraid of anybody or anything and believe me you will be a great success!"

"You are so very kind Julia, I do hope all the people I meet will be like you." She smiled shyly at her.

Julia suddenly felt a wave of pity, and a strong affection was born in her for this girl whom Larry had found so strangely. And she determined for Mitsi's own sake as much as for her love for Larry she would do her best to make things easy for her.

"Everybody'll like you," she replied briskly. "Anyway you have Larry to look after you in London."

It was not to be expected Mitsi could fully realize the enormity of the undertaking Larry was planning for her. Certainly the future held promise of excitement. But the practical part of her was foreseeing, she would have plenty to learn. Plenty to worry about. As Julia told her she must learn to exploit her new-found personality. She must learn to be, to act the part of a glamorous lady as well as look one.

"Larry is paving the way for you," said Julia. "You've got to follow. Use your common sense and your imagination."

"I like Larry so much," Mitsi murmured.

Mitsi was only dimly understanding what Julia had been saying. The only solid thing she felt she could hang on to in the future was Larry. She felt that reminding herself of him gave her strength and confidence.

"Everyone likes Larry," Julia said. "Leo and I have known him for years. We're very fond of him."

She turned away to gaze out of the window.

"I am—I am a little hungry," Mitsi said a little hesitatingly.

"All right, we will have lunch first."

And Julia redirected the taxi.

They stopped at a small restaurant where outside little tables invited them. The bright sunshine glanced off the polished glasses and made patterns on the gaily checked table cloths.

"I think Paris is so beautiful," sighed Mitsi.

"Leo and I can't live anywhere else. Of course Leo works better here...shall we sit over there in the corner? I always like a corner table or a side table. I hate sitting bang in the middle of a restaurant, don't you?"

Julia marched towards the chosen table and sat down opposite her. She gazed at the golden head, at the piquant, wistful, lovely face.

Well, well, she thought to herself, it just shows what a beauty parlour and some lovely clothes can do! Wonder what Larry will think when he sees her again? Wonder if he will realize I've done all this for the sake of a few words of thanks from him? I like her enormously. I want to help her, but I'm really doing all this for him. I want him to know this lovely creature's my job. That I made this girl beautiful. I want him to admire my taste.

She sighed. But actually I know he won't think of that. He'll just be knocked over by her and will be worrying himself over this crazy stunt of his. Well, so long as he concentrates mainly on his stunt I suppose I mustn't mind!

"What did you say, Mitsi?"

"What about the songs I will have to sing? Will I sing in English or in French?"

"Larry's fixed all that, my dear. He'll exploit your continental personality as much as possible. Don't you worry."

Mitsi laughed softly. "Continental! That is so funny because I am really more English than French!"

"You are much more marketable as Parisian, I assure you! So useful being able to say, 'I do not understand,' at odd moments when you don't want to!"

Mitsi laughed.

"Would you like to try some wine?" Julia asked.

"Please I think not. I am not used to it."

"Then you'd better *get* used to it! For I can see a long stretch ahead of you when you'll have to dig into the stuff every night and be expected to take it." She smiled. "I'll get Leo to give you a few lessons on lowering liquor when you get back!"

The *garçon* brought a bottle of Sauterne. Mitsi stared at it with wide eyes.

"What a big bottle it is!"

"You're only going to have half of it so you needn't get excited. Tell me how you feel about life when you've had some of this."

She poured the pale amber liquid into her glass.

Timidly Mitsi lifted it to her lips. "It is a very pretty colour," she said. She sniffed it delicately. "And what a *lovely* smell!"

"Bouquet, my dear," Julia corrected her. "Not—smell."

"But bouquet is for flowers?"

"It's also the name for the aroma you're sniffing now," explained Julia.

Mitsi looked puzzled and Julia changed the conversation by suggesting she drank, which she did. It tasted very pleasant and she drank a little more. Julia eyed her critically.

"Take it easy," she warned.

Mitsi set down her glass. "A cabaret singer is not a very—nice thing to be, is she?"

"Good Lord! That's a very old-fashioned idea! Nowadays it doesn't matter what you do. Sing in a cabaret—perform in a circus—so long as you make money. You'll get asked to supper by all the right people, my dear! They'll only be too thrilled to meet you! And after all, even a cabaret singer can be an artist at her job. Plenty of the really big stars are very talented people. They can make you believe the sickly sentiment about Moons and Junes is something real."

Mitsi was leaning forward earnestly, her forehead puckered, as she tried to understand what was being said to her. Julia noticed her glass was now empty. With a faintly lifted eyebrow she refilled it.

"It's up to you," she went on. "Don't lose your sense of perspective. Or your sense of humour. Give the best you can—but there I go, I am preaching at you!"

Mitsi gave her a little dreamy smile. Her face was now firmly supported by her hand as she leant across the table.

"For this suddenly to happen to me, Julia, I cannot understand. For me to suddenly meet people so kind, so good as you and Leo and Larry—it is too much. I cannot believe my happiness. I cry sometimes. My mother would be so happy to know I have such friends as you.

Before I felt so hopeless—so lost and lonely. I did not want to live. You see there was nothing to look to in the future. Except that to keep myself I must get some work—somehow. I loved nobody, and there was no one loved me, or even cared about me…now it is as if all my worries had been taken away from me. I think I have been too lucky. I think that surely something must happen to punish me for having so much—so easily. I hope it is always like this for everyone who is unhappy and alone. I think there must be always someone perhaps to help everyone?"

Julia looked across at her. She was quite moved. And there were tears in Mitsi's eyes. Emotional, highly strung, the girl was quite tragically beautiful now.

"My dear, you're being morbid! Never feel you're alone any more. Leo and I and Larry are your friends." She laughed a little shakily. "Any friend of Larry's is a friend of ours! Besides, we like you anyhow so there's nothing to be grateful for." She helped her to some more wine.

Mitsi tried to say something, but choked, her heart too full for words.

"And don't ever let wine make you cry," Julia admonished her. "I know it is such a lovely, miserable feeling, but tears are to be used only on certain useful occasions! They're *valuable!* Much more valuable if they are not too often evident. But you wouldn't know what I am talking about...how d'you feel now?"

Mitsi gave her eyes a quick dab with her handkerchief. She smiled expansively.

"I feel happy, very happy! The sun is beautiful. The world is beautiful. Paris is beautiful, and you are the most beautiful of all, Julia! Now all the colours are brighter and things are farther away—the traffic—the cars seem to murmur in the distance. I am drunk with happiness—aah!"

She leant back and stretched out her arms as if to embrace the entire world. Her glorious hair streamed out behind her as she laughed up at the sun.

"Humph!" said Julia. "*Do* relax dear, but mind the waiter with the soup behind you!"

6

"What must we buy now, Julia? I do not feel like buying anything at all. I feel so much like lying in the sun and perhaps sleeping a little."

"Sorry to disorganize your inclinations, but we've got to buy shoes. We haven't too much time you know. You've hardly seen Paris yet, and you must be able to talk about the place."

"You talk so nicely, Julia," Mitsi said with sleepy complacency. "You have a most pleasant voice. I like listening to it—so far away—so distant..."

"*Garçon!* The bill," said Julia.

She hurriedly paid and hailed a passing taxi, and her steadying hand helped a now slightly nonchalant and reckless Mitsi into a place of safety.

They completed their purchases with a certain amount of difficulty. Julia had not bargained for the extraordinary effect two or three glasses of Sauterne could have on her charge.

Never again! she decided. Never again unless I've got someone with me. She's lovely when she's tight, but completely hopeless. It'll be absurdly difficult for her if she can't get used to it. Dear, dear, Larry's got a job on his hands!

"I shall be most successful if I can drink this Sauterne everywhere before my performances," declared Mitsi. "I shall perform well then! Julia, thank you for my lovely mood. I am so happy, so very, very happy. I wish Larry were with us. I must give him this Sauterne sometimes too! Can you buy it in London?"

"Yes, anywhere my dear. But I think Larry would much prefer a bottle of whisky any time!"

"Is that so?"

"Yes. You see, he's a newspaper man and they always prefer Scotch."

"And does Scotch make him happy, too?"

"It helps, so I'm told."

"Good, good! Then I must give Larry some Scotch...you know Julia I am particularly fond of my stockings which we bought yesterday. I think they are very becoming. They have an effect on my legs which my own do not—do you not agree, Julia?"

They were being ceremoniously bowed out of a shoe shop. Oblivious of the instantaneous effect upon the male passers-by Mitsi proceeded to display her legs for Julia's inspection. Even to her critical eye they were very lovely. Long and slim in their sheer silk. Not unnaturally every passing man stopped to admire this delectable vision. Julia foresaw their immediate arrest for obstruction. She made a sudden grab at Mitsi, quickly bundled her into a taxi, and directed the driver to her apartment with all speed.

"Here we are. Don't forget the parcels." Julia tumbled out and conveyed the various packages into the hall.

Mitsi followed her dreamily, clutching one small parcel tightly to her. Julia took it from her, and she wandered into the studio. There Leo was working feverishly to catch the last of the evening light. He did not look up.

She stood quietly in the doorway suddenly sobered by seeing him, who had first given the beauty that was now hers colour and form. She gazed round the studio.

Already it had grown familiar to her. Not by time but by happy associations. The small daïs on which she had posed for Leo. The painted screen in the corner. The long, low, fireplace. The well-lived-in atmosphere of the quiet attractively shabby room. On the hearth stood a large vase of yellow flowers. By Leo's easel was a low table on which stood a big earthenware saucer. It was filled with tobacco ash and ringed round with a variety of his pipes of all shapes, sizes and kinds. Now he was smoking a calabash, busy sending fat clouds of smoke towards the ceiling. The mellow afternoon glow streamed through the windows.

Mitsi sighed deeply.

For a long time to come she would look back upon this intimate, homely security, enjoyed so briefly. Suddenly she was filled with panic and distress. She was to leave all this. To go to something about which she knew nothing. In this room she felt safe—but away from it…?

"Leo," she said urgently, and moved towards him.

"Don't disturb me, my dear," he said.

"No, I just want to stand here."

She saw he was putting some finishing touches to her picture. Fascinated, she stood close to him. Breathed in the foul smoke from his pipe as if it were incense. This was real. She was safe here with Leo and Julia.

The rest was tomorrow and other tomorrows.

Leo turned to her, putting down his palate and brushes. He gazed hard at the picture and muttered: "Can't do any more today—light going."

"It's wonderful, Leo. You have made me so beautiful."

"No more beautiful than you are now," he said gruffly. "I am only sorry they are making you into a damned cabaret moaner!"

She stared at him a little frightened for a moment. He noticed her expression and patted her kindly.

"You see, they'll spoil you Mitsi, and it's a pity. But then there's no room for people like you in the world today. You're too old-fashioned."

"I do not feel old-fashioned any more. These beautiful clothes Julia has bought for me to make me feel so different. I feel very chic—that is the word? I do not feel the same person. I am like a picture in one of those fashion books."

She pirouetted before him.

"Don't you like me? Aren't I like the Mitsi Linden you painted?"

Leo eyed her frowningly.

"Hum... I'm not so sure I didn't like you better as you were before."

She paused and faced him.

"But I am the same really. It is only the outside of me that is different."

"Well, let's hope it'll always be that way."

"But of course." She took his hand with a strange little childish earnestness. "You see... I shall be glamorous only to those who do not know me. To those who do I am an ordinary little girl from Zurich."

"All right then. Come on, let's find some tea."

Leo led her as if she were a child towards the sitting-room. At the door Mitsi turned to him laughing.

"Julia says you must teach me to drink!"

Leo looked at her. "Drink?"

"Yes, yes... Sauterne! It makes things seem so far away, so much happier."

Leo growled inaudibly and they went out of the studio to find Julia unpacking parcels and strewing their exciting contents about the room.

7

After dinner that evening Mitsi left Julia and Leo arguing together.

Leo had some theory of painting in coloured clays. He was expounding at great length, trying to convince his sister clay could be a more interesting medium than oils. The conversation had been clean over Mitsi's head and she crept unobtrusively away while Leo bellowed his ideas across the table at Julia.

Mitsi stood quietly for a moment in the darkened studio.

Then crossed quickly and snapped on the one standard lamp that stood in the corner by the piano. She began to play softly.

The music was quiet and mellow as the room in which she sat. She was not an experienced pianist but there was a certain quality about her playing that was attractive. Presently she began to sing softly. To sing softly to herself snatches of little French songs.

From the other room Leo's voice still raised in argument came faintly. It was the voice of the present mingling with the voices of the past.

Again her thoughts drifted. Her fingers wandered down the keyboard, and soon she was picking out the melody of *"J'attendrai."*

A little later the door opened and Julia stole in noiselessly. She stood listening for a moment as Mitsi, unconscious of her presence, sang in her quaint, husky voice. Then she turned and saw her. She broke off, smiling shyly rather like a little girl caught playing some forbidden game.

"Go on my dear, that's lovely!"

Mitsi smiled delightedly.

"But I do not play or sing so very well."

Julia moved over to her.

"You don't have to worry about your playing. Your singing will do."

Mitsi left the piano.

"I would rather you played and I sat quiet and listened to you."

Julia patted her head. "That's a pretty little compliment, my dear!"

She sat down and ran her fingers along the keyboard with her expert touch. Mitsi watched her admiringly. To her Julia seemed the unattainable personification of sophistication. The smart cut of her dark hair, the broad, intelligent line of her brow. She loved, too, the way she manoeuvred her cigarette in its long, slender holder as she played and talked.

Julia, conscious of her gaze, turned to give her a quizzical glance.

"Anything wrong with me?"

Mitsi stammered and blushed.

"N-no…I was just wishing I were like you, Julia. You seem so clever, so assured. As if nothing that happened in the world could ever hurt you."

Without taking her fingers off the keys Julia eyed the other with a faint smile. "I have got my troubles," she answered lightly. "Life is not all beer and skittles even for we clever and worldly-wise people!"

Mitsi stared at her, puzzling over her words.

"What is beer and skittles—?"

"Oh, it's just a sort of game."

Not understanding her in the slightest Mitsi nodded. "I see," she said slowly.

"Anyway, don't wish too hard you were like me—or any other woman who looks as if nothing could hurt her. Many an 'Arden' face hides a broken heart!" She turned back to the piano. "Come on, now, sing something."

She started playing *"Parlez-moi d'amour."*

Mitsi broke in: "Oh, I know that song. I have heard it often."

"It's a pretty little thing," said Julia.

Mitsi sang, her funny, low voice giving the tune a wealth of sentiment.

"You ought to have something like that to sing in London," said Julia.

"Yes, yes…it is very attractive."

"You'll have to find a tune you must make quite your own. One nobody but you can sing. A song that'll always be associated with you. That's what the big cabaret stars have done."

Mitsi laughed excitedly.

"That would be lovely, to have a song of my own! So that when it was played in restaurants and by dance bands everyone would say 'that is Mitsi Linden's song'."

"That's the idea!"

Julia was suddenly thoughtful.

"Yes, my goodness," she exclaimed with emphasis, "it is the idea." She turned to Mitsi quickly. "I think we can find somebody who can write just that sort of song for you," she exclaimed. "Wait just a moment, I'll talk to Leo."

She hurried out of the studio calling for her brother.

She was back in a moment.

"Leo is trying to get him on the telephone now."

"Who?"

"Max Cooper is his name."

Julia laughed.

"Probably playing some world-shattering symphonic movement on his old tin piano at home!" she went on. "Leo's going to try to get him right away. He is quite mad, but brilliant really. An Englishman who writes highbrow music and finds Paris the cosiest city in which to starve! He'll do anything for Leo."

At that moment Leo bawled from the other room: "He's coming round now, Julia."

"Where did you find him?" Julia yelled back.

"In his usual restaurant!"

"I hope you didn't interrupt his supper?"

"Bringing it with him," Leo roared.

Julia turned to Mitsi laughing.

"You see? That's the sort of man he is," she said, spreading her hands. "Strange people we know, don't we?"

Mitsi said nothing. She wondered what this mad musician friend of Leo's would be like.

In a few minutes Leo brought him in.

Mitsi thought he looked much more like a boxer than a musician. Short and thick set with massive shoulders. His nose, high-bridged, jutted out aggressively. He carried a large plate filled with spaghetti which he was eating as he entered. He waved his fork wildly at Julia, and his mouth full of spaghetti, muttered to Mitsi: "Hello, how are you?"

8

"You've got to compose a lovely song for her," said Julia. "She's got to sing in a cabaret and she wants a tune like—oh, '*Parlez moi d'amour*'—you know."

"Impossible," retorted Cooper, his mouth full. "Can't lower myself to such a thing! I write music—not twaddle!"

He gestured wildly with both hands. Mitsi was fearful the spaghetti would spatter them all. Miraculously it didn't.

"Now don't talk rubbish," Julia said calmly. "You've been brought here to write her a song, and write her a song you shall!"

"I'm afraid you'll have to, old man," said Leo sympathetically. "You know what Julia's like when she makes up her mind. Look at this child for instance!" He pointed dramatically at Mitsi. "When she was first brought here she was quite beautiful. Then Larry—"

"That mad journalist fellow?" queried Cooper.

Leo nodded.

"Decided to make her into a cabaret star!" He snorted. "Julia, of course, backs him up, has had the poor girl's hair dyed, her face pushed about, and dressed her up in these ridiculous clothes!"

The man who looked like a prizefighter threw back his head and roared with laughter. It filled the room and was very infectious. Mitsi looked at him wonderingly, and without knowing why started laughing too.

"I see nothing funny in it at all," said Julia severely, "and do mind where you are throwing that spaghetti!"

Cooper stuffed a forkful into his mouth, still laughing.

"I can see Julia has been having a marvellous time," he choked. "Getting a vicarious pleasure, transforming a human being into some incredible doll!" He wagged the fork dangerously near Mitsi's nose. "Now you want me to write a song for her?"

"You've got to," declared Julia.

"I see. Cabaret. Iddi-um-tumty-tum-boopa-doop-hiii-de-he stuff!"

He broke into a hideous imitation of crooning. Mitsi's expression was painful and Julia put her fingers to her ears. Leo roared at him to shut up. Cooper subsided.

"We want something pleasantly tuneful," explained Julia, "you know perfectly well what I mean, Max. Don't be difficult."

"All right," he answered resignedly. "Let me finish my supper first." He threw himself into a chair. "And let's hear the girl sing."

"Well, I'll leave you to it," said Leo. "Do your best Max." And he slammed out of the studio.

Julia played again and Mitsi sang *"Parlez moi d'amour."* Cooper sat back, his eyes closed, and ate greedily. When she had finished singing he said without opening his eyes:

"Not bad! Not good, of course, but not bad!"

Mitsi looked at Julia who hastened to reassure her. "Don't take any notice, my dear!" She crossed over to Max and dragged him to the piano: "Play yourself into a more charming temper," she said.

"Yes," Mitsi put in, "do play some of your own music."

Cooper gave her a sidelong glance, sniffed and sat down.

Beginning very quietly his music resolved itself into a weird but curiously attractive melody. Beautiful sound filled the studio. Mitsi sat enraptured. It reminded her of times when her mother had taken her to concerts. If Mother were here now, she thought, how she would have loved it.

The music died and Cooper's hands came to rest once more on the keyboard. He turned round to her and Julia. Laughed sardonically.

"All the audiences I ever get are played to for nothing! Thanks for listening."

"It was beautiful," breathed Mitsi. "It reminds me so much of—"

Cooper leant forward to the girl. "Did you ever hear Schnabel?"

"Yes," she said. "Once with my mother. He played Beethoven."

She hummed the thin thread of the tune of the "Moonlight Sonata."

Cooper swung back to the piano again and picked out the melody as she hummed it.

"You mean like this?"

"Yes, yes," she agreed.

He went on playing. Again Mitsi and Julia were drowned in magical sound.

When it had finished he came across to her.

"Why must you be a cabaret girl?" he asked. "You are quite intelligent."

"Now come on, Max," Julia interrupted. "Let's do some work."

He went back to the piano. Mitsi leant against it watching him. Julia stood over his shoulder as if forcing him to do what was required.

"Well, what do you want to call your song?" he asked. "D'you want a French title, or an English one?"

Mitsi and Julia thought for a moment.

"I think English would be best, don't you?" Mitsi suggested.

Julia nodded her head in agreement. "I think so too."

"All right, then think of something," and Cooper's fingers rippled along the keys. "It's got to be a love song, of course?"

"Of course!" from Julia.

"Something cheaply poetical," sneered Max.

Mitsi bit her lips in thought, and Julia wrinkled her brow. Cooper looked up at them, an amused grin on his face. Mitsi hazarded two or three suggestions. None met with Julia's approval.

"No, no, it must be something romantic—sentimental."

"Well, you suggest something," said Mitsi.

"How about 'Moonlight in Montmartre?" offered Cooper.

Julia shook her head.

"Why not 'Midnight in the Morgue'?" he said, heavily facetious.

Mitsi giggled, but Julia glared. "I've got it!" she exclaimed excitedly. "'Orchids in Paris!' How about that?"

"Lovely!" cried Mitsi.

Cooper let out a derisive hoot.

"All right! Let's see, it should go like this…"

For two hours the three of them—interrupted and aided by Leo with suggestions and drinks—worked on the song.

To Mitsi Max's skill was uncanny as he traced the melody, evolving a fascinating lilt. He tinkered with it, fitting in harmonies. Making up the lyric to suit the tune, altering the tune to suit the lyric.

And so "Orchids in Paris," Mitsi's first song—created specially for her—was born.

9

"You won't know her my pet!" Julia spoke into the telephone

"Good!" came Larry's reply over the wire from London.

He had telephoned at midnight, just after Max Cooper had left. And the studio seemed strangely empty, bereft of the fascinating music of "Orchids in Paris."

Mitsi had gone to bed, both excited and exhausted. Leo, too, was asleep. Julia had been lounging deep in an arm-chair, too tired to move. This glamorising business is wearing, she was thinking, when the telephone rang. But it seemed worth it to have Larry's thanks.

"It's grand of you Julia, my dear! Bless your heart!"

"How have you been doing your end?"

"All right... I have kidded Raymond she's the biggest sensation Paris has ever known!" He chuckled. "He'll be mad with me when he finds out, but it'll be too late then!"

"You haven't seen Mitsi yet," retorted Julia. "Believe me, he's going to be *grateful* to you—she is a sensation!"

"That's comforting. Anyhow I'll put her over big with the newspapers."

"It's amazing how the child's blossomed out. Her personality's changed. She really has got glamour! And the voice is most attractive too. We've got a new song for her—"

"Oh?"

"Yes. Max Cooper's written it—"

"That mad composer chap?"

"He's written a grand song for her anyhow."

"What's it called?" Larry did not sound very impressed.

"Orchids in Paris."

"Hum...*not* bad," he went on crisply. "I've been fixing things about her songs. Got Al Young working on something for her right now. He'll be her pianist for the show, too. Maybe we can use 'Orchids in Paris' all right."

"Don't be so damned condescending," snapped Julia. "I tell you it's a lovely song. Just right for Mitsi..."

Larry's laugh placated her.

"Darling," he told her, "you've been perfectly marvellous about all this. I appreciate it enormously."

"It's a pleasure, Larry," she mocked him.

"Please, can I speak to him—?"

Julia turned with a start to find Mitsi at her elbow. Her lovely hair was tousled, her eyes sleepy. She made an incongruous picture as she stood there in her own very unglamorous nightgown and one of Leo's old dressing-gowns clutched round her.

"The telephone ringing wakened me up," she explained huskily. "I guessed it might be him so I came out to see."

"You ought to be fast asleep. You've got another hard day tomorrow!"

"What's that?" It was Larry's puzzled voice.

Julia turned back to the telephone, laughing.

"I was talking to Mitsi," she explained. "She's here. She's got out of bed to come and talk to you."

"Very nice of her," said Larry. "Pity I can't see her though in all her new glory!"

Julia eyed Mitsi quizzically.

"I'm afraid her night attire would not meet with your approval!" she answered. She described it to him.

Larry chuckled.

"We'll put that right tomorrow," Julia said. "Filmy black lace...all very transparent and fetching!"

"All right!" laughed Larry. "It won't worry me anyhow. I'll only see her in business hours!"

Julia did not smile.

"Here is Mitsi," she said, and handed the telephone to her.

Mitsi took it gingerly. "Hello, Larry! How are you?" His voice, distant but warm, filled her ear.

"Fine! And I hear you're looking very handsome!"

Mitsi said simply: "I am very like Leo's picture which you admired so much. Julia has been wonderful. I do not think you will recognize me when we meet."

"So I'm told. Are you enjoying it?"

"Yes. But I am afraid also. That is why I wanted to talk to you now. Because when I know you are going to be with me in this strange, exciting new world I do not feel so afraid."

"You'll be all right," was the reassuring reply. "Everybody's going to be kind to you. Help you to be a great star. Make you happy."

Mitsi sighed.

"Now hadn't you better get back to your beauty sleep? Must take care of yourself."

"All right, Larry. When will I see you?"

"I'll come over and collect you in a day or two."

"*Au revoir*."

"'Bye!"

Julia took the receiver from her. Noted her expression. Her eyes had complete faith, utmost trust in them. She was smiling with quiet serenity to herself.

Julia gave her a little push. Without a word—as if hypnotized by Larry's voice—Mitsi went back to bed.

"You know Sadie Harris, don't you?" Larry was saying. "I want you to take Mitsi along to meet her. Do her good. Give her some right ideas."

"*Right* ideas?" queried Julia. "Sadie's just about the toughest woman in town!"

"That doesn't mean a thing. She's a grand person. I knew her well in the old days before she retired from being America's Queen of Song. Tell her all about Mitsi and my stunt. You know she'll be very helpful."

"All right, Larry. I'll fix up a meeting tomorrow. We'll go along to one of her mad parties. Initiate Mitsi into life as lived by gay Americans in Paris! Anything else I can do for you?"

"No...just keep up the good work!"

Larry and Julia chatted for a few more moments. It was mainly about Mitsi. He spoke of how his plans were progressing for her reception in London. He was quickly building up an interest in this new glamorous song bird who was to alight in London to thrill the nightlifers.

Her arrival would be greeted with a fanfare of publicity.

He hoped she would stand up to it all right. "She'll do her best," Julia told him. "And if she lets you down you'll only have yourself to blame, dragging an unknown child into the glare of limelight she doesn't want!"

"It'll be fun for her!" he argued.

"Fun for *you!*" Julia retorted. "You know you don't give a hoot for her feelings. You're just a hard-boiled newspaper man out on the spree!"

Larry laughed. Then advising her to follow Mitsi's example and climb into bed, he hung up.

It was only just before she fell asleep Julia wondered if Larry did indeed give the smallest hoot for Mitsi's feelings. The thought absorbed her, but she was too tired to worry about it. A slight frown did, however, mark her brow as she slipped into oblivion.

Next door Mitsi slept.

Her lips parted in a little smile. It was the same smile she had worn after speaking to Larry.

10

Mitsi had never seen such an astonishing looking woman in her life before. She had brilliant red hair, brilliant black eyes, and a dead white skin. She was startling in every way. She wore a black dress which Mitsi thought revealed far more than was absolutely necessary.

"Let me look at you, honey!" hoarsely gasped America's ex-Queen of Song. She put her bejewelled hands on Mitsi's shoulders and gazed at her intently.

Her eyes, though they are too heavily made up are really very kind, thought Mitsi. I like her.

Sadie Harris turned to Julia.

"Yeah!" she laughed throatily. "I guess she'll be a riot in London all right! Trust that son of a gun Larry to pick a peach!"

Mitsi blushed. The American woman chortled. "Look! Her face is red! Isn't she the cutest thing?"

Julia took Mitsi's hand.

"I'm afraid she's very shy," she explained.

"Sure, sure…I'm sorry!" apologized Sadie. "Now come on, have a snifter and meet the folks!" She smiled kindly. "Relax, my dear, relax!"

She led the way into a large room.

"What is a snifter?" queried Mitsi wonderingly.

"Lubrication for the old tonsils," grinned Sadie.

"She means a cocktail," Julia explained gently.

The room was surprisingly furnished with green hangings and light wood furniture. To Mitsi it looked like a cool, green cave. The traffic outside in the Boulevard Montparnasse sounded like gentle waves. About a dozen people were present. Most of them were clustered in a far corner of the room where was the cocktail bar.

Mitsi suddenly felt very shy. She turned to Julia who smiled back at her reassuringly. Sadie left them for a moment to get some drinks.

Julia whispered: "Hold tight, my dear! Sadie's got the kindest heart in the world. If she likes you there's nothing she won't do for you."

"She is beautiful!" breathed Mitsi. There was a wealth of meaning in her tone so that Julia gave her a quick glance. I do believe the child's got a sense of humour! she thought.

Sadie came across to them, bearing glasses. "John's latest cocktail mixture!" she cried.

Julia took hers and looked at it suspiciously. It was a sinister green colour containing a large, scarlet cherry.

"It's positively poisonous," Sadie went on. "But you don't notice after the first six!"

She raised her glass.

"Mud in your eye!"

They drank.

Mitsi thought her throat would explode. Fortunately she saved herself from choking, swallowed, and felt better. The cocktail after the first shock had quite a pleasant taste, she decided. Some of the people came over from the corner to Sadie. She introduced them.

As a tall, loose-limbed, ugly young man shook hands with Mitsi, Sadie said: "This is John Foster. He made your cocktail, but don't be too hard on him!"

"I mean well," the young man grinned disarmingly.

"I am liking it," said Mitsi.

"Good for you!"

"There you are, John," Sadie laughed. "You've made a friend. Lucky you!"

The long American was very friendly. Mitsi liked his voice—slow and with a pleasant tang—unlike Julia's crisp, concise English. He gave her another cocktail. The room began to have a queer, dream-like quality.

She heard as if in a dream the young man talking to her. Others broke into their conversation. Sadie shouted something to which she answered without knowing what she said. Julia smiled at her and to the best of her belief she smiled back. The room was filled with the buzz of chatter.

She found herself talking with unbelievable ease to this man called John. Her shyness vanished by magic and she began to enjoy herself. As she talked she looked round at the others. Her companion pointed them out. Writers, artists, musicians. There was a big, fat man talking to Julia. He was an American newspaper man.

"The same as Larry?—"

"Friend of yours?" queried Foster.

Mitsi nodded.

"Great scout!"

Mitsi felt this was something highly complimentary and she smiled with pride.

Presently Sadie walked across to a white grand piano. She opened the lid and called out to John:

"If you can tear yourself away from her," with a mock scowl at Mitsi, "you might pound the ivories for me!"

Foster grinned an excuse to Mitsi and went over. He sat down and began to play. The music mingled with the hubbub of talk. The rhythm insinuated itself through the sound of voices. People began to hum and then quite suddenly everyone seemed to be dancing. Only Mitsi was left alone. Julia was dancing with the fat newspaper man.

Sadie was leaning over the top of the piano staring at Foster's fingers as they moved over the keys and beat out a rhythmic melody.

Mitsi felt strangely stirred. This music—there was something about it. Sad, sentimental. Julia and her partner passed by, both dancing skilfully. Mitsi found herself sitting in a corner watching the dancers, listening to the music. In turn two men came up and asked her to dance. She shook her head, smiling:

"Please, I so much enjoy just watching and listening."

Both men were understanding. They stood one on either side of her. One of them gave her a cigarette. She took it unconsciously and smoked. The cigarette had a pleasant, harsh tang about it which she liked. It was different from the one or two with which Julia had initiated her into the art of smoking.

Suddenly a voice, so lovely, so rich and warm broke into the music. The piano sank into a soft accompaniment. Sadie Harris was singing. Mitsi caught the words of "Body and Soul." Sadie leant against the piano staring straight in front of her. Her body was quite still. Everybody stopped dancing, one by one, and listened. Mitsi sat hypnotized by the voice of this strange woman—a voice so much more beautiful than her own, with its deep resonant quality. And the melody seemed to her to be the saddest thing. Even she realized that Sadie gave the words a significance and a reality which was very moving.

The song came to a close but John Foster continued playing. He drifted into another tune—"Smoke gets in your Eyes." Sadie shook her head, but he looked up at her and smiled:

"Please, Sadie."

The others took up his pleading, so Sadie sang.

Mitsi looked up to find Julia beside her. She took her hand.

"Enjoying it?" Julia queried.

Mitsi nodded.

Julia glanced across to the piano and Sadie.

"She was the toast of Broadway three years ago."

"She is beautiful. I wish I could sing like that."

"Well you can try. If you are only *half* as good it'll suit."

Mitsi listened intently as though she would absorb some of the other's magic. The song ended and in spite of repeated demands Sadie left the piano. Another man took Foster's place and he came over to Mitsi.

Now another tune, gayer and swifter, filled the room. People were dancing again. Foster gave Mitsi a little burlesque bow—clicked his heels and twisted an imaginary military moustache.

"Dance? Yes?"

She moved into his arms.

He danced very slickly and a sudden mood of happiness lifted her up. Presently she felt a tap on her arm and turned to find Sadie beside her.

"Pardon this cut in, John, but I want to talk to her myself."

Mitsi's partner pulled a face at Sadie and released her. She found herself with the American woman in a clear corner.

"Julia tells me you're going to sing in London. Larry Curtis is boosting you up over there. Lucky to have him looking after you, though you ought to do pretty well anyway by the look of you."

She scrutinized her narrowly.

"Got what it takes all right you have," she muttered. "With your accent and that glamour which to us most foreigners have anyway."

"I am half English."

"That so? You don't look it. If I were you I'd forget it."

"That's what Julia says."

"Julia's right. She tells me you have a nice voice, too."

"Not so—exciting—is that the word?—as yours."

Sadie laughed harshly.

"Ha! Gone to bits. Haven't sung properly for years."

"Why not?"

Sadie gave her a long look.

"I hit the toboggan I guess."

"I do not understand."

"Slid," the other explained succinctly.

"Lost my grip. With the racket you're going into you'll have to hang on hard."

She paused to light a cigarette. Mitsi watched her curiously.

"Julia thinks I might be able to give you a bit of advice," the other went on through a cloud of smoke. "Help you a bit. Well, I guess I can give you plenty of that! But if you listened you wouldn't remember anyway. You have to find out for yourself, I reckon. When you are in a bit of a jam listen to your own heart. Do what that tells you."

She gave Mitsi a smile that was full of surprising gentleness, and said:

"Tell you what I will do though—I like the look of you and I know you must have something or Larry wouldn't be all het up about you—! Ever heard of Sam Levinsky?"

Mitsi shook her head.

"Well, he's the greatest little song writer both sides of the Atlantic!"

She nodded towards the piano. The man was playing a slow, lazy tune with an infectious rhythm about it.

"That's one of his numbers."

Mitsi listened to the tune as Sadie spoke about its composer.

Sam Levinsky occupied the premier position among America's purveyors of tuneful sentiment. Hollywood paid him colossal sums. The radio plugged his tunes to millions of listeners. Tunes which he churned out with incredible speed while maintaining an originality and charm which was unique.

"He's only to write one song for you to set the seal on your fame," Sadie concluded.

Sadie's enthusiasm thrilled Mitsi.

"He's in New York now but on his way here. I'll tell him about you, and if he's interested maybe he'll knock out a song for you."

Mitsi tried to thank her, but she silenced her.

"Sam won't do a thing if he doesn't like you, so don't thank me!"

At that moment she saw Foster bearing drinks making his way across to them. He was laughing as he dodged through the dancers. Somebody threw a cushion at him which he ducked.

"The party's livening up, I guess," Sadie muttered to Mitsi. She screamed at him: "John! Look out! If you spill those cocktails on my floor they'll burn a hole clean through it!"

11

Three days later—and Larry expected from London.

He was due to arrive at Le Bourget about four o'clock that afternoon. Julia and Mitsi went to the airport to meet him in.

Julia was relieved Mitsi did not recoil from the scene of her sudden, stark meeting with the news of Henri Tallier's tragic death. She would have been surprised—except that Mitsi had all along apparently completely pushed to one side any thought of Tallier and his suicide.

Ever since she had spoken of it to Larry in the airport waiting-room, she had made no further reference to it. It might have been a nightmare which she had dismissed from her mind on waking.

Julia concluded that was, in fact, how she had treated the tragedy which might so easily have had a more drastic effect on her personally.

But for Larry.

She's not so helpless as she seems, Julia had decided. There was much more to her than showed on the surface. An infinite capacity for taking bangs on the chin, to come up smiling. And obviously, faced with thrilling future, pushed on to her out of the blue, she had simply resolved to forget—as much as possible—what she did not want to remember.

Another thing, Julia reflected. She's had no time to think of anything but her overnight metamorphosis from an insignificant, destitute nobody into the gorgeous creature she had become.

Today Mitsi was filled with keen excitement at the prospect of seeing Larry again. Longed to learn his reaction to her new appearance.

She wore a very plain, exquisitely tailored suit of a soft brown shade. It accentuated her blondeness. Contrasted with the deep blue of her eyes, and her faintly golden skin. With it she wore a jaunty brown felt hat, with a gay yellow feather stuck through the crown.

Julia smiled at her with affectionate admiration.

"You are a peach to dress. You do the utmost justice to your clothes—put on a thousand francs to the original price!"

"I never thought I might ever wear beautiful clothes like these... But it is you who have been so clever to choose them for me."

They were standing on the tarmac, waiting for the plane.

The sunshine was bright and warm. Mitsi seemed to have absorbed some of its quality into her own personality. Her eyes were bright, shining with excitement. Her skin glowed. Her voice had a warm, husky quality. She was a thrilling, vital creature. Everybody stared at her. Turned round to look at her as she passed.

Mitsi was deliciously conscious of the stir she created. She preened herself, laughing at Julia's mild criticism.

"It is *beautiful* to be stared at—so! I like it so much!"

"Try to be more blasé, though. As if you're used to it, and bored by your own beauty!"

Whereupon Mitsi stuck her nose in the air and surveyed everyone with haughty disdain. Julia was more amused than impressed.

Presently the airliner was sighted.

Mitsi watched it, her fingers tightly entwined, her lips parted as she thrilled at the sight of the roaring machine circling above. The plane swooped lower…its wheels touched the tarmac, bumped gently. Then it taxied towards them and stopped.

"There he is! There he is!"

Mitsi was pulling at Julia's shoulder, and pointing to the familiar figure as he hurried down the wooden steps on to the tarmac. He saw them, and waved, barked something at a steward, and came quickly over to them.

He did not seem to be looking at Mitsi. His eyes were smiling at Julia. Mitsi bit her lip in bewilderment. He hadn't seen her. She was dumb.

"Julia, my dear! It's grand of you to meet me!" And then with a glance at Mitsi: "Where's Mitsi?"

Julia stared at him.

Mitsi found her voice. "Larry!"

He looked at her coolly.

"Who's this?" he asked rudely.

Julia was laughing. Mitsi, too, was not sure whether to laugh or cry. Her relief was almost unbearable.

"You did not recognize me!" she cried gleefully. "Oooh! You did not know me at all!"

In an ecstasy of excitement and joy she flung her arms around his neck. Larry looked a little taken aback by this demonstration. He caught Julia's eye and winked at her mischievously. She realized he *had* recognized Mitsi, of course—he was just kidding her. What a baby he is! she thought, and flashed him a tender smile.

But he didn't see it. Mitsi was holding him close, laughing throatily. He was forced to hold her to save himself from being pushed backwards. He caught the scent of her hair. It was attractive. He felt the warmth and softness of her young body. A thrill danced down his spine.

Gosh! She's *attractive*, he thought—then took a grip on himself.

"Hey! Hey! Young woman—you're strangling me!"

With a growl he pulled her arms from about his neck, held her off, and surveyed her. Took in vital, brilliant loveliness that was now hers.

"My, My! How you've changed!"

"Do you approve? Please say 'yes'!"

He nodded to Julia.

"You're a *genius*, my sweet!"

Julia could not help blushing a little with pleasure. He did appreciate her cunning, expert hand in the fashioning of the picture.

He was kidding Mitsi:

"How *could* I have known you? Why, I don't know you, now!" He held her from him, and scrutinized her.

"You mean to tell me, you're that grubby, plain little piece I left behind?"

Mitsi, delighted—and apparently quite deceived by his play-acting—nodded vigorously. (Julia had a shrewd suspicion she wasn't being fooled at all, really. But was obligingly entering into the spirit of the thing!)

"I am the same Mitsi Linden!" she cried. "Only the outside of me is different—!"

Larry pushed his hat farther back on his head than it was already shoved by Mitsi's onslaught.

"Well, you certainly look the part all right, now!"

He saw the slim lines of her figure, her slender legs, bewitching in their transparent, silk stockings. Saw the chic moulding of her suit, emphasizing the beauty which had been hidden before by her ugly clothes.

His eyes travelling up from her smart shoes, noting how well she wore her clothes, met her eyes. For an infinitesimal flicker of time, they gazed fully into his. Unconsciously registered his masculine admiration. Without any coquetry, without knowing why, she lowered her lids.

Then he was catching Julia by the arm. Taking Mitsi's arm, too, he propelled them both towards the Customs barrier.

Going back to Paris in the aerodrome bus, Mitsi—aided by Julia—gave Larry an account of all that had happened since he had left with instructions to make her look "like a million dollars."

He learned of her success with Sadie Harris. That pleased him. And he was particularly glad when she told him of Sadie's promise to talk to Sam Levinsky about her.

"Get him to write a song for you, and—!" He banged the palm of his hand with his fist.

"Let's hope Sadie doesn't forget about it," said Julia cautiously.

Larry laughed. "I'll see to that! I'll talk to her tonight on the phone… She knows I'd chew her up, if she ever let me down! Besides she's not that sort."

Mitsi told him about John Foster. How he had spoken nicely about him. Larry knew him slightly, and remembered him when she described him to him.

"He said you were a good—something… I forget what it was now. But it sounded most complimentary!"

"It had better!" was Larry's rejoinder, in mock sternness. "If anybody ever says anything nasty about me to you—*don't tell me*…. But just put poison in his drink next time you see him! See?"

Mitsi nodded seriously.

"Just as you wish…"

Larry and Julia looked at her amusedly.

When they got to the apartment, Larry declared that both of them, and Leo, should dine with him at Prunier's. He wanted to see what Mitsi looked like "all dolled up" in the white evening gown which had just arrived from the modiste's. It was one of the many which Julia had selected for her.

Then Larry talked at great length, and with avowals of even greater affection, to Sadie Harris. Mitsi and Julia left him to it, while they prepared themselves for a "gay, hilarious, happy and hectic Parisian Night!"—as Larry put it.

The telephone conversation over—"Phew! But Levinsky's as good as written a song for her already!"—Larry repaired to the bathroom, whistling with cheerful confidence.

It was in the taxi en *route* to Prunier's that he mentioned quite casually he was taking Mitsi back to London the following morning.

"But her packing," protested Julia.

"Tomorrow morning—Mitsi says 'So long' to Paris,'" insisted Larry firmly. "Everything's set for her arrival—we're crossing by train—it might spoil the glamour idea if she got air-sick and green in the face…" He smiled at her. "The Channel's very smooth—you'll enjoy this trip much more than your last one!"

Mitsi gave him a grateful look.

"So, young woman, it's London for you tomorrow…and the dazzling life of a night-club star!"

Mitsi did not speak. Her mind was a sudden turmoil of thoughts, fearful, exciting. Thrilling and apprehensive.

"When does the club open?" asked Julia.

"Four days' time. She'll have plenty on her mind. Songs to rehearse. Press photographers. Interviews. All the fun of the fair!"

Mitsi was staring at him.

He didn't see the helpless, frightened look in her eyes. But Julia did. She grasped Mitsi's hand firmly, gave it a warm squeeze which said: Don't worry…

"Damned, footling nonsense, I call it!" grumbled Leo into his beard.

"Ah, but it's grand fun…"

And Larry chuckled—still not noticing Mitsi's worried face.

12

It was ten-thirty next morning and the time of Mitsi's departure was near.

Leo and Larry had already gone on ahead in a taxi that was bursting with Mitsi's luggage. Julia and Mitsi gave the flat a hurried last minute's look round to see nothing was left behind. Clutching a travelling case she and Julia piled into the taxi.

"*Gare du Nord, aussi vite que possible!*"

"*Bien, Madame!*" the driver grunted mournfully through his beard and they shot off with erratic speed. They made the station with a quarter of an hour to spare. The Golden Arrow was due to leave at eleven o'clock.

Followed a swift altercation between Julia and the taxi-driver over the size of her tip after which she emerged blushing but triumphant. A porter grabbed Mitsi's case. Julia enquired for their platform.

"Vous avez une place reservée, Madame?"

"Yes, yes." The seat was reserved.

"Très *bien, Madame*," grinned the porter and led the way.

The train was already in—much to the amazement and excitement of Mitsi. She had never seen a boat-train, let alone the famous Golden Arrow, in her life before. To her this massive, puffing engine with its line of luxurious carriages meant a gateway to the world. She turned excitedly to Julia:

"It's so exciting!"

Julia glanced at her as they hurried to their compartment.

So smart, so pretty she looked. Julia thought she had never experienced such an extraordinary combination in one person as she found in Mitsi. She had no knowledge of the things that to Julia were simply part of life, of which she had never been without—such as boat trains, the hub of stations and the hustle of travel.

But Mitsi could thrill at these things yet look so beautiful, so *soignée,* as if she had just left the Rue de la Paix.

The porter found their compartment. They saw Leo and Larry haranguing other porters with methodical aggressiveness.

Suddenly Mitsi clutched Julia's arm:

"I don't want to go!"

"Don't be silly," said Julia firmly. She watched anxiously for tears. "Why, it's all going to be grand! It's going to be lovely I tell you!"

Mitsi shook her head miserably.

"I don't want to leave you now."

"Come on, cheer up! You can come over and see us again very soon. And I expect I'll be over to see you some time."

Julia patted her gently on the shoulder.

Mitsi looked up into her face. This woman had befriended her, helped her, sympathized with her as her mother might have done. She couldn't bear to think that she was leaving her for new faces, strange—perhaps unkind—people. There was Larry, she knew. But he was different. He was terribly kind and understanding. But he was rougher, harder—like Leo, only more so. And so far she was not sure how much Larry liked her.

She was sure Julia did.

Julia was saying:

"You'll make plenty of new friends. Everyone will be kind."

"I don't want to make new friends. Suddenly I am so afraid of this new life. I do not like this change now. I am not settled at all—"

"My dear, be thankful you've got a job and this chance to be a howling success! It's a chance that comes to a girl in a million."

Suddenly she put her arms round her and kissed her.

"Write to me often," she told her. "Tell me all about it. I'll love to hear from you."

The easy tears came to Mitsi's eyes.

"Thank you, thank you, so much dear Julia," she said huskily. "I shall write to you very often."

Leo bellowed to them. Mitsi gave her eyes a furtive dab with her handkerchief:

"Is my make-up spoilt?" she enquired of Julia anxiously.

Julia shook her head, took her arm and they went towards the compartment.

Larry had already settled himself in a corner and there was an opposite corner for Mitsi. There were magazines and newspapers scattered on the seat. Larry gave her a quick smile.

"All right?"

She nodded.

There was a sudden bellow from behind.

Mitsi turned to find the tall young American, John Foster, waving an enormous bunch of orchids.

"From Sadie," he explained, "with her best love."

Mitsi clutched them to her.

"Oh, how kind of her! Please thank her for me often."

Foster waved her thanks away casually.

"She thinks you're cute! So do I!"

He turned to Larry: "Guess I may be able to get over pretty soon. Can I ring and make a date?"

Larry eyed him.

"With me?"

"Hell, no!"

"Ask her then."

Foster turned to Mitsi questioningly.

"I shall be very glad," she answered simply.

Larry cut in crisply:

"Bring Levinsky over with you."

"Sure!" the American said. "I'll bring him before he goes down south. Gee! You ought to see his place at Cannes. It's swell!"

"I've seen it," Larry said quickly.

Julia spoke to him. "I say, doesn't Mitsi's luggage look nice?"

She pointed to the rack where two cases of heavy pigskin and two shiny block hat boxes rested.

"And that's not all of it. You should see the stuff in the luggage van!" Larry exclaimed.

Leo added a cynical observation:

"She might be an American heiress—if she were not so pretty!"

"Say, that's a slur on the American race," laughed Foster.

"I like Americans," said Mitsi. "They are so kind."

"Atta-goil!"

They laughed.

Julia said, "How's that for diplomacy?"

A round-faced man in a cap and gold braid bustled up.

"En voiture! Prenez vos places, Messieurs, Mesdames!"

"You're off! You're off!" cried Julia.

She kissed Mitsi quickly.

There was a confused buzz of hurried farewells. Doors slammed. Leo pecked Mitsi's brow, his beard tickling her face. Simultaneously Foster gripped her hand.

"All the luck in the world! And no sea-sickness!"

He followed Julia and Leo out of the carriage.

Mitsi hung out of the window desperately fighting back her tears. Behind her was Larry shouting his good-byes to the others into her ear.

The engine gave an effeminate "peep," peculiar to French trains, and then began to move.

Foster yelled something and Mitsi just caught the words.

She turned miserably to Larry.

"They are so lucky! They are lunching at Prunier's," she said.

13

Larry took a look at Mitsi's tear-brimmed eyes and tremulous lip and rang for the steward.

In a moment a smiling, white-coated chap appeared.

"A White Lady and a large Scotch, quickly, George!"

"Oui, oui Monsieur!"

"Make you feel better," Larry smiled at her.

She murmured her thanks inaudibly.

I hope she's going to be all right, he thought. On the surface she's got everything. But whether she's really got the guts to go through with it is a different matter. There are some surprising twists to her character.

She had sung to him last night. She had been talking enthusiastically about "Orchids in Paris" during dinner at Prunier's. He had been sceptical. Said all right, let's hear it when we get back to the apartment.

He had been quite amazed by her air of assurance as she stood by the piano. Then that throaty voice of hers singing what he had to admit was a darned attractive song. He remembered how alluring she had looked. Her hair glittering like champagne under the soft lamp light. Her figure slim and very lovely in the simply-cut white gown.

Yes! She looked *and* acted all right then. As she sang she had smoked a cigarette—and the contrast between this sophistication and the *naïveté* of her eyes gave her an odd appeal that was fascinating.

The steward appeared with the drinks.

"Here's to crime!"

He raised his glass.

"What is that?" she queried, puzzled.

"Oh, another way of saying 'Cheerio'!"

She raised her glass.

They drank.

Mitsi glanced out of the window at the swiftly passing scenery. They were tearing through the fields and woods of Chantilly.

"This is where there's the famous race-course," he told her. "Chantilly."

"Where the women wear such wonderful clothes?"

"They do have some racing, too!"

She laughed, wrinkling her nose at him. She was brightening up. She glanced at the magazines and papers beside her and took up one of them.

"Is there anything here in English I can read?"

He gave her a glossy magazine.

"You can get an idea of London night life from this. It's filled with nothing but pictures of celebrities and big shots."

She started to look at it.

He immersed himself in a newspaper.

Presently he said: "You know you must be careful to talk as if you knew all about places like Chantilly."

She looked at him earnestly.

"There is Longchamps, Auteuil, Le Touquet, Cannes…"

He rattled off a list of names to her. "You're supposed to know all of them. So once you're in London don't ask questions about 'em. If you're not sure, keep quiet or you'll give yourself away. When you hear other people—as you will—talking about these gay spots just *look* as if you knew all about 'em too. But say nothing. You're a well-known nightclub star from Paris. You've been around places. But you can't talk much because your English isn't good." He burlesqued: "I not ondairestand! Get the idea?"

She seemed highly diverted.

"I think it is all going to be a wonderful game!"

"It will be if we both play it properly. I think I'll manage my hand all right, and if you play up—as I know you will—we'll pull it off."

He glanced at his wrist-watch.

"Like lunch now, or on the boat?"

"Oh, on the boat, please."

A sudden thought struck her and she leant across to him, her face wearing a serious expression.

"There is a thing I want to ask you," she began hesitantly.

"Hmmm?"

"This money that is being spent on me. All these lovely clothes. The beauty shops—all so terribly expensive!" She frowned. "Travelling in this grand style…eating nice food, drinking nice drinks…it is all costing such a lot—and I—"

He gave her a level look.

"Listen. You don't have to worry about any of these things. Though it's nice of you to. I appreciate it." He smiled at her seriousness which was almost comical.

"Know how much Bob Raymond's paying you?" he asked.

She shook her head.

"Two hundred pounds a week!"

He gave her a surprised glance. She did not seem very impressed.

"Did you hear? Two hundred pounds."

She looked puzzled. "How much is that?"

"Oh, gosh! In francs?" He explained how much.

She gasped.

"It is tremendous money!"

"Well, don't forget you've got to live up to it! Swell hotel. Private suite. Maid. Dresser at the Club. It'll cost you plenty."

She nodded understandingly.

"But all those francs!" she murmured, and added: "a week!"

"You'll get that for three months anyhow," he said briskly. "And the contract has an option on you for a further three. It's waiting in London for your signature."

She was only half listening.

She was still trying to grasp the magnitude of the sum he had told her was to be her salary.

He realized she was overwhelmed, and prodded her arm sharply with a businesslike finger.

"And this is where the money I'm spending on you comes in. So listen. I reckon you'll have cost me round about five hundred. So I'm taking twenty per cent of your pay for the first three months. Forty pounds a week. Understand?"

She thought for a moment.

"That means I shall then receive one hundred and sixty pounds?"

He nodded.

"Smart girl!"

"Still such money is enormous for me!"

"If you go on with Raymond—or move to another club—after the three months, all the money you make is yours. See? I'm making no profit out of the deal—but I'm going to get a *lot* of fun!"

He grinned at her.

"I am still in a dream," she whispered. "I know that suddenly I will wake up to find you, who are so good—so wonderful—to me are not here at all."

She paused, then went on: "And I am just"—shrugging pathetically—"a nobody, with no one to care…"

He gave a little laugh that was embarrassment, touched by her words.

"Read your magazine," he said gruffly, and reached for his newspaper.

14

The Golden Arrow drew into Calais, and porters swarmed on to the train, a mass of blue blouses and red badges.

Mitsi surveyed them wide-eyed.

A sudden torrent of French poured on them, and she watched a wild-looking individual grab their bags. He swung them dexterously on to his back, and they followed him. Larry yelled instructions after him.

"Passport ready?" he asked her as they chased the receding figure of the porter.

She produced it. Clutched it tightly.

"Thank God you're British really! It saves a lot of trouble—only keep it to yourself!"

She nodded.

"Our luggage is registered through to London—so we don't have to worry about that."

She had been wondering what happened to the bulging trunks which held her magnificent possessions.

They reached the quayside. Followed the usual preliminaries and they passed up the gangway on to the steamer.

The sun was shining brightly. The sea was blue and calm. Larry looked out to where the horizon and sea merged in a pearly haze.

"Going to be a good crossing."

He glanced round the deck. Noted with pleasurable pride that many of the other passengers were giving his companion appraising looks.

"Don't see anyone interesting on board, as yet," he said. Then added with a wink at her: "Except ourselves!"

She laughed excitedly.

She was watching the quayside. It swarmed with activity, as the luggage and freight was hoisted noisily aboard.

"Most of the big shots—so called!" he went on, a touch of cynicism in his voice, "hop about by plane, these days. You'll have to try that way again, too, later on. Maybe it'll be nicer when you've got more used to luxury living!"

"I am so excited to see England. I was always told by my mother how beautiful it is."

She leaned back against the rail, turning her head to gaze out to where England lay beyond the horizon.

Soon the gangways were cleared, the steamer's propellers churned. Ropes snaked from the quayside, plopped into the sea, were hauled aboard.

"You'll be seeing the good old white cliffs of Dover in an hour's time," he said.

He thought she looked quite painfully lovely as she stood there with the sun shining down on her. Her excited eyes sparkling with the zest of life and adventure.

She wore a navy blue travelling suit. A cherry-coloured hat was perched cheekily over one eye. The freshening breeze blew her skirt tight against her delightfully slim legs.

Larry sighed.

Well, you hard-boiled egg, he thought. If that's the way she gets you, she'll tear 'em up in London! Suddenly another thought struck him. He frowned. He glanced at Mitsi as she leant over the rail, watching the frothy, creamy wake.

Wonder how she'll strike *him*? he asked himself. Or how he will strike her?

He shrugged, leaving both queries unanswered.

"Come on down, and we'll see what's for lunch."

She gave a backward glance at the receding docks of Calais. Then she took his arm and they went down into the saloon.

He chose a table. She was too excited to give any real attention to the menu. He helped her order her lunch.

When the steward had gone he said:

"Hhmm!… Must admit I don't mind looking across a table at you, young woman!"

She blushed a little.

"I like looking across a table at you."

"Yes? But you must learn not to blush when men say pretty speeches to you. You've got plenty of them coming your way, believe me, and you've got to pretend you've been hearing them all your life."

"That I shall find difficult," she said simply.

"Oh, I expect you'll soon get used to it. You'll find lots of gay and charming men making love to you over a cocktail with a slickly put phrase and a twinkle in their eye. Some of 'em will mean what they say and some of them won't. By the look of you I reckon most of them *will* be anxious to prove their words by actions!"

Mitsi held a spoonful of soup poised over her plate.

"All that you say is difficult for me to understand," she said, "but then that is because I am not yet what you call sophisticated. Yes?"

"Something like that."

"When I have learned all these things I *shall* be sophisticated? I shall learn very quickly." She gave him a mischievous smile. "Then I shall not blush so easily."

She drank her soup.

"Don't overdo it. Don't try to learn too much. You know you're very sweet right now and I don't want you to get tough and tiresome like so many of the women one sees around."

He ordered drinks. He was enjoying himself. He relaxed while Mitsi was bright and happy. They joked and laughed.

He told her stories about the people—famous, celebrated and notorious—whom she would meet in her new life. The eccentric inhabitants of Chelsea and Bloomsbury. Actors and actresses, writers and artists. The Society crowd—and the hangers-on. All the odd mixtures who contribute their posturings, grimaces and witticisms to the ceaseless whirlpool that was London's life.

He talked easily and vividly. She thought he was the dearest person in the whole world.

When they had finished their lunch, they went on deck once more.

Presently the thin, white ribbon that was the cliffs of Dover cut the blue of sky and sea.

"England!"

She gazed fascinated as the cliffs drew nearer, until soon they were dazzlingly white, topped with green against a blue unclouded sky.

"Here we are—nearly there. Then a short train run up to Victoria. I'm parking you in a swellegant hotel—the Norchester—until you've found your feet. You won't be lonely there, anyway. It's a nice, gay spot. You'll have newspaper reporters of all shapes, sizes and sexes barging in on you for the first few days, but don't let 'em worry you."

She nodded and he went on:

"Say as little as possible—except the old one about the Englishmen!—that won't hurt you, I reckon. The boys and girls'll make most of it up anyway! I'll be around, too, to help you cope with them. So you see you've got nothing on your mind at all, really."

He smiled reassuringly at her. He was hoping to heaven she'd not panic, and give the show away.

"Raymond will be at Victoria to meet us. Expect there'll be some photographers hanging round, too."

"I hope he—this Mr. Raymond—will like me." A doubtful look showed in her eyes.

"He likes you *already*—don't you worry!" He laughed exuberantly. "I've seen to that!"

She smiled vaguely.

Wondering what this man whom she had heard so much about, with whom she would have to come into contact so much, was like.

Julia had said he was handsome and charming. Larry liked him. But Leo was openly rude about him. Though, as Julia pointed out, her brother had only met Raymond once.

She was both thrilled and a little frightened at the prospect of meeting him.

15

On the way up from Dover to Victoria Mitsi, suddenly tired, fell asleep.

It was only just as they steamed into the station that Larry gently shook her. She awoke with a start. Gasped.

"Here we are."

She stood up and hastily glanced at her face in the mirror, fixing her hair and dabbing her nose with powder.

"Amazing how you girls get the hang of it so quickly," Larry grinned.

She pulled on her hat and they got out.

A porter was tackling their bags while Larry gazed expectantly down the platform.

Suddenly he turned to her.

"Here he is!"

She saw a tall, distinguished looking young man with a clove carnation in his buttonhole walking swiftly up to them.

"Hello, Larry!"

He turned to her with a charming smile.

"Welcome to London, Miss Linden."

Larry introduced them. Then asked her for her luggage keys. "Bob will look after you while I see your stuff through the customs."

She smiled her thanks, gave him the keys and turned shyly to Raymond.

As she did so there was a sudden flash which momentarily blinded her. "Oh!"

Raymond chuckled.

"I know, they always make me jump, too!"

He took her arm sympathetically.

She stared up at him without the faintest idea what he was talking about. Saw he was looking past her. Turned to follow his gaze. She was just in time to see two or three men, hats on the backs of their heads, ranged a few feet away from her.

Each held a square-looking box affair surmounted by what appeared to her to be a large glass eye. As she stared at them the three eyes exploded simultaneously. Another blinding flash which nearly made her jump out of her skin.

She cried out.

Raymond's hand tightened on her arm.

"So sorry," he apologized. "You must hate it, but the press must have their pictures too!"

One of the men came up to him.

"Can we have one of Miss Linden alone?"

"Go ahead."

Just at that moment Larry hurried up, pushing his way through the knot of people who were watching the scene. He shoved the keys into her hand.

"That's that. Everything all clear." Then with a glance at the photographers, he grinned.

"Oh, the boys have started on you already, have they?"

The man who had spoken to Raymond said:

"We've got some of Miss Linden and Mr. Raymond. We just want one of her alone."

Larry nodded.

"All right. Let's make a pretty picture, shall we?"

Quickly he and the other photographers piled up some luggage. In a daze, still blinking from the effects of the flashes, Mitsi found herself posed on this impromptu perch.

"Smile!"

She bared her teeth in an artificial grin. One of the camera men lifted her skirt still higher, exposing as much of her knees as he dared.

She gave her legs a nervous look, but was too overwhelmed to protest.

Somebody else shouted: "Wave!"

Her arm was lifted up in an attitude of greeting.

"Hold it!"

Once more the cameras flashed.

"All right. One more, please!"

She remained rigid. The glass eyes exploded again.

There was a babble of thanks from the photographers and they turned tail and rushed away.

Her eyes aching, seeing nothing but myriads of wildly jumping spots, Mitsi was helped from her seat, and found herself hurrying between Larry and Raymond.

"I've got the car here," Raymond said to her. "I'll take you straight to your hotel."

"Are the reporters waiting there?" Larry cut in.

"Yes."

"Good!"

The porter had gone ahead with their bags, and in a moment Mitsi was in Raymond's luxuriously cushioned large black car.

They purred off.

Raymond turned to her conversationally. Asked her all the appropriate questions: Had she had a nice crossing? Was the train full?

She answered automatically.

"I'm afraid Miss Linden finds it all a bit strange, Bob," put in Larry. "And her English is not too fluent."

He laughed at Mitsi, at the same time surreptitiously squeezing her arm.

"So go easy on your questions," he said.

Raymond quickly apologized.

Fortified by Larry's presence she plucked up enough voice to say:

"I am afraid I am a little tired also."

Raymond smiled sympathetically.

They swung into Hyde Park Corner.

"That's our famous Hyde Park, Mitsi."

Larry waved vaguely to his left.

She looked out at the confused combination of buses, policemen, railings and bright green trees.

They swept through the gates and then she saw some people on horseback, rows of deck-chairs, people walking and sitting in the sunlight. Glimpses of flowers. A child bowling a hoop, and acres of grass stretching away.

"It is very nice," she whispered to Raymond.

He smiled back at her.

The car shot into Park Lane and a moment later they drew up at the huge white edifice which was the Norchester.

Larry shepherded her through the vestibule and up a short flight of stairs. Raymond followed behind. "We're going to talk to the reporters now," Larry was saying. He managed to add in a whisper: "Don't worry. You'll be all right!"

Raymond caught up with her.

"It won't take long, Miss Linden. I hope you don't mind."

She shook her head.

"She's used to it," said Larry quickly.

Inspired by his tone Mitsi braced herself confidently.

When Raymond asked her: "Are you not too tired?" she gave him a dazzling smile.

"They're in here—holding up the bar!" and Larry led the way into a sort of buffet lounge.

She saw a handful of men and women. Some standing, some seated, but all clutching drinks.

As they entered a concerted movement was made towards them.

"This is Miss Mitsi Linden, who's popped over from Paris to brighten London's night life!" Raymond announced. There was a welcoming buzz.

Larry steered her to a chair. Simultaneously Raymond asked her what she would like to drink.

She hesitated for a moment.

"I think you'd better have a brandy," advised Larry. To Raymond: "She's very tired."

In a moment a glass was in one hand, a cigarette in another and people were standing round her all asking questions at once.

Larry stood behind her and she felt the pressure of his hand on her shoulder. Raymond stood on the other side, his attention divided in watching and listening to her and the journalists.

"This is the first time you've been in England, Miss Linden?"

"You speak English quite well? How did you learn it?"

"Where were you appearing before?"

"How long have you been a night-club singer?"

"What made you become a singer?"

"Are you married?"

"What are your views on love?"

"Do you think a woman can manage a husband and a career at the same time?"

Mitsi gulped at her brandy and tried to answer some of the questions as they were fired at her.

She could deal with only a few of them. But Larry answered for her with a glib efficiency and charm. She did manage to reply to the question about her speaking English.

"I do not speak English well. I am very sorry. I do not understand very much you are saying. But I hope to speak it very well soon. Then I would like you to ask me these questions again."

This won her a murmur of sympathy from her inquisitors. But they continued with their questions.

A smartly dressed young woman, furiously smoking a cigarette, snapped at her:

"Who is your favourite dressmaker?"

Mitsi goggled for a moment gulping the remainder of her brandy.

"I have no favourite," answered Mitsi. "I have just bought some new clothes in Paris, but I do not choose only one *couturière*. I think a woman can be so much more—how you say?—individual, if she does not have always the same person to dress her."

"That's interesting," snapped the woman reporter. "Thanks."

Larry whispered hoarsely in her ear:

"That was marvellous, my dear! Splendid!"

Another brandy was put in her hand and the questions continued.

A mannish looking middle-aged woman with a figure like a barrel asked her:

"Have you any beauty hints to give me for the readers of the *Daily Telegram?*"

"It is difficult to think of them now—I always use soap and water."

"Thanks."

"Would you like an Englishman for a husband or a man of your own country?"

An untidy looking individual shot this query at her over his glass of whisky.

Question and answer... Question and answer. Until she thought she would collapse.

She turned to Larry imploringly.

"All right boys and girls, that's the lot for today. Miss Linden's very tired. She's had enough."

Mitsi thanked them. Raymond was at her side and he led her away. Larry followed, answering a few straggling questions as he did so. As he left them he turned, grinning cheerfully.

"Thanks everybody. You've been grand. Give yourselves another drink. I'll be seeing you."

He joined Mitsi and Raymond at the lift and they were shot upwards towards her suite.

As she entered the sitting-room she gasped with pleasure and delight.

"It is so charming! I shall like this very much."

She snuggled down into a soft cushioned chair and pulled off her hat.

Raymond said anxiously:

"I hope you'll be comfortable here—if there's anything I can do...?"

She gave him a smile.

"It'll suit you for a week or two," said Larry. "Then you can make other arrangements, if you like."

"I am sure I shall be very happy here."

Raymond wore an anxious expression on his handsome face.

"I'm afraid they've tired you."

"No, No! Only I get so muddled because I forget my English... I hope they understand?"

He was looking straight at her.

She thought how tall and dark he is. His clothes, too. They look so nice on him. He is so different from Larry. So smooth—so distinguished—so debonair.

While Raymond was thinking how lovely she was. So soft and quiet. Not harsh and strident as he had expected.

Larry caught the steady look Raymond gave her.

He glanced at Mitsi as she gazed up at the other. It seemed to Larry a faint intimate note had been struck by these two. Something in the lift of Raymond's eyebrow, the little smile that played across his mouth. Something in the brightness of Mitsi's eyes.

He said to himself irritably: "You're getting imaginative in your old age! And anyhow I expect they *will* fall for each other sooner or later, so what the hell!"

Raymond was saying: "So *au revoir* for now."

He took her hand.

"Yes. I am going to rest," she said.

"You'll have dinner with us, Bob?" asked Larry.

The other gave him a swift smile. "I'd love to." He turned to Mitsi. "If you won't be too tired?"

"No, no. Please do!"

"Thank you."

With a nod to Larry he went out.

Mitsi leant back in her chair.

Her eyelids dropped drowsily. Larry was saying something. But his words seemed to come from so far away. She longed to go to sleep. He looked at her sympathetically. Her eyes flicked open for a second to talk to him. Then closed again.

He stole quietly out of the room.

In a moment a maid entered and woke Mitsi gently.

"You wish to rest, Madam?"

She nodded sleepily.

In a moment the maid helped her slip off her dress and into the coolness of a *crêpe-de-Chine négligé*. The curtains were drawn for her, making her bedroom dim and restful.

The moment her head touched the pillow she was asleep.

Her last thoughts were of dark eyes gazing deeply into hers.

16

Half an hour before dinner Larry sent the maid to wake her. Presently a message from Mitsi reached him. Would he go up to her room?

She was looking refreshed and very lovely in a black tulle gown. Her fair hair shone almost silver under the softly-shaded lights. Her figure slimly outlined was delightfully moulded and softly curved in the exquisitely cut dress.

"Feeling better now?"

"Yes," she replied smiling. "I like you in your evening clothes," she added.

He wore a double-breasted dinner jacket and a soft turned down collar.

"You look all right yourself."

She knew by his expression he was admiring her, thinking she looked beautiful. Involuntarily she thought: I wonder how the other will like me?

"Bob should be waiting for us."

She started; it was as if he had read her thoughts. But he only smiled at her.

"Shall we go down?"

They found Raymond in the vestibule with drinks, waiting for them.

In the restaurant, as they crossed to their table, many eyes were turned upon them.

Mitsi felt exceedingly proud as she sat down and surveyed her two companions. Raymond's dark head was turned to the *maître d'hôtel*, who stood obsequiously at his elbow. She noted with a little thrill his finely chiselled profile, cleanly cut mouth and chin. Both he and Larry helped her to choose what to eat.

"Thank you. I do not feel very hungry. I think I had so much to eat at lunch. I have no hunger now."

"Perhaps *Lobster a la Norchester* will sharpen your appetite?" suggested Raymond. "It's very good."

"I'm damned hungry!" put in Larry. "If she doesn't want her lobster, I'll eat it for her!"

"The sea air has given you an appetite," she laughed.

She turned to Raymond.

"It was so very beautiful on the steamer today," she told him. "The sun was so warm and the sky was so blue. And the water was blue and very quiet. It was lovely."

He glanced at her sharply.

If anyone else had said that, he thought, I'd have been sick! But somehow with her it was just right. She looks lovely in that dress. I really think she's the most attractive person I've ever seen.

The dance band began to play a sentimental, treacly tune. It was the melodic hit of the moment.

Mitsi's heart melted.

A gentle, dream-like feeling crept over her. The scene was perfect she felt. The unobtrusively lit restaurant, the quiet, unobtrusively efficient waiters, the chatter and little splashes of laughter, the beautifully dressed women and immaculate men around her. Outside the rumble of London's traffic up and down Park Lane seemed to blend with the dance music.

She gave a tremulous little sigh. How happy I am! I have two of the nicest-looking men here with me and I think—yes, I am almost sure—I am the nicest-looking woman in this room.

"Would you like to dance?"

Raymond's voice broke into her thoughts.

She gave a quick glance at Larry, but he was not looking at her. She felt Raymond's hand on hers and she turned to meet his enquiring gaze.

"Thank you," she said.

He rose and took her in his arms.

As they moved together a new feeling she could not quite analyse set her heart beating more quickly. She looked at his hand clasping hers and thought: How nice this is. I like him to hold my hand. I wonder if he realizes that I do?

They danced to a slow fox-trot.

He smiled down into her flower-like face.

Her eyes are the bluest I've ever seen, he thought. They reminded him of the sea at Capri on a summer night, with the violet sky and the stars swinging overhead. So frank, almost childish, they were too.

"I'm longing to hear you sing. When can I?"

"I shall be rehearsing all tomorrow at your club—so you can listen all day if you wish!" She laughed at him. "Though I warn you when I am rehearsing I am not at my best, you understand?"

He nodded his complete understanding.

She couldn't help wishing Larry had heard her say that. He would have been delighted at the professionally casual way she had answered him.

"I hope you will like the club," Raymond was saying. "It's been a terrific rush to get it ready in time... I like its name, don't you?... The Gardenia?"

He watched her face, anxious for her approval. Smiled quickly, with boyish pride at her enthusiastic reply:

"I think it most—how do you say?—smart!"

"It was my idea..."

"So clever of you."

He told her about it.

How it was in a little street just off Piccadilly. Originally it had been a private house, then a restaurant which failed. He had taken it over, and completely converted it. It had been an expensive job.

"I'm sure it will be a great success."

"I'm lucky you're with me," he answered simply. "I know it'll make a grand start with you."

He smiled at her again and both were suddenly silent.

Larry watching them thought: What a pair! The best-looking pair in London!

Then Raymond made a sudden pause as they danced, to wave excitedly over towards the restaurant entrance, where some people were coming in.

Mitsi looked over his shoulder at them.

Two men and two women, the women very beautifully dressed, the men young and tall and immaculate. There was something about these people—so easy and confident.

She suddenly felt small and unimportant. She murmured:

"I am a little tired. We will dance again perhaps a little later. Besides Larry is left all alone."

He nodded sympathetically and steered her across to their table. Said to Larry:

"Jessica Horton's just come in with the Countess Dalvanya—jolly useful woman for the club. Knows everybody in the American and Continental crowd. If you'll excuse me, I'll just go across and get matey."

He turned and looked at Mitsi. His eyes sparkled into hers and she smiled back.

"I won't be long," he said.

"Do you think he guesses anything?" she asked Larry, as Raymond hurried away.

"Nobody ever guesses anything as far as I'm concerned. They know me well enough not to try and guess anything that's my business."

"I'm so glad. He is very nice to me. I hope I shall not disappoint him."

"You *won't!*" he snapped. "Come and dance?"

She danced with him, and when they returned to the table Raymond was installed there once again.

"She's bringing a big party on the first night," he announced triumphantly. "Wealthy American canned goods merchant's daughter married into Hungarian impoverished but impeccably good family. Bought her title and is run after by everybody."

She nodded wisely.

"Charming, charming!" observed Larry.

Raymond laughed and reached for his drink. Mitsi began to feel happy. Larry fooled about, being irresistibly funny. Making amusing remarks about the people at the tables round them. Raymond added his own light-hearted comments. She danced with him, and with Larry again, until suddenly it was twelve o'clock.

He addressed her with a parental air.

"Time for shut-eye. You've got a long, arduous day of rehearsal to-morrow."

She pouted.

"But I am at last waking up! I like this hotel, I am in love with this band, and I find my two gentlemen so charming!"

Bob looked across at her laughing eyes. Lovely lady, he thought.

"Must you go?"

"She's on her way," Larry cut in quickly.

She pulled a little face at him and rose. They escorted her to the lift, when she was swallowed up and shot towards her suite.

Larry looked at Raymond as they returned to the restaurant.

"Nice girl."

"She's marvellous! I'm terribly grateful to you for getting her over here."

Larry muttered something and lit a cigarette.

He gave the other a narrow, speculative look through a cloud of smoke. Bob Raymond was far away, a happy smile upon his lips. He gave a little sigh. Larry grunted, prodded his arm.

"Come on! Let's have a drink."

In her sitting-room Mitsi found the evening newspapers. Larry must have sent them up there as a surprise for her. One of the papers carried her photograph in the gossip column. One paper reproduced a large picture of both her and Raymond, and there were interviews with her.

She could not remember having said a word she saw printed, but it was all very eulogistic and charming. She scrambled into bed and read what they had said about her carefully. Gazed at her picture.

She was clutching the crumpled newspapers to her as she fell asleep.

17

It was the morning of her debut at the Gardenia.

At eight o'clock Mitsi's bedside telephone rang and woke her.

It was Larry.

"How are you feeling?"

"Very well. But not quite awake."

"I'm going to be pretty busy all day, so Bob's taking you out to lunch. He'll call for you. I'll be round to collect you this evening. See, you're rehearsing this afternoon, aren't you? So I'd take the morning off and forget all about the show. Just relax. See?"

"That I shall find very difficult, but I shall try."

"Yes, do. Al Young will see you at the club at two-thirty. 'Bye!"

"Good-bye."

She snuggled down again into the bedclothes. She could not believe that tonight she was to be face to face with the climax of these hectic days of preparation. She could not think of it coherently, believe it was true. She only knew a grave terror which seemed to numb her brain. But this ordeal now so close upon her was almost too big for her to comprehend. She seemed mesmerized. Unable to give way to her fears. Compelled to go through with it no matter how frightened she might be. And there was an inner courage, too, characteristic of her, which she called upon when it seemed her terror would swamp her.

Grimly she determined to do her utmost to succeed.

She rang the bell, and when the maid appeared ordered breakfast in bed in her most autocratic voice.

Then the telephone rang again.

"Good morning, Mitsi."

She thought the way he said her name was delightful.

"Bob?" She said it shyly.

"You know my name sounds so much nicer when you say it!"

She laughed huskily. He was charmed.

"Larry tells me he's going to be a hard-working journalist all day. So I suggested we might lunch together before your rehearsal?"

"That is so nice of you."

"When shall I call for you?"

"I am almost dressed," she lied. "I have my hat to put on and I will be ready. Perhaps at half-past ten?"

She pulled her knees up in her excitement, nearly having disastrous results with the breakfast-tray which began to slide on to the carpet. She saved it just in time.

"You're going to take a long time putting on your hat! I've practically arrived at the hotel now. Shall I come up and wait for you?"

"You must not do that at all," she cried in alarm. "At half-past ten you may."

"See you then." He rang off.

She sank down into the pillows again and gazed dreamily at the ceiling.

Then she remembered her breakfast tray. She poured herself out another cup of coffee, drank it down quickly. She bounded out of bed and raced through to the bathroom, turned the bath on. While it was running she went through her wardrobe and decided with puckered brow to wear her black suit.

The bath only a quarter full, she immersed herself in it, powdered herself until the perfume must have asphyxiated anybody passing outside her suite, and threw her clothes on.

Dressed, she surveyed herself. Black suits me I think, she said to herself. The black hat, without the veil I think.

She looked slim and lovely in the severe perfectly tailored suit. She went out of the room and rang for the lift. It was five-and-twenty to eleven.

He was waiting for her in the lounge.

"Every time I see you you manage to look nicer."

"Thank you."

He led the way to his car parked outside. There was no chauffeur today. He helped her in and took the wheel. Soon they were driving through the traffic towards the country. They cut across Westminster Bridge and he pointed out the Houses of Parliament and as they drove through the drab streets of Waterloo

Bridge and Lambeth she remembered her life in wandering round France and Italy with her mother, when they lived poorly, shabbily. She thought: if he knew what I am really—he would hate me perhaps.

He talked pleasantly all the time. When they left London behind them and drove out into the woods of Surrey, she felt happy once more.

The little hotel at which they had lunch was a beautiful old place which had originally been a country house. They sat at a table by french windows which opened out on to gardens and faced a view of richly wooded hills.

"England is very beautiful. It is smaller—I mean the scenery, the beauty—smaller than France. Here it is all so very friendly."

He looked at her wondering again whether she really meant what she was saying, or whether she was only playing a game. Trying to impress him. She says the most extraordinary things for a woman in her profession, and yet I think she's sincere, he said to himself.

"I've spent some wonderful times in France. I can't say I know Paris well, but I know Cannes and Nice and Brittany. Used to go there almost every summer," he said.

She had to be in London soon after lunch.

Bob drove swiftly and expertly. He suddenly felt contented and quiet with this girl. Something he had never known before with any woman.

18

She rehearsed with Al Young for two hours.

Al was thin, pale-faced, and wore loud suits with heavily padded shoulders. He had a nasal voice, was a brilliant songwriter and played the piano quite marvellously.

Larry had first thought of taking him into his confidence about Mitsi. Then decided to wait until the first rehearsal before doing so.

He was glad he had kept his mouth shut.

To his surprise Al thought Mitsi was the greatest thing since Sadie Harris. He had been completely carried away by her throatily lovely voice as she sang "Orchids in Paris" to his accompaniment, at that first rehearsal.

Bob Raymond, who had heard her later that day, was tremendously impressed. Here he felt confident was someone who would draw them in their hundreds to the Gardenia, his club on which he had banked so much. This lovely little person with her beautiful, sad voice made him long for something he had never wanted before. Something almost indefinable, of which he knew now, dumbly felt, was reaching out to him through her song.

At this final rehearsal Al succeeded in convincing her that "Orchids in Paris" would be more attractive played in fox-trot tempo. It had been written as a sort of waltz ballad.

"It's lovely, all right, but honest you'll ruin it singing it straight!" insisted Al. "It's grand like this. Listen again, will you?"

He beat out the tune with expert rhythm.

She agreed. Perhaps after all it would be better that way.

She went through the routine for the last time before the evening show. Her act consisted of five numbers: opening with a song Al had written for her, then "Orchids in Paris." Two more of Al's, and finally Gershwin's "The Man I Love."

Waiters were hurrying about in their shirt-sleeves as she sang. Electricians fiddled with spot lights and the microphone which she had learned to master so that it enhanced the quality of her voice to a remarkable degree. The dance orchestra lounged about smoking and chatting, waiting for her to finish so they could also rehearse.

Presently she was through and went back to her hotel to rest. She was feeling very jittery but she managed to sleep.

It was eight o'clock when the telephone shrilled her awake. Drowsily she lifted the receiver.

"How are you feeling? Jumpy?"

It was Larry. He asked the question casually, but she could detect the concern in his voice.

"I feel quite all right."

"Good! Take it easy. I'll be round to give you some food in about an hour's time, then we'll wander along to the club and you can get used to the atmosphere till your show at midnight. How's that?"

"Yes."

"You're wearing the white dress, aren't you? The new one. Julia told me you'll look *most* expensive in it!" he chuckled.

She murmured something and he rang off cheerfully.

She lay back for a few moments to try and collect herself. Then she turned on the bath, loaded it with bath salts and lay back in the warm water feeling soothed already. Everything seemed secure here. She did not want to move, to go out and face a crowd of strange, critical people and sing to them. It was strange how she became attached to places—Julia's apartment in Paris and now even this hotel—a place which no one could call "home"—but it appealed to her with all the security of a home at this moment.

She began to hum Max Cooper's song the way Al wanted it to go.

Suddenly she knew with an inner conviction that it was not quite right that way. Then it occurred to her how effective it might be if she sang it first as it was written and then gradually changed into the other tempo.

Excited with this new idea she hurried out of the bath, and slipping on a dressing-gown she ran to the phone.

She got Al Young at his flat. Told him her idea. He was impressed.

"Yes, there's something to it. Can I come round and go over it with you?"

(Mitsi had had a baby piano installed in her sitting-room so that she could practise alone.)

"I'll be ready in half an hour."

"Okay."

She continued leisurely with her dressing. She did not call the maid, preferring to be alone.

She began to make up. She had quickly acquired the knack of applying creams, lotions, powders and mascaras. When she had finished she gazed with pleasurable satisfaction at the radiant face that stared back at her from the mirror. Her hair shimmered, freshly fixed the day before.

Her cheeks were smooth and fresh. Her eyes sparkled starrily. Her mouth was a crimson petal.

From the wardrobe she took the white gown she was to wear. It was a magnificent sequin model, truly Parisian, very expensive looking. She slipped it over her head. It shimmered over her shoulders.

She pushed her slender arms through diamanté straps. It clung to her, a glistening sheath. A deep V revealed her beautifully modelled, almost childish back. She moved across the room watching herself through the mirror, noting how the long skirt clung heavily to her slim, long legs.

"I wonder if he will like me in this?" she thought. She was thinking of Bob. I think I look sophisticated in this dress. Perhaps that is why Julia knew I should wear it tonight. It makes me feel braver, more confident. I do not look real. I look like a woman that has been artificially created.

The telephone pealed.

"A Mr. Al Young is waiting downstairs."

He stared at her as if overcome as he entered the room.

"You'll certainly knock 'em back in that!" he murmured.

She smiled and he followed her to the piano.

He sat down and rippled the keys.

"Straight first, then put on the heat? Eh?"

He began playing and she sang "Orchids in Paris" through as Cooper had written it.

She had a sudden homesickness for the apartment in Paris. With Julia and Max Cooper at the piano, and Leo sitting looking on passing sarcastic remarks. Everything so friendly. She remembered again the shabby, comfortable, beautiful room. The yellow flowers on the hearth. Leo's pipes.

Al swung into the faster rhythmic tempo.

Now she saw another picture. A man's dark head bent over a wine list. Immaculate evening dress, a gardenia in his button-hole.

"I think it's a great idea," agreed Al. "We'll do it that way."

"I am glad. I found the idea in the bath!"

He nodded approvingly.

"I get ideas there, too! Dunno why."

She turned to him urgently.

"I feel frightened—!"

He patted her elbow sympathetically.

"Don't you worry," he reassured her. "They'll be full of drink! And *that* makes 'em very responsive!"

He rose.

"I'll be seein' you!"

As she closed the door after him there was a knock and a page appeared bearing an enormous basket of flowers which he set before her on the floor and disappeared with a cheery grin. She buried her face in the masses of roses of every conceivable colour that overflowed the green wicker basket with a huge handle. They were magnificent.

She looked for a label, but could find nothing. Then she found a small envelope buried deep among the flowers. She opened it and found a visiting-card: "All my thoughts and best wishes for your success tonight. Bob."

She looked at it for a long time then smiled secretly and put it away in her evening bag.

A moment later two telegrams arrived. Then another. Then more, until she had an array of them. From Julia, from Leo, from Max Cooper—wishing her success for them both. From John Foster and from Sadie Harris.

Then Larry came in.

He handed her a long slim box with a nonchalance that was rather overdone.

"Thought maybe you'd like to wear these."

She opened the box and found a magnificent spray of tawny yellow orchids.

"Like 'em?"

"They are beautiful! I love them. It is a thing that I thought I should never in my life do. Wear orchids! They are the first I have ever had! They look very wise, a little cruel too, but very chic."

She smiled at him and pinned them on her diamanté shoulder strap.

"Do you like my dress?"

He scrutinized her critically.

"Hmmmm… You look very sophisticated and worldly wise. Not sure I like it personally, but I have no doubt it'll create the desired effect on the Gardenia patrons!"

He gave her a kindly, semi-sardonic smile. Then he spotted the basket of flowers.

"Who on earth sent you those?"

"Bob!"

"Oh! The perfect employer!"

"I think it is so very kind that everybody has remembered me," she said hastily. "Look at all these telegrams I have received tonight?"

"You see how confident everybody is of you," he said. With a wry smile he glanced from her to Bob Raymond's flowers again.

They had a quiet dinner and sat long over coffee. His quiet assurance calmed her and soothed her nerves. She arrived at the club with him feeling confident, all conquering.

* * * *

The lights dimmed.

The chatter and laughter at the crowded tables hushed expectantly. A match flickered here and there, cigar-ends made little red blobs, cigarettes winked like so many fireflies.

She stepped through the door behind the dance-band platform. In front of the orchestra a white grand piano glimmered. As she moved forward towards it, a spotlight blazed on it circling it with amber.

Al sat at the keyboard, glancing off in her direction. He was smiling a fixed smile.

She saw he was deathly pale, little beads of perspiration showed on his forehead.

She almost broke into a laugh. It seemed so incongruous he should feel so terrified, while she...she couldn't tell how she felt. She was an automaton.

She made out the packed people in front of her; white blurs of faces, glimmering shirt-fronts and the creamy arms and shoulders of the women.

The silver and white walls and ceilings reflected the light of the spotlamp, and seemed to make a mysterious haze over the gloom of the darkness out there where her audience waited.

She stepped into the circle and blinked.

There was a clatter of polite applause. Whispered comments, a subdued murmur greeted her. She was smiling. She turned quickly to Al. He muttered something. She didn't hear what it was. She stood against the piano, smiling easily now, wondering at the coolness of her brain. Marvelling that she didn't turn tail and bolt. A queer indifference enveloped her. Though it failed to quell the racing of her blood, the thumping of her heart.

Al's hands fluttered across the keyboard. He glanced up at her, muttered beneath his breath: "Here we go, Baby!"

She opened her mouth and nothing happened.

19

Al glanced at her panic-stricken. Quickly he went back over the introduction. There was an embarrassed coughing from the audience and one or two snickers of laughter.

Larry had come out of her dressing-room and stood taut as a bowstring.

She's failed! he told himself. She's let me down with a wallop! He shrugged. Ah, well. It wasn't her fault, poor kid. He'd asked too much of her. He wondered what Bob Raymond was feeling about it. It was going to be pretty grim for him. A wry little smile flitted across his face as he realized that he, himself, was going to have quite a job talking himself out of the spot he'd got poor old Bob into.

And then, suddenly, some voice was croaking the words of *"J'attendrai."*

It was someone in the audience, singing in French. Larry moved forward quickly to see who it was. He spotted a grey-haired, somewhat dissipated-looking man, who had stood up and was beating time with his fork as he sang.

With amused smiles, the people round him began to join in:

> *"J'attendrai,*
> *Le jour et la nuit…"*

"A drunk!" Larry muttered to himself as he stared at the grey-haired man. He caught, from the tail of his eye, the agonized blur that was Bob Raymond's face at the back of the Club. Then, suddenly, Al was picking out the tune on the piano and urging Mitsi to sing it.

"Sing! For Pete's sake, sing!"

He pounded *"J'attendrai"* at her.

"Go on!" he implored. "Sing it!"

Automatically she began to murmur the words. The overwhelming stage-fright that had paralysed her voice began to slip away. Once again that feeling that was almost indifference took command. Her voice became louder, and with at least half of her audience backing her up she began to sing as she had never sung before.

"J'attendrai toujours, Temps retour, J'attendrai."

Al was playing like someone possessed. Now her low, husky voice began to reach out above the thread of melody plucked by his fingers.

Began to reach out above the voices of the people out in front, of the grey-haired man beating time with his fork. It reached out across the faces which seemed like flowers in the gloom, across to where Bob Raymond was standing, tense and taut.

Mitsi remembered afterwards that it was of Larry she had thought during those terrifying moments. And then, when she had found her voice, it was Bob she remembered.

"J'attendrai, Temps retour!"

The applause broke over her in a great wave.

Al was crouched over the keyboard, staring up at her, almost weeping with joy.

The applause rolled on.

Al, laughing uncontrollably, started to play "Orchids in Paris." Her voice carried the melody without a tremor. Its rhythm was smooth and effortless, quiet and lovely. Now there was complete silence. A hush over the tables crowded so close to each other. Al's face became serious once more as the air filled with the soft over-tones of sadness.

Her voice died, then as the applause started Al plunged into his rhythmic arrangement of the tune. Mitsi kept her body quite still. Al sat, like some crow carved from stone, only his long arms swinging up and down the keys as he beat out the rhythm.

Simultaneously, the spotlight began to turn, throwing all the colours of the rainbow upon them. The effect was sensational. The motionless figures, one white and shimmering and straight, the other black, crouched over the white piano, and the changing colours. The throbbing melody, the infectious lilt of that throatily alluring voice.

As the last chord faded, a storm of clapping broke out. There was a frenzied babble of excited talk. "Orchids in Paris" was a smash!

Mitsi bowed, smiled. Bowed, smiled.

She turned to Al, her eyes shining.

"Okay?" he grinned at her, then turned to grin at the clamouring audience.

She sang two more songs.

At the end of which Bob Raymond was wondering how the roof managed to stay on. He would never have believed the blasé sophisticated crowd could be so affected.

Larry had gone back to her dressing-room, where he sat hunched, the door opened wide, seeking to judge the applause—its sincerity and spontaneity—with an expert ear. In the room with him, wearing an equally anxious expression, was Hattie, Mitsi's dresser. She was a tubby little Cockney whom Larry had engaged to watch over Mitsi and mother her generally.

Larry turned to her.

"What d'you think of it? All right?"

"It's *luverly*, dearie! *Luverly!*"

Larry's expression relaxed.

She'd clicked! In spite of that disastrous start she'd got away with it. Mentally Larry blessed the grey-haired little drunk who'd started her off with *J'Attendrai.*

Another wave of applause. Excited voices screaming: "Encore! Encore!"

Hattie beamed expansively.

"Hear that, dearie! *Luverly!* Bless 'er!"

He sighed.

He'd done it. Dragged a nobody, a lost, frightened kid out of nowhere and boosted her into fame overnight!

He recalled her wan, insignificant face, her mousey hair, shabby clothes. Smiled to himself.

And tonight! Applauded by a mob of London's top socialites and celebrities. He wondered what they'd feel if they knew they were cheering the crazy, impulsive idea of a kind-hearted newspaperman!

The spotlight had changed to a pale, shimmering blue.

The applause had died once more—and the well-known opening bars of Gershwin's "The Man I Love" stole among the listeners.

Bob Raymond thought: It's impossible that this curiously sophisticated, yet sometimes childish, almost naïve creature could sing this with such a wealth of passion and sadness.

She seemed so untouched. Though for all he knew she may have had a score of lovers. But he couldn't believe that, somehow. In spite of the veil of mystery and allure about her, there was an ingenuous something which contradicted it all. She was extraordinarily intriguing!

Al gave a sign to the orchestra leader behind.

"The Man I Love" welled, with the added depth of the dance-band. Mitsi's voice lifted a fraction. Then the band stopped. She sang the last phrase but one in a husky whisper:

"I'm waiting for…"

Her whisper was caught up as the music rose…

"The Man I Lo—ov—e!"

It was over.

The lights came up, the applause beat and crackled again and again. Bows. Smiles. Bows. Smiles. A broken, shaky little:

"Thank you. Thank you so much—"

A cool, detached Larry awaited her, seemingly quite unimpressed. Hattie was murmuring round her. Al was saying: "Marvellous!" every other second. As if from a distant dream came into the dressing-room the murmur of the dance-orchestra as it started to play a popular fox-trot.

Suddenly Bob burst in. His face was radiant. His white tie askew. His hair rumpled.

"My God, what a triumph! *What a triumph!*"

"*Marvellous*!" Al said again.

She saw Larry smiling happily. He said, hiding the shakiness of his voice with a little gruffness:

"How d'you feel?"

For answer, she suddenly flung her arms around his neck and burst into tears.

20

"Have you seen the papers?"

It was Bob's voice over the telephone.

"No. I am not awake yet!"

Mitsi looked at her bedside clock. It was nearly midday.

Bob was saying:

"You've got smashing write-ups from everybody. Oh, my dear, I am so pleased about it all!"

His voice almost sang with excitement.

"I will have them all sent up with my breakfast," she laughed.

"I was hoping we could read them together."

The disappointment in his voice touched her.

"I will dress quickly and have breakfast with you downstairs! Then we can read all about ourselves together."

Half an hour later she was sitting beside him in the lounge, her breakfast-table strewn with newspapers.

The gossip-columns and entertainment pages had given the opening night of the Gardenia plenty of space.

Mitsi found herself described with adjectives ranging from "gorgeous" to "orchidacious." Three newspapers dubbed her "the magnificent Mitsi." One or two newspapers carried photographs of her. She was famous all right!

From being a mere nobody she had become a name upon thousands of people's lips.

Bob was like some excited schoolboy.

"I am glad for you that it is such a success," she said to him.

He took her hand and pressed it warmly. "And I owe it all to you!"

She shook her head.

"No, no! It is a delightful club. So smart—so attractive. People will always want to go there whether I am there or not."

He smiled at her. "Well, all I can say is—don't you ever leave me!"

Her eyes were very bright as she looked at him. He is such an exciting person, she thought. So nice and he says such very charming things.

A group of people passed through the big swing doors into the lounge. There were two men and two women. One the bronze-haired woman to whom Bob had spoken that night in the restaurant as they had danced together. Countess somebody or other. Mitsi tried to recall her name, but couldn't. The other woman was tall, fair and very lovely.

It was she who saw Bob first and she came over quickly to him.

He glanced up at her with surprise.

"Carol! Good heavens, I thought you were still in New York!" He stood up and gave her an intimate smile.

"I got back yesterday. Almost in time to come to the opening of your quite crazy club. But I was very tired and went to bed early. I'm so glad it's been such a success."

Her voice was very cool and assured.

Mitsi saw she had a delicately chiselled nose. Her head was almost on a level with his as she smiled secretly at him. Mitsi felt these two knew each other very well.

He turned, as if only just remembering her.

"This is Miss Linden." He introduced them. "Miss Lewis."

Carol Lewis looked down at Mitsi and smiled distantly as if not in the least interested. Mitsi felt very small and shy.

"We've just been getting excited over the newspapers," he explained, indicating the untidy mass. "Miss Linden's made a great success."

"I'm so glad. Countess Dalvanya was there. She enjoyed it immensely. You know her, don't you?"

"Slightly."

At that moment the other woman joined them, the two men accompanying her.

"Hello there! I think your club's the swellest place both sides of the Atlantic!" she gurgled at Bob.

"Thank you."

"And as for you, my dear," turning to Mitsi, "you're grand! Absolutely grand! Can't think where I've heard you before—maybe Paris? Well your voice, the way you sing certainly reminds me of somebody or something."

She laughed frankly at her.

Mitsi, though embarrassed at all this attention showered upon her, felt a strong wave of gratitude to this little American woman with her generous praise. So warm and kind and friendly. Involuntarily she contrasted her with the tall Englishwoman.

The men were introduced, and Carol turned away with Bob, talking to him at a little distance from the others.

The Countess sat down and patted a chair next to her for Mitsi to sit beside her.

"Have a drink, my dear." To one of the men:

"Lionel, what about an Old Fashioned? I always feel they put you right with the world about this time o' day. You'll have one too, won't you my dear?"

Mitsi nodded automatically. The other went on:

"Of course! Now, my dear I know! Sadie Harris! That's who you reminded me of. Sadie's a great friend of mine. Ever since she left the States and got married, and though we somehow drifted away from each other we are still great pals. I always go to see her in Paris. She's American, too, you know. Of course there's absolutely nothing about you really that's like her, but still you remind me of her. Don't you think so, Lionel? Jack?"

The two men muttered a reply.

"I met her in Paris," Mitsi managed to put in. "I heard her sing. I thought she was very beautiful. You have paid me a great compliment."

"Such a cute accent the child's got! Now, if Paul—that's my husband—had an accent like that I guess we'd get along better together. He's a Slav, you know, or something—so temperamental! All the same he's the sweetest thing. Isn't he Jack?"

"Yes, Louise."

The drinks arrived.

"Now this is an all-American cocktail and it's the best yet!"

She handed a glass to Mitsi, who sipped it and smiled at her companions. She glanced over to where Bob was standing in apparently earnest conversation with Carol. The other followed her glance.

"Just look at those two!" She laughed lightly. Then to Mitsi:

"They were engaged once, you know. She's just come back from the States—they've both been trying to forget each other or something. I guess now they are finding out if they have forgotten or not!"

Mitsi forced an answering laugh to her lips. She felt suddenly cold. The excitement in her blood died away. Everything seemed flat.

"Would you care to join us for lunch, my dear? Lionel is staying here, you know, and we are all feeding with him. I know he's been simply dying to ask you, but hasn't been able to put the words together!"

Mitsi smiled at her and at her companion. She hesitated. Earlier on Bob had murmured something about lunching with him. And now with Carol Lewis monopolizing him it seemed unlikely he would remember it.

"I am not sure yet. I have to wait for a telephone call about luncheon." She made up the excuse quickly. "If I am free I should very much like to join you."

If Bob had forgotten she would not have made it awkward for him.

At that moment he turned and came across to them quickly, Carol Lewis following.

"Forgive us muttering to each other like that," he apologized. The others laughed understandingly. He turned to Mitsi.

"What about lunch?"

"I am waiting for a telephone call from Larry."

He gave her a quick look.

"Oh, I see."

The Countess rose.

"I'll see you again my dear, I hope," she said to Mitsi. "Can I phone you here?"

"Please do!"

She moved away towards the restaurant, the two men following her. Carol turned to Bob.

"Don't forget to telephone me then, darling. I'll come along probably tomorrow night. Good-bye Miss Linden—so looking forward to seeing you!"

And with a cold smile she followed the others.

Bob smiled brightly, if uncomfortably, at Mitsi.

"What's this about Larry phoning? You know you're lunching with me."

"Countess Dalvanya asked me to lunch and I had to make an excuse," she said simply, "in case you had forgotten."

He looked at her a little puzzled.

She returned his gaze frankly, trying to fathom what he was thinking. Suddenly he laughed.

"As if I *could* forget! Run along now and get your hat. We'll drive out into the country, shall we?"

"Yes." She felt a sudden desire to get away from her surroundings.

As she was shot upwards in the lift she wondered: Why do I feel so awkward with some people? I am prettier than she is but she is so cold. The Countess is so kind. She likes me. But the other does not. She resents my being with Bob.

He was sitting in the car, staring moodily in front of him when she joined him a few minutes later. When he saw her he gave her a warm smile.

She knew somehow he was glad she was there.

21

"You're such a restful person," he told her as they steered out of the traffic on to the Watford By-pass.

Neither of them spoke much until they found themselves with lunch spread before them in the little coffee room of an old-fashioned inn. The french windows opened on to a sunny garden.

"Carol Lewis and I were engaged once, and then we broke it up. She's terribly jealous, and I'm not a very good person to be in love with really. Can't concentrate very well."

He smiled at her.

He went on: "I like being in love, in fact I seem to have the reputation of never being out of it! But I just don't think I've ever been *really* in love. There's something about Carol—I don't know—let's not talk about it."

He crumbled his roll in his fingers.

"You were the one who spoke of it."

"I know. I'm a fool. I'd got so settled and happy about this club and then she comes along and interrupts everything. Makes me irritable."

"Are you now in love with her?"

He looked up and suddenly saw the expression in her eyes.

"You funny little person. Definitely not."

His hand reached out across the table and took hold of hers. She looked at them clasped across the white cloth, and again felt the surprise and excitement run through her that she felt every time he touched her.

He gazed at her tenderly. Then laughed softly.

"To think you thought when I'd already arranged to lunch with you I'd break it off for her! It'd need a Helen of Troy to make me break a lunch date with you my dear!"

He was suddenly serious.

"Haven't you realized by now I like being with you and taking you out?" he asked her.

"It is kind of you to say this."

Something that had been tense and repressive seemed to go out of the air.

They felt happy and carefree once more.

After lunch they went out into the garden of the inn, with green smooth lawns, and borders of chrysanthemums, a green painted garden seat. They sat in the sun and looked at each other. He leant back and threw his arm across the back of the seat.

"You are so lovely to look at."

"You say so many nice things to me. I hope that you believe all that you say."

"I do."

She is lovely, he thought. So quiet and unexpected, so different from Carol and the others like her. She is variety for every moment I spend with her.

"I am expecting to meet Sam Levinsky very soon," she said. "He is to compose me songs. He is a brilliant song-writer. Larry is to arrange it. He does everything. Larry is very—how do you say?—trustworthy man, I think?"

He laughed. "Trust Larry with anything anywhere."

She looked at him. She thought: I think perhaps you are not trustworthy. One could not trust you unless one were always with you. You would be unfaithful. You look so very youthful now, with your hair ruffled by the light breeze. You look human, real, which you do not always look.

Bob looked at his flat, gold wrist-watch and whistled.

"We must leave this lovely peace and go back to the mad rush of town and the eking out of one's existence! Come on."

He pulled her up and for a moment held her close to him. Then he released her and led her towards the car.

They were very silent on the way back. Town once more seemed too near to both of them. The country was an escape from everything—escape from themselves. They were real and individual—just two people when they were together. But at the hotel, at the club, there were so many others to spoil things, to interfere, to interrupt this intimate bond which drew them together.

Suddenly she felt she needed Larry.

He was so uncomplicated. He was so much associated with the happy things in her life from the day he had befriended her at Le Bourget.

She felt safe and friendly with him.

She had never been so ecstatically happy with him as she was with Bob. But she was always more at ease, more confident that she was with a friend. Larry is like a rock in my life, she thought.

When she arrived at the Norchester, and after Bob had left her, Larry telephoned her from the *Courier* office. Told her he would be able to accompany her to the club that evening, if she felt she still needed his moral support to back her for her show.

She was happy he was going to be with her.

"I have wanted you to speak to all day."

His chuckle came over the wire.

"What've you been doing? You didn't stay in all day, did you?"

"I went into the country and had lunch with Bob."

There was a tiny pause. Then: "I'll bet that's the first time a girl has ever wanted to speak to me when she's been out with him!" He chuckled again. "Don't you like him?"

"I like him so much—but with you it is different—because you are my friend."

Pause, while he thought that one out.

"Well, you'll have the pleasure of my company at ten-fifteen this evening! Can't make it before—got masses of work to get through here."

She rested, after arranging to have dinner sent to her suite. This new life was not agreeing with her, she decided. I'm too quiet a person. I was never made for a life like this. This life does not make me happy.

Her thoughts whirled round and round, until finally she fell asleep.

She was awakened by the sounds of dinner being laid in the small sitting-room. The scent of Bob's roses met her as she went in. They were heady and strong.

She noticed they were already drooping.

She dined leisurely, enjoying the quiet and peaceful solitude of her room. She dressed and prepared herself for the show.

Presently it was time for Larry's arrival. She remembered he was coming from a very hard day's work to take her to her job. She rang and ordered drinks to be sent up.

He arrived a little late and cheerfully apologetic. He glanced gratefully at the whisky bottle and syphon that stood on the table and poured himself out a drink.

"Thoughtful person."

He is nice-looking, she thought. *Kind* looking, very masculine. I don't think he really likes women, but he is sorry for me. Still treats me as a child, that's why he is kind to me.

They made their way downstairs and the commissionaire hailed a taxi for them. Larry lay back in the cab all the way to the club. His eyes were closed, and she could see the tired lines round his mouth. He shouldn't do it, she thought. I must tell him that I can come here alone now. It is not necessary for him to come too.

A spray of magnificent gardenias lay on her dressing-table. There was no inscription on them. Larry picked them up and smelt them.

"Bob?"

Hattie helped her to pin them on to her shoulder. The perfume was beautiful.

Then the door opened and a waiter came in laden with bouquets and baskets and sprays of flowers of all descriptions. Hattie beamed with excited pleasure—they might have been for her.

"I've been keeping them alive downstairs," the waiter said. "Most arrived earlier on and I thought they'd die if I left them 'ere."

Mitsi was overwhelmed by such magnificence.

"Whatever shall I do with them all?"

"Take some back to your hotel, leave the rest here to decorate the club. Shows what your public feel about you!"

Larry grinned at her somewhat sardonically.

Secretly he was elated. This was a sure sign of her triumph. That she had made a hit.

22

The days that followed her triumphant opening at the Gardenia were very full.

Rehearsals—she was eager to consolidate her success by improving her technique, by learning all the little tricks which helped her put her songs over.

She listened—in the privacy of her own room—to all the records of past and present stars. Lucienne Boyer, Hildegarde, Grace Hayes, and of course, Sadie Harris. Sadie she worshipped. Did all she could to model herself on her lines.

Al was a fervent admirer of Sadie's too. He had every record she'd ever made. He'd seen her in New York countless times. Knew her every trick and gesture. Mitsi found him very useful. Without his in any way realizing it, she contrived to pump him about her. For his own part Al was only too glad to talk about Sadie, and was delighted Mitsi was ready to listen. And learn.

Experience had taught him most stars thought they knew everything, and regarded their contemporaries as "hams," and the old favourites as "has-beens."

Mitsi was something unique, refreshing in his life. He thought she was the grandest person he'd ever met.

Her post-bag was enormous. Letters from would-be managers and agents. From press-agents, wanting to devise publicity stunts for her ("Make you ride through the streets on an elephant!" surmised Larry cynically.) There were those intriguing little bundles of press-cuttings which seemed to overflow all over her dressing-room. There were journalists wanting interviews. Song-publishers begging her to sing their hits. Gramophone recordings to arrange, broadcasts to fix up. And so on.

She enjoyed it all enormously.

Even Larry's cynicism, as he expertly rejected or considered the various letters—weeding the wheat from the chaff—could not damp her excitement over all the notice that was being taken of her.

Only the begging-letters depressed her.

She would have paid away most of her salary. Here again Larry managed to persuade her something like a mere two per cent of the letters were sincere.

It was during all this excitement that John Foster telephoned her. He was in London and might he call on her?

She invited him for dinner at the hotel and decided to take him on to the club afterwards to hear her sing. She knew that she had vastly improved since their meeting at Sadie Harris's. She now had self-confidence, and a certain amount of acquired showmanship, and she wanted him to be quite sure about her voice and capabilities, before introducing her to Levinsky.

He came, tall and friendly, with his drawl, just as she remembered him.

"Got dozens of messages from Sadie and Julia for you! And Leo. Just can't remember what they all are! Guess they weren't important any of them except to let you know they've been checking up on all the time since you left, and send their love."

"How are they all? Is Julia well? Leo? And Sadie? Some people over here say I sing like her."

"Is that so?"

"I want you to come along to the club this evening after dinner. It is so nice there. Perhaps you would care to bring someone with you? It is dull sitting alone."

"But won't I go along with you?"

"Of course. But I shall be singing for a little while."

"Then I guess I'll still come along with you. It isn't everybody that's complimented by escorting you any place. Besides about the only woman I know in this burg is Louise Taylor—she's Countess Dalvanya or something nowadays."

"She is nice. I have met her."

"What's she look like as a countess? Used to be a great toast at baseball matches at Yale, but I just can't imagine Louise having any dignity at all!"

"That is her friend over there. She is often having meals with him here. He is also an American."

Foster looked across the dining-room towards the table she had pointed to and where sat the man to whom she had been introduced as Lionel.

"Don't know him from Adam."

Foster turned to her.

"Guess you've changed a heap since I saw you first in Paris. I thought you were just a quaint sort of kid then. Couldn't believe you were one of these song-birds!" He laughed frankly. "Now I guess I could believe anything you wanted to tell me. Gee! You're so slick looking."

He glanced admiringly at her slim fairness.

Presently she said tentatively:

"Sadie was so kind as to say she might introduce me to Levinsky... he has come over with you?"

He gave her a look. He'd had instructions on how to "handle" Levinsky from Sadie (who'd had her instructions from Larry). He realized Mitsi knew nothing of the machinations at work to bring her and the song-writer together for her benefit.

"Why sure! It's all set. That's what I wanted to see you about too. I'll get him along tonight."

"No—please. I would rather *you* first saw me."

He nodded without saying anything. He knew what he had to do.

After they had dined he made an excuse to leave her and telephoned Levinsky at his hotel.

"Well! Well! So it's you is it? What can I do you for?" Levinsky bawled across the wire.

"First cut those corny cracks of yours," Foster told him. Then casually:

"Just thought you might like to come along with me to a new club that's opened called the Gardenia. Supposed to be the smartest dump in town."

"I've got a coupla lads up here now. If I can get rid of them, maybe I'll come along. But I don't feel like listening to any of the acts. I've heard enough of them to last me for years with jokes I can tell my grandmother."

Foster smiled to himself.

"We can walk out before the show comes on."

"Oke. Where'll I pick you up?"

"I'm at the Norchester this minute. If you'd like to come along here—"

"Can't! What about meeting you at this club? Where d'you say it is?"

Foster thought rapidly.

"Just off Piccadilly. Tell you what. I'll come and fetch you, Sam. Just after eleven—that'll be after the show's through and we can booze up then."

"Oke! Be seein' yuh."

He went back to Mitsi's sitting-room.

"Piano! Come on honey. We'll practise!"

He grinned at her, and sat down at the instrument. His long thin fingers picked out a lazy tune on the keys.

She dropped down on the divan and watched him playing. They didn't speak for long. When Foster found a piano, he simply played. Most of his conversation was music of the especial kind he played. Like Mitsi he rarely had much to say for himself.

"Do you only play this kind of music?"

"You ought to hear me play Bach—It's rich!" he told her.

"You mean that you play Bach well?"

"I mean we don't speak! He's got different ideas of music from me. Guess I don't like his ideas on rhythm! Quick and sharp and sort of mathematical. I like this kind of soft, careless rhythm and the treacly tunes that go with it! My people used to take me to hear the Philadelphia Philharmonic when I was at college. They wanted me cultured, but I disappointed them a lot when I started a college ragtime band!"

He laughed at her, and plunged into "Alexander's Ragtime Band."

She listened and told herself: This can't be me—Mitsi Linden—sitting here listening to a young American telling me about music and playing the piano to me. This can't be me, who should have gone into a drapery store in Paris.

"When does your act come on?"

"At midnight."

"Would you mind if I left you just after eleven to meet a pal of mine? Thought I might bring him along back with me. He's having a party now, and he wants to see me. Would you mind very much?"

"Please do that."

Shortly after that they left for the club. On their arrival, she looked round for Bob, but couldn't find him in the restaurant.

"I would like you to meet him," she said to Foster. "He will look after you while I'm singing."

"Sure. I'd like to meet him." He glanced round critically. "Done it pretty well. The interior's great. Pretty near as good as you can get in New York," he laughed. "Funny how we always think England can't be slick like we can."

Mitsi led him upstairs towards Bob's room and tapped gently on the door. She could hear voices inside and wondered who was with him. Presently he came to the door.

"Darling! Can you give me a few moments? I'll come to your room when I'm through with this."

He looked worried and she thought a little guilty.

"Of course. I have a friend here tonight. I wanted you to meet him."

"All right, my dear. I'll come along in about two minutes."

He closed the door gently.

"What's happened?" asked Foster as she turned towards him.

"He's busy. I think he is interviewing somebody. He will come to my room in a few minutes."

They went to her dressing-room, where, as usual, she was greeted with flowers.

"Say, let's go into business! You get these flowers, and I'll have a stand and sell them the next day, huh?"

She started to laugh, then heard footsteps down the passage.

As they passed her door which was slightly ajar, she saw a glimpse of a blue dress and a white ermine coat flit past. Someone—the person who had been with Bob? Then he came along and knocking on the door, entered.

"This is Mr. Raymond—Mr. John Foster," she said hurriedly.

"Glad to know you."

"How d'you do." Bob glanced at him, wondering where Mitsi had found him.

"He is a friend of mine from Paris," she explained. "I have brought him to the club, and I would like him to be looked after when I am singing."

"Let's go and find a table then shall we? We can all sit together perhaps?" Bob said.

He led the way down to the restaurant and found them a table, then he ordered drinks.

They sat down, and Bob turned to Foster. Mitsi felt somehow he was avoiding meeting her eye.

"Are you over here for long?"

"I mostly live over here. I'm supposed to be in the family business, but it doesn't take much doing. When everybody else's job is done, there's not much left for me to do."

"Wish I had your life."

Mitsi wished to goodness they would each break the ice that seemed to hover over them. They were so formal, so careful with each other. Didn't they like each other?

And then she stared straight across the restaurant. Saw the woman in the blue dress and the white coat sitting at a table with the Countess Dalvanya.

It was Carol Lewis.

23

Bob anxiously followed her glance.

He knew he ought to be sitting with Carol, but he wanted to know who the young American was. Obviously somebody with money—but who? And what exactly was he to Mitsi? She had known him in Paris and he knew nothing of that chapter of her life.

Then Foster spotted the Countess.

She saw him, too, suddenly waved furiously at him and came hurrying across the floor, dodging the dancers, to their table.

"Well, John Foster! Why didn't you tell me you were over? Of all the luck in the world—to find you here! Gosh, it's good to see an old Yale baseball face again."

They almost wept in each other's arms, and Bob became even more suspicious of the young American.

The Countess asked them all to join her at her table.

"Say—I'm sorry Louise, but I've got to get along to collect a fellow. Maybe I'll bring him over later. He's coming here afterwards."

He rose, nodded to Mitsi and Tony.

"Promise?"

The Countess walked back across the room with him, and Mitsi and Bob were left alone. He leant across the table towards her.

"Is he the person you're in love with darling?"

"In love—with him? Of course not."

Things seemed to be going wrong tonight. Bob was strange, and distant, and restless, as if his thoughts were elsewhere.

"I only wondered," he said lightly.

"I do not love anybody."

He regarded her for a moment, his expression enigmatic.

"I'm sorry I had to keep you waiting this evening," he said at last. "I had a very difficult interview in my office."

"I thought perhaps it was something like that. You must not say you are sorry to me though. It was all right. We are friends, and things like that must happen sometimes."

"Are we friends? Really?"

He was suddenly earnest, suddenly serious.

"Of course."

"I want us to be. I want—oh, I don't know! I'm all out of gear at the moment. Everything's going wrong. I wish I knew whether you really liked me."

She stared hard at the tablecloth.

"I do. Please always believe that."

She felt sorry for him. He looked unhappy, and different from the man she had always pictured him to be—gay, gallant, and so self-assured.

"Thank you. You know Mitsi, I'm not sure I don't love you. I feel happier with you than with anybody. This all sounds silly. I've said it before, but never really meant it. This time I do."

His dark eyes met hers, and suddenly she smiled.

"I do not know what to say," she said.

"Don't say anything. Just always look like that when you're with me."

"There are so many things I would say, but I cannot."

"Tomorrow—let's go out into the country again. We haven't been out for such ages have we?"

She nodded.

"Tomorrow."

"It always seems to be tomorrow with us. I wonder if it'll ever be today. Everything's such a hell of a mess!"

He dropped his head in his hands.

"But the club is doing well is it not?" she said. "You have nothing to worry about, have you?"

"The club's all right. It's—just complications—that's all. All the blessed worries I've ever had seem to be cropping up now. Anyhow, they're nothing to concern you about. Let's forget it."

She glanced round the room, wondering whether anyone was noticing their earnest conversation. There seemed to be the usual chatter and laughter, and the dancers on the floor successfully hid all the tables from a too prolonged view of each other.

"I'll stay here until your friends come back," he was saying. "Then I'd better make myself sociable to some of the others. If you weren't here, I'd never come near the place now it's established. I'm sick of it all."

"You must not make yourself unhappy because of me. If you wish to go away, then you must not stay here for me. I am all right now. People know me. It is not so difficult. Please be happy."

"I'm only happy here. I'd simply long for town and the club and you if I went away—just as I long to get away when I'm in town!" He laughed shortly. "I always want something I can't get."

She patted his hand. He smiled at her more cheerfully. His conversation became lighter.

Presently he reminded her it was time for her to prepare for her show. Not once had he given a look at the Countess's table. But as she left him, she caught a quick glance in that direction.

Foster brought Levinsky into the club, just at the moment that Mitsi's show was due.

"You rat!" Levinsky whispered hoarsely. "You've timed this nicely. I'm going. I'm not staying here to die of yawning!"

He rose, and the other tried to stop him. His little ruse had failed after all.

Levinsky, seeing the worried expression on his face, sat down again.

"Oke. We'll just laugh at the bits that aren't funny. I guess there'll be something to laugh at anyway—even if it's only an imitation torch-singer—poor little soprano forcing her guts out trying to be another Helen Morgan!"

"Don't laugh. After all, we're Raymond's guests here. He's standing just back of you."

"To hell with him!"

And Sam gulped down his drink and lit a poisonous cigar.

The restaurant was almost in darkness now. Suddenly a white wraith of a girl slipped across in front of the band. Then as the spotlight drenched her, Al began to play. Levinsky shook his head as he heard the opening bars of "Orchids in Paris"; played straight.

Mitsi started to sing and he still shook his head, unimpressed. Then she went into Al's version, and he leant back in his chair and gazed distantly but not distastefully at her.

She sang "*J'attendrai*," then came to "The Man I Love."

Foster turned and looked enquiringly at Levinsky. He stifled a yawn, but said nothing. Foster wondered what he was thinking, but decided to keep quiet.

The orchestra crept in, building up to the climax of Mitsi's show.

Levinsky still gazed distantly before him, glancing every now and again under his bored, lowered lids at her.

When it was over, he turned and remarked:

"Pretty little wench, isn't she? Foreign goods, eh?"

"Yes. French, I believe."

Foster spoke with complete disinterestedness.

"Not laughable—quite. Fairly good for a London joint, huh?"

"Just fair…"

"Don't happen to know the dame, huh?"

Levinsky put the question elaborately casual.

"Sort of. Seem to recall meeting her at Sadie's in Paris."

Levinsky shot up in his chair and eyed Foster.

"You mean this is the girl Sadie spoke to me about? Who's being put over by that newspaper guy?"

Foster nodded.

Levinsky smiled urbanely at him. "Doin' a little trick stuff with me, eh?"

Suddenly he guffawed, slapped Foster heavily on the shoulder.

"What an old trickster you are! And Sadie, too... I see her scheming in this! And that newshawk playing me for a sucker! Bah! I get it—tryin' to sell me this Parisian doll in a big way, huh!"

He guffawed again, then was suddenly serious.

"What about asking her over for some supper?"

He leered at Foster, shooting his cigar from one side of his face to the other.

24

"Somethin' to drink? Or some ham and eggs, lady?"

Levinsky addressed Mitsi as he would any Broadway blonde. To him all women in show business were alike. Feed 'em and make a fuss of them was his motto.

John Foster winced, but dug his foot against Mitsi's under the table, warning her not to worry about the song-writer's eccentricities.

Bob had joined them, sitting next to Mitsi. His mood had changed. Now he was very gracious and casually tender towards her. She knew from the little smile that played about his mouth when he spoke to her that she was making him happy.

Now he rose and left her with the two Americans, sensing Levinsky wanted to "get acquainted" with her. He flashed her his dark and secret smile.

She turned to Levinsky, smiling in her heart.

"So you're French, huh?"

Levinsky glared at her ferociously over a precariously balanced piece of egg on a fork.

She nodded, amused by the vulgar vision opposite her.

"Nice folk—the French. Very musical. I appreciate musical people."

"Yes," murmured Mitsi, feeling that the conversation wasn't going too well.

"Done any new songs lately, Sam?"

Foster threw in the question casually.

"One or two I'm quite pleased with. But I'm mostly concentrating on pictures now. Bigger dough, and you get your name in lights too. Ever made any pictures, Babe?"

He turned to Mitsi.

"No. I have only been in England a few weeks."

"Make any in France?"

"I am a night-club singer. I cannot act."

"You're pretty enough to get by all right." He said suddenly: "So you'd like to sing my numbers—huh? Think you could?"

She looked at him, not knowing whether he was serious or not.

"Sure she could!" chimed in Foster heartily.

"What do you know about it?" Levinsky glared at him.

"Oh, nothing—nothing."

"Well anyhow, I guess it's a sort of an idea, huh? Say, like to dance?"

"Thank you."

She wondered how he danced. He was so little and fat.

The little composer took her in his arms and swept her into a fox-trot. He danced beautifully, and she realized that this man was, after all, a genius of rhythm and melody.

"You know, I like your voice. Reminds me of Sadie Harris."

"She was very kind to me in Paris."

He nodded absently.

"You know, you've chosen a queer profession. Guess there's more sort of unhappiness in a showgirl's life than any other. Why didn't you stay at home and learn shorthand?"

"I have always wanted to do this," she lied.

"Yeah. Glamour and all that. I like a girl who stays home and don't go in for anything exciting. You're a homey sort of a girl to know—guess you don't *look* so homey though."

They finished the dance. He brought her back to the table and Foster. They talked for a few minutes, then he said:

"Well. I'm going along back now. Feel kinda tired."

Foster said he would see her back to the hotel, and drop Levinsky on the way. When they got to Levinsky's hotel, he asked them to come in. Although Mitsi felt like refusing, Foster accepted for her. They went up to his suite.

He poured out drinks for them and then he sat down at the piano and began to play.

Foster looked at her significantly.

"Come over and try this one."

She went over and stood beside Levinsky at the piano.

He was playing from a manuscript. Even had she been able to read music she would have found it difficult to follow the markings and scorings on the sheet. She shook her head, puzzled.

"Okay, Babe! I know it's bad. Still, I'll play it over to you and then we can go through it."

He played the tune—a smart, slick, clever tune that delighted her.

She began to hum it.

"I haven't got the words yet. I do all my own lyrics you know—but I wanted to call it 'Towers in the Sky'—New York you know. Guess I'm feeling homesick. Like it?"

"It is a marvellous tune."

She was still humming it as he played.

"Like to sing it?"

"It would be wonderful!" Suddenly she realized what he meant. "You mean—to sing it before anybody else?"

He nodded vigorously.

"Break it in for me."

"Please—please Mr. Levinsky! Let me do it. I would like to so much!" she begged.

"See how she recognizes my talent boy!" he grinned at Foster.

"Sure she does. It's one of the swellest things you've done yet!"

"I know it! I know it!"

He turned to Mitsi. "Okay, I'll let you do it. I like you—you're a high-class sort of a showgirl. We'll get along together all right I guess. I don't think much of your voice—there's plenty as good—but you got something—personality, and you get a song across. That's all that interests me."

Foster rose.

"We won't keep you out of bed Sam. You're tired."

"Okay boy. Tinkle me up. I might want you to help me with the spelling if I do this lyric to-morrow." He turned to Mitsi. "*Au revoir, chérie*—guess that's all the French I know!"

He didn't rise to see them out, but remained seated at the piano, playing softly all the time. Working out new harmonies, new rhythms, new phrases.

They left him.

"And he won't get to bed until four o'clock in the morning either," said Foster as they walked downstairs.

"Hope the people in the room next door don't hear him and be kept awake!"

"That wouldn't worry him!"

"What shall I do about that song—to remind him he said I could do it? He will forget. Or perhaps he was only making fun of me?"

"He'll remember all right. You'd better bring Larry along next time and get him to come to some sort of arrangement with him."

He hailed a taxi and took her back to her hotel.

"Well—thank you for the evening," he said. "I enjoyed it a heap. I'd like to telephone you again—er—not so much on business' this time! May I?"

"Please. I am so grateful to you for doing this."

She went upstairs.

It was very late. The hotel was quiet. Not a soul stirred. The corridors with their thick carpets, the golden wall lights, the doors of the bedrooms, all seemed to echo: "Sleep. Sleep. Sleep. Quiet. Quiet. Quiet."

Involuntarily, she tiptoed into her room and flung her evening clothes off. She was desperately tired.

Somehow, Levinsky and Foster and the club didn't seem to matter. Her work, this new career which Larry was trying to build for her—didn't matter.

All that mattered as she laid her weary head on her pillow, was Bob's secret smile as he left her at the club that night.

And tomorrow she would see him—be with him again—away from everything, from everyone, in another different world peopled by only him and herself.

25

And so Sam Levinsky came into Mitsi's life.

He wrote songs for her, and when she sang them slanged her for spoiling them, until she wept. Then he called her again and for hours played tunes over to her and asked her advice about them as if her criticism was the most valuable in the world.

Larry was delighted when he heard she had been successful with Levinsky. He wrote a big newspaper story about her, how the song-writer was writing songs for her instead of returning to Hollywood.

Mitsi was again in the news.

One morning the telephone woke her and she picked up the receiver to hear Larry's voice on the line.

"Will you lunch with me today?"

"I am so sorry but I cannot. I have already made arrangements to lunch with Bob."

"Julia's arriving this afternoon and I thought we might go on and meet her."

"Julia is arriving? How wonderful!"

"Can you meet me on Victoria station at two-fifteen this afternoon? Come along after lunch."

"But certainly I will. It will be so nice to see Julia. Will she stay at the hotel?"

"She'll probably stay with me."

"Oh."

She somehow felt vaguely jealous that Julia should stay with him. She had never been to his flat, which was somewhere off Baker Street, and where a housekeeper looked after him.

"See you this afternoon," he was saying. "Julia will be expecting us both. Hope you enjoy your lunch—but for God's sake don't take Bob too seriously."

He's annoyed—or jealous, she thought as she hung up. Of course I shall take Bob seriously. We are in love. Larry does not know what that means.

It was a drizzling wet morning, grey and dull. But she felt tremendously happy. She looked through her wardrobe and chose the green suit for it looked gay on this drab day.

When she had dressed with even more especial care than usual, Bob was announced. She was surprised he should have come up to her sitting-room, for he usually waited for her in the lounge. He came in, radiant, and gave her a gardenia to wear in her coat. She pinned it on the lapel of the little green coat and turned to him smiling.

He put his arms round her. She leant against him, her heart completely full and feeling exaltedly happy. He raised her chin and looked deep down into her eyes. Then he bent his head swiftly and kissed her.

He released her, laughing.

"Let's go, darling! I want to get you away from everything and everybody. Let's go miles away somewhere and spend the whole day together."

They went down and into the car. "Where shall we go?"

He turned to her.

"I do not know. You must know England better than I do!"

"I'd like to take you to Scotland, but I don't think we'd quite do it somehow—even in this car!"

They sped out North and found themselves on the Oxford road.

"Don't want to go to Oxford particularly, but there's one or two nice places along the road we might pick on for eats."

They had finished lunch and Bob ordered coffee.

"What'll we do now? Would you like to go on to Oxford? Or what? It's such a beastly day it's difficult to know what to do."

"It is not a 'beastly day'! It is most beautiful," she said dreamily.

Bob looked at his watch. "Two-thirty."

And then she remembered.

"Julia!"

"Julia?"

"She was coming over from Paris—you know, she's Larry's friend. I promised to be with him at the station at two-thirty to meet her."

"She won't need to be met by you particularly will she? If Larry's there, it's all right."

"It is not. She is my friend. She was very kind to me in Paris. I love Julia, and now I have been so very rude."

"You can make up tons of explanations between now and when you see her darling. Don't think about it."

"I must go back immediately;" and she began to collect her bag and gloves.

He stared at her with surprise.

"Don't be stupid, darling. We're nearly forty miles from London. It'll take us some time to get back. You've done it now. You can explain we went out into the country for lunch and couldn't get back or something—anything. All that matters is we're here. And we're going to stay away from London until you have to get back for the show. It's the only time we really have together—and today of all days."

He folded his hand over hers on the table and she looked up at him, worriedly.

"I do not want Julia should think I am rude or that I do not wish to see her. I am so pleased she is in England again, and I wish to tell her so."

"Where's she staying? You can telephone her if you like, but I simply refuse to take you back now."

"She is staying with Larry."

"Oho! Old Larry. Well, who would have thought it!"

His tone annoyed her. She resented the insinuation about Larry and Julia.

"So Larry's falling at last?"

"He is not in love with Julia. He is her friend."

"I was only fooling."

A wave of irritation went through him. She hasn't any sense of humour, he thought.

"I must telephone and arrange to see her this evening," she said.

"Darling, surely we can spend today together without letting other people interfere? Tomorrow may be too late." He smiled at her. "We may have fallen out of love by tomorrow. And I am so very much enjoying the pleasant state of being in love."

She looked at him.

"I shall be in love with you all my life."

"So stay with me now."

"I am fighting a battle inside me. I will tell you when it is over."

He sat silent, half-laughing, half-angry with her. He realized he really didn't understand her or know anything about her, so why should he get so het-up over her sudden capriciousness?

She drank down her coffee and turned to him resolutely.

"We must go."

They went.out.

The little hall of the inn was momentarily empty. Suddenly he turned and putting his arms round her pressed his mouth down on hers.

26

On the platform at two-fifteen Larry waited for Mitsi.

He was early. He went into the buffet and ordered some coffee while he waited. He reflected how many coffees and drinks were ordered not because people wanted them but because they had to do something while they waited. It's waiting for a woman drives a man to drink, he thought. Just a Scotch while you waited. Then another, then another. Then the girl arrived or didn't as the case might be.

Presently he walked out to the barrier but found no Mitsi.

He thrust his hands in his pocket and paced up and down impatiently. If she let him down now, he couldn't ask Julia to wait for her after her journey across from Paris. Scatty little devil. Yet she'd never been late before. Lunching with Bob was, of course, an absorbing business.

She's fallen like a ton of bricks for him, and he seems to have fallen for her—temporarily. Bob always did fall heavily for a little while, then he seemed to tail off. His women, like his enthusiasms, never lasted. Except of course, the Lewis girl. He still seems to be involved there, Larry decided. Suppose he'll marry her some day. She's got money and her father's got influence.

The train steamed in.

He felt a wave of fury that Mitsi should have let him down—and Julia. After all, dammit, we're older friends than Bob Raymond is.

Julia threw her arms round him, suit-cases and all. They bumped on his back as he hugged her in turn.

"It's grand to see you," he said.

"It's grand to see you. Leo let me get away only just in time, but I made it!"

She looks pretty marvellous every time I see her, he thought. She was dressed in blue, and her olive skin was set off amazingly well by the colour. Her black hair peeped out beneath a chic hat set on the back of her head.

"You're not looking so good, Larry," she said. "Shadows under your eyes, lines round your mouth, and I believe I see a grey hair sprouting just above your left ear."

"Never felt so fit in my life!"

"How's Mitsi?"

"Damned annoying brat! She promised to be here to meet you."

"She's got a lunch date she can't get away from I expect!"

"Lunching with Raymond. He's probably taken her out on one of his famous rustic drives!"

"Does he do things like that?"

He led her towards a taxi and gave it his address.

"What about work, Larry?" she enquired as they swung out of the station.

"Taking the afternoon off. I arranged we'd have tea at the flat."

They were silent for some minutes, then she looked at him.

"Worried about Mitsi?"

"Good Lord, no! After all, I only found her the job. I've no further responsibility for her."

"Quite."

After a few minutes he said:

"But I'm damned annoyed she hasn't turned up."

"Don't worry about me, dear. I don't mind a bit. I didn't expect her to meet me really. It was frightfully nice of you to come. I hope I shall see her tonight."

"We'll go along to the club shall we—and hear her do her stuff?"

"I'd love to. But you look tired. I can ring up John Foster and ask him to take me if you'd like?"

"Hell, no! *I'm* coming with you. We can ask Foster as well, if you like."

Julia knew then.

He wants to see Mitsi. He's in love with her and she's in love with Bob. It's all so silly. Poor darling Larry. I wish I could make him happy.

His housekeeper, a tubby little Scotswoman, with a rich Scots accent, showed Julia to her room.

Julia was somehow always surprised at the quiet good taste which was evident in the flat. She had visited it before, each time felt the same quick surprise at the comfort and ease of the place. There were flowers in the lounge and in her bedroom—large tawny chrysanthemums on the dressing-table.

She took off her hat and coat and after running a comb through her hair, went into the lounge. She joined Larry over the fire, where a tea-table was invitingly laid.

"When you're looked after as well as this, you hardly feel like getting married I suppose?"

He nodded with mock gravity.

"You're the only woman who's absolutely dependable and reliable."

"Give me some tea, darling! I'm getting passée and compliments no longer have any effect on me!"

"You're the most attractive woman I know."

"I'm hellishly thirsty!"

Julia knew he was worrying about Mitsi. Although she felt he was only half-listening to her conversation, she talked of Leo and Max Cooper, and Sadie and all the others he knew in Paris.

Presently he asked her: "Like to go out and have a drink somewhere?"

"Why drink? You know I don't very much or very often."

"I feel like one."

"You mean, you feel like several."

"All right. I feel like several!"

"How about removing the tea and replacing it with a whisky-decanter and a syphon and a glass and get down to it right here? You don't have to go out."

"That's certainly an idea," he said. And acted upon it.

Over his glass-rim he shot at her:

"Why on earth you haven't got married I don't know, Julia."

She gave him a non-committal shrug.

Why, I can't tell you, my dear, she thought. I might have done, once—twice. Instead I seem to have existed to meet you and feel lonelier than ever when I'm not with you. This hour—the firelight, the dusk just creeping down outside, and you sitting opposite me—it would be perfect if you loved me.

She smiled at him casually and her thoughts went on: You're miles away thinking of somebody else. I'm here and you're glad, but you wish I were someone else.

He half-smiled back at her and started to light his pipe. He crossed his legs, puffing away comfortably.

There was silence for some minutes, then the telephone bell shrilled through the flat.

He rose and crossed to his desk.

"Hello? Yes, all right."

After a few moments, he leant eagerly against the desk.

"Oh, hello, Mitsi."

She caught the elaborate casualness in his tone. It didn't fool her for an instant. She wondered if Mitsi saw through it.

"Don't mind in the least. It was just rather rude to Julia. Nice people don't break appointments, especially when they're supposed to be meeting trains and people like Julia... It's quite all right, she can see you tomorrow if you're free. Don't bother, my dear girl—not tonight—it isn't worth it. Good-bye."

He hung up and came back to his chair sucking his pipe furiously.

"Don't you think you were a spot abrupt with the child?"

"Do her good. I don't like you being treated like that." He added: "Damn Bob Raymond! Kept waiting just because of him!"

Julia stretched up a hand and touched his. He grasped it and looked down at her with a quick smile.

"Larry—we've been friends for years—let me help you. Just tell me one little thing."

"Yes?"

"Are you in love with her?"

"Well! I certainly didn't expect a frontal attack like that!"

"Tell me—"

"I really haven't analysed my feelings about her, but she gets me in a sort of way. I feel terribly sorry for her, sort of responsible for her. She was such a lost kid when I found her at Le Bourget, and I've more or less made her what she is. I suppose I feel a proprietary sort of right in her. But I suppose that'll pass. It's unlike me to feel this way over a girl."

He suddenly bent his head against hers. His arms went round her. He turned his face to hers and looked into her eyes.

"Julia, I'm a rat!"

"No, darling. You're only a fool."

"I suppose I am."

He drew away from her slowly.

"Please don't. It's comforting. I'm a lonely type, too."

He gathered her close.

"Darling Julia. I like you so very, very much."

She laughed a brittle little laugh.

"I suppose when you get to be my age—when you begin to feel life's gone by you and you've lost a lot of things—you only begin to miss them."

He kissed her softly and kindly on the mouth.

She clung to him suddenly as if she never wanted him to leave her.

"I'm being a fool now. Forgive me," she whispered.

It was thus he discovered she loved him.

Inwardly he cursed his stupidity. I *am* a swine! I've been telling her all about this damned silly business with Mitsi, and she's in love with me.

"I'm so sorry," he muttered.

She clung to him, then smiled up at him. Her eyes were very bright.

"I'll always remember this, Larry."

The door-bell rang.

"Say I'm not in," yelled Larry through the door to the housekeeper as he heard her hurry to answer the bell.

They heard voices vaguely.

"She's a marvel—the way she keeps people out of my way," Larry said.

The door burst open, and framed in the doorway was Mitsi. Behind her the figure of Bob. "Oh—!"

Mitsi stood there staring at them and there was a knowing little smile on Bob's face.

27

"Sorry old man. Didn't dream you'd be engaged," broke in Bob apologetically. "If we're—er—in the way we'll get along."

"Cut it out," Larry snapped at him. "Come in and have a drink."

He crossed and switched the lights on. Julia smoothed her hair. Mitsi recovered from her surprise, rushed towards her and threw her arms round her.

"I am so sorry that I was not at the station. I have been so happy that you were coming to London."

Bob came over and Larry introduced them. Bob smiled his all-conquering smile at her.

Julia appraised him with new interest. He certainly is charming, and terribly good-looking. And he'd knock Mitsi sideways, inexperienced as she was in the ways of young men like him.

Attractive woman Larry's got hold of, Bob was thinking. Larry handed round drinks.

"Like to have some food here you two, and then go on to the club?"

"I've got to get back and change. Snag about running the place—always got to put in an appearance all smarted up!" said Bob.

"It's now seven-thirty. We can have dinner by eight and then you can cut along. So can Mitsi. We'll be coming along to the club tonight. Julia wants to hear Mitsi's show. But we'll get along later of course."

"Let us stay here and eat," Mitsi said.

She looked at Larry. I cannot understand him, she thought. He will not look at me or smile at me. He keeps looking at Julia. What has happened?

After dinner Bob left with Mitsi for the hotel.

When she got back to the hotel, she rested for a few moments and went over the events of the day.

She could hardly bear to remember Larry's voice on the telephone—curt and short and rather rude. It had somehow spoilt things.

All she had wanted then, was to get back to him and Julia and explain to them. The feeling that she had been disloyal—and for no good reason—worried her then, and worried her still.

Then Julia and Larry together—in each other's arms—she had never understood that things were like that between them. It made a cloud fall over all Bob's tenderness. Why it should make her feel depressed, she couldn't understand.

She chose the white dress because of Julia—the white, shimmering sequinned dress. She surveyed herself in the mirror. She felt a little surge of satisfaction as she gazed at her reflection. She patted down the golden wing of hair brushed back from her brow.

I wonder how long this will keep gold, she thought. I must ask the hairdresser. It would be terrible if it suddenly went darker again. Bob would not like that.

Not that Larry would mind, she reflected. He wouldn't really care how she looked. He doesn't care how anybody looks.

She reached the Gardenia feeling refreshed and hoping that Julia and Larry would already be there. Instead, she found Levinsky and John Foster sitting at a table near the door. Levinsky grabbed her arm.

"Don't forget, you're singing my new number tonight."

"I could not forget that," she smiled at him. "It is such a marvellous number."

He laughed.

"Come and have a drink. I guess John's just dying for you to talk to him. He dragged me here tonight I guess by sheer brute force. Making some pallid excuse about 'I must hear you sing my number'. Guess I wasn't particularly interested in hearing it, but there you are. Can't let a pal down!"

John brightened up when he saw her and pulled out a chair.

"Louise is throwing a party afterwards," he greeted her. "Come along to it? She asked me to bring a crowd if I could."

She thought quickly. Perhaps if Bob and Julia and Larry came it would be fun.

"I have three friends—may I bring them? You know, Julia is here. She arrived today and is coming here tonight with Larry. Perhaps if I could bring them and Bob Raymond—?"

"Bring the whole lot. It's not my party! Anyhow I think Raymond's been asked already. His girl friend's going along—you know Carol Lewis."

She didn't bat an eyelash.

"I see. Then Julia and Larry and I shall come with you."

"That'll be fine. I'll look out for Julia and Larry."

He smiled at her as if the whole world was fine.

She hurried away.

So Carol Lewis was going? People thought then that she and Bob— but he belonged to her, now. She wondered what he would do about his past love and his present love at the same party, when everyone thought that the past love was still his present love?

She went to her dressing-room and sent Hattie away.

She sat alone there. It seemed there was something wrong in her loving him.

Then the door opened quietly and he came in. He raised her out of her chair and held her close to him.

"We are going to the party," she said.

"So am I," he said. "Let's all go along together."

"I am taking Julia and Larry and we are going with John Foster and Levinsky. You will not want to come with all of us."

"Why not? I'd rather go with you alone—but Louise's parties are wonderful. She has a colossal house and if you get bored you can always hide away somewhere where nobody will find you. That's just what we'll do, darling!"

She looked up at him.

"I have been sitting here alone. Getting my thoughts sorted out."

"Fighting another battle inside?" he teased her.

She looked at him gravely. "You really do love me?"

"More than I've ever loved anyone before."

"Will you stand at the back where you always do, tonight?"

"Why yes, darling."

He gazed at her with a somewhat mystified expression.

She hurried out of the room and down the corridor and left him still looking after her.

She sounds as though she's contemplating suicide. What's the matter anyway? he puzzled. We're in love—it's so damned silly to take it all so seriously. Love is a thing that ought to make you happy. I hate being serious and ponderous about it. Damn it all!

She sang Levinsky's song and it went over big, as Sam himself put it. She was given two encores at the end of her show.

But there was a heaviness in her heart. She didn't know quite what it was—as she sang to a figure standing at the back of the restaurant. A tall figure in evening dress.

Julia turned to Larry as the rich warm voice swam out across the tables towards them.

"She's come on all right, hasn't she? Her voice is really lovely now. And she looks beautiful. So lovely and fragile in white. She sings that stuff as though she really felt it."

"That's the reason why she gets by."

"Yet she can't, she can't know anything about love. Not the sort of love that—" She broke off. "She's so young."

He looked across at her.

"Always wanting to protect people, aren't you?"

She replied briskly: "I need all the protection I can give myself at the moment."

He grinned and glanced at the slender, white shimmering figure with the gold aureole of hair and the almost incredibly beautiful face.

He remembered the shabby little girl at the aerodrome outside Paris and he thought: I haven't done right to bring her here and give her this life. She's too soft for it. She'll get knocked about and hurt, and she won't be able to stand up to it.

He looked at Julia and tried to forget how much he loved Mitsi.

"The words of these songs are such utter hokum!" Julia exclaimed.

He nodded.

"Somehow, when you're feeling mellow after a few drinks you go for the stuff all the same. They help, sort of."

Mitsi's song ended and Julia joined in the applause vigorously.

"She's very good."

"Wonder what she'd be like anywhere else?" he said judiciously. "Got a feeling that when she's surrounded by friends and a friendly audience, people she knows and believes in—she's all right."

He paused and knocked the ash off his cigarette.

"But in Paris or New York where she'd be strange, I don't know," he went on. "You see, everything's been made pretty easy for her. She's had me to call up when she's felt lonely. She's had Foster to help her with Levinsky, she's been taken up by Louise who'sit through Foster again. Bob's in love with her and she with him. Everything in the garden's lovely!"

He paused, then continued:

"But when he gets tired of her as he will inevitably—he'd get tired of Cleopatra after a few weeks—God alone knows what'll happen to the poor kid. She'll cave in I think. She relies so much on other people. I don't know—I don't think she's grown up yet enough to know how to rely on herself."

He took a deep breath and looked worried.

Julia said slowly:

"I believe you. Anyhow, if anything does happen let me know immediately and I'll come across and fetch her. I think she rather looks on Paris as home now—because Leo and I made her feel at home during that first week."

Mitsi's show was over.

Larry felt he must see her. Julia went across to John Foster's table while he was gone and John asked her to come to the party.

Larry found Mitsi in her room sitting dejectedly in front of the dressing-table staring at her reflection.

"Bad for little girls to look at themselves too much in the mirror."

She turned and smiled at him.

"Larry! I thought you were angry with me."

"Of course I'm not. I was just feeling a bit irritable over this afternoon."

"I'm sorry."

"Come and have something to eat—or at least, something to drink."

"I will. I need something."

They went back to the table where a gay party consisting of John, Levinsky, Julia and Bob had gathered.

Julia and Levinsky were wisecracking at each other.

Mitsi danced with Bob first, then with Levinsky and lastly with Larry.

"Dancing with you reminds me of that time we danced together in the flat in Paris. Remember after I came back looking so different with my hair all changed and my face made up? You liked me then?"

"Little Miss Two-Face," he grinned at her. "I remember. But I'm not sure that I didn't like you better before."

"You are afraid of me like this! You ask yourself: 'Who is this woman with the yellow hair and the lipstick with whom I dance? I do not know her. She is strange and sophisticated!—'" She broke off to ask, "Do you think I am sophisticated?"

"I think you're lovely. But you talk too much."

28

Louise's house was gaily lit up, and the sounds of the orchestra could be heard faintly in the street.

Bob had arrived first, knowing London and its short cuts better than Foster did. They were waiting in the car for the other two. They all got out as they heard the roar of the exhaust of Foster's car turning the corner on two wheels.

Bob looked round ostentatiously.

"No policemen! Good! Can't afford to be involved with a driver like Foster now I've taken on the club. I'm suspect now!"

"Haven't you always been?" inquired Larry innocently.

They hurried into the house. Louise broke over them like a sea roaring up the sands with her genuinely effusive welcome.

"Go right along in and you'll find a buffet and drinks. The band's in the ballroom at the back, and the garden's all lit up. And so are some of my friends!"

"Sounds like a swell party!" said Bob, with enthusiasm.

As they entered the large and beautifully flower-bedecked ballroom, he turned to Mitsi. Swung her into a slow fox-trot the band was playing. Without a word they danced for a few minutes while he held her close in his arms.

He steered her towards the large windows which opened out to the soft, warm night. The lights strung along through the trees which lined the high walls of the garden, invited them.

He danced out through the windows with her on to the lawn, and when they felt the soft carpet of the grass beneath their feet, he bent his head and kissed her.

In the ballroom Larry said to Julia as they danced:

"He's up to his famous tricks again, is old Bob. Taking the impressionable young child into a garden all lit with fairy lights!"

As they reached the doorway again he led her upstairs towards the buffet.

"What's that, Larry? Looks too fruity to be much good to me."

Julia was peering into the glass where floated all manner of fruit and vegetable.

"Try it, Baby! It's potent."

It was the voice of Levinsky from behind a double whisky. Foster was beside him.

"Oho!... So you got here first?"

"For an old-timer like me, a bar's the only place holds any excitement."

"They're playing one of your tunes, Sam," broke in John Foster.

"We ought to have Mitsi here to sing it. She's pretty hot at some of my old numbers now. Guess she's learning something from old Sam. Don't you agree?"

He turned to Julia.

"She certainly has changed since she came from Paris," said Julia guardedly.

Larry was worried. Where was all this going to lead Mitsi? Why had he bothered about her in the first place? Wouldn't she perhaps have been better if he had left her alone? He turned back to Julia and saw Bob and Carol Lewis come into the buffet.

Where was Mitsi?

Then he saw her enter the room behind them, looking ineffably small and bewildered. He saw Bob turn and take her arm and lead her towards them. Carol Lewis walked on in front, apparently determined to take no notice of Mitsi's presence.

On an impulse Larry went straight over. Looking at Bob, he said distinctly:

"I'll give Mitsi something to eat, Bob. Our party's waiting for her."

He led her back to Julia. Mitsi looked at him gratefully.

Julia looked at her face. Saw the light now gone out of it, and glanced across at Bob and Carol Lewis.

"Mitsi, dear, would you like to go?"

"Oh, no. I am enjoying it so much."

"Little liar," laughed Julia softly. "You're not happy at all. Tell me," she continued, "are you jealous?"

She glanced across the room, then at Julia.

"I do not think so. Because he loves me. So I should not be jealous, but she makes me feel unhappy. She does not like me, I think."

"I know she doesn't!"

"I am sorry."

"No need to worry over her. They've been friends for years and years and always will be. Very few women like Carol. She's what's commonly known as a cat my dear, and she's fond of men—any kind of men."

"She is fond of Bob?"

"She was once engaged to be married to him."

"That is why he must be so nice to her I suppose."

Julia looked at her carefully.

"Don't take him too seriously my dear."

She said it lightly. She knew Mitsi would not heed any warning from her. What does one do when one sees a rabbit go straight into a trap? she asked herself. Why doesn't Larry do something? Just curses himself for bringing her over here, but that doesn't do any good.

He came up at that moment and led Mitsi away. Bob miraculously left Carol Lewis high and dry and asked Julia to dance.

"How did you manage that?" she smiled at him.

He smiled back at her.

"I just did. Some people are a bit tricky, aren't they?"

Deliberately she misunderstood him.

"Especially when they're young, and have to be taken care of and not hurt?"

He eyed her as they danced.

"Are you warning me, Julia Green?"

She didn't answer.

"I wouldn't do anything to hurt Mitsi for all the world."

"I believe you—I think."

They danced on.

"You really will think of her happiness now and again, won't you?" she appealed to him as they returned to the others.

He clasped his hand over hers.

"Trust me."

Larry returned with Mitsi. She seemed happier now, her eyes were shining again. Bob walked possessively across to her.

"Enjoying yourself, darling?"

As she turned to him, a waiter hurried up.

"Miss Lewis has gone sir," he said to Bob. "She said would I inform you she was tired and has left early. She wished me to say 'good night' to you for her and to ask you to telephone her in the morning."

Bob nodded and Julia saw his mouth tighten at the corners. He looked as if he had had enough of Carol Lewis.

He turned to Mitsi again. Smiled his little intimate smile at her.

"Shall we dance?"

29

For the last several nights Mitsi had noticed the same crowd of noisy youngsters at the Gardenia.

They drank a great deal too much but were otherwise harmless. Bob Raymond harboured no loving feelings towards them, but he appreciated their apparently unlimited spending capacities.

They cheered Mitsi's performance tremendously. Like other habituées of the club, she became used to them and their raucous reception each night.

They made no attempt to make her acquaintance as so many of the others did, however. Until one night when they were accompanied by a middle-aged man of a kind of shabbily distinguished appearance.

He seemed to spend most of the evening pointing out various celebrities in the club to the members of his party. Dining before her act, she found herself curious about them and wondering who the man might be.

Her show over, she was waiting in her dressing-room for Larry who was calling to take her back to the hotel. A page-boy knocked on the door and told her a gentleman would like her to join him at his table for a few moments.

"He says he knew your father very well."

"My father?"

"Yes, Miss Linden."

It seemed impossible anyone could know her father. She would not know him herself—could not remember him. And if he were alive—wherever he might be—it was unlikely he would have identified himself with a daughter who was born to him so many years ago. When he deserted her mother.

"Shall I tell him off?" The small page pursed his lips and looked judicially at her. "Maybe he's tryin' a new way to get to know you?"

Mitsi laughed.

"Mr. Curtis will be here shortly, anyway. I might as well find out what this man wants. Send him to me."

The boy disappeared. Returned with the man who was with the party of youngsters. He came into her dressing-room and smiled a little nervously.

"I felt I must come and see you, I've read so much about you lately in the papers. You seem to be a great success."

"Thank you."

"Linden is not a very usual name."

He hesitated, his voice tailing off.

She studied him.

His hair was thinning and grey at the temples. His evening clothes looked somehow as if he wore them little.

"It is nice of you to come and see me."

"You will think it strange perhaps. But a great many strangers wish to know you after they have heard you sing I suppose?"

He smiled slightly.

She wondered where she had seen that smile before. There was something familiar about it—the lift of the lips at the corners. It made a rather uninteresting nondescript array of features attractive.

"I understand you knew my father?"

"I know him very well."

He was watching her carefully now.

"I have not heard of him for many years. He is still alive then? I did not know—"

He nodded.

"I know he had a daughter called Mitsi. His wife was French."

It was strange that she should suddenly possess a father. She wondered what he was like.

"He has fallen on very bad times I am afraid."

He was speaking again, slowly, cautiously almost.

"You mean—he is ill?"

"I think he would like to go back to his wife."

"My mother is dead."

The other started and looked up.

"Really? When?"

"About three months ago."

"I am so sorry. So terribly sorry. She was a charming sweet woman."

"You knew her?"

Mitsi leant forward eagerly.

He nodded.

"She was very like you. Her colouring was different. She had brown hair, soft and the colour of beech leaves in the autumn, but you are very like her apart from that. I recognized you at once."

"There is so much I would like to talk to you about—but I don't know where to begin!"

"Your poor father felt it very badly that he had to leave you both. You were so very small at the time."

His voice was trembling emotionally.

"I am afraid I feel very bitter about him. My mother was so very wonderful. I have no memories like that of my father."

He broke down quite suddenly.

"I am your father."

"You!"

She was utterly bewildered by this sudden revelation. She stared at him.

"There is a time in everyone's life—however bad they may be—when they regret and wish to make some sort of reparation."

His voice was choked with humility.

She felt a great wave of pity for him. She tried to forget the misery he had made of her mother's life. There must be some sort of bond between them. In spite of everything he had done to the mother she loved.

"But we do not know each other. You are a stranger to me and I to you."

"I know what you must be thinking about me," he said. "I want you to forgive."

Impulsively, she took his hands. She remembered he had said he was ill and poor. She saw more clearly the stamp of need upon him.

"Come and lunch with me tomorrow," she said. "I'm staying at the Norchester Hotel. I would so much like to help you."

She paused shyly, almost not knowing what to say to this ghost of the past.

"It is difficult to believe I have found my father," she murmured.

He smiled at her. He was about to say something as he opened the door to leave, and then Larry stood in the doorway.

"Hello?"

The other made to leave. He did not appear anxious to make conversation with Larry, who stood in his way.

"Larry—this is my father."

Larry's expression remained poker-like as he held out his hand.

"Really? This must be quite a surprise."

To Mitsi, with a geniality that was charged with cynicism: "You weren't even sure he was alive, were you?"

"No. It is a great surprise."

She smiled at her father, trying to make him at ease.

"Well—I'll leave you now my dear. I shall hope to renew our relationship tomorrow."

"You did say your *father*?" queried Larry as he closed the door firmly behind him.

"Yes."

She answered him doubtfully. She couldn't yet sort out her emotions properly.

"How do you know it was him?"

"He told me."

"Remember your father at all?"

She shook her head slowly.

"But there is a resemblance between us, don't you agree? And he spoke about my mother. Of course, it's my father, I'm not worrying about that. What I *am* worrying about is that I don't feel anything about him at all. Except I am sorry for him. He looks so poor. I wonder how he got here—with that party of people."

"They're the type who know all kinds of odd people and drag them along on their sprees without being too particular who they are or where they come from."

Mitsi looked at him sharply.

"You are being rude."

"Only careful. I'm suspicious—naturally—of a father who suddenly turns up out of the blue to see a daughter he's not known since she was a baby. Especially when she's successful and making a great deal of money."

"You couldn't think that!"

"When are you seeing him?"

"Tomorrow at lunch."

"Going to give him money?"

She did not answer him.

"Are you?"

"He looked so broken—"

"You are a complete fool."

"Would it be so wrong—when I would wish to help him?" He shrugged his shoulders.

"Go right ahead and see what you'll get yourself into."

"Let's go. Forget about it. I am ready. I may not see him ever again."

"You'll see him all right—and pretty soon too. He'll never be off your doorstep now."

As he left her at the hotel, he said:

"I may be around tomorrow about lunch-time. I'll drop in for a few moments."

"I'd much rather you didn't."

"All the same—I still will!"

He hailed a passing taxi and got in before she could reply.

30

The following day her father turned up for lunch.

He was wearing a slightly threadbare brown suit which made him look more nondescript than ever except when he smiled and his face took on that strange individuality—almost a distinction.

It was a peculiar lunch. There seemed nothing to talk about. He asked Mitsi eagerly about her career and how she had become a cabaret star. She told him, telling him about Larry.

"The man you met last night. He's a newspaper writer."

"Oh—on a newspaper?"

He looked, she thought, slightly ill at ease.

"The *Courier*."

He was silent for a time. Then presently he leant forward and said nervously and confidentially:

"Your mother was always telling me how I could never deal with money. She always said I would never have any. Because I didn't know the value of it. I don't. I'm broke now—"

He crumbled his bread between long fingers, the nails of which she saw were ill-kept. He went on gropingly.

"And shortly I'll be sued and probably imprisoned for not being able to pay my debts. It would be terrible if I was put in prison, wouldn't it?"

He raised his eyes and stared at her.

She was only dimly comprehending his words. The word "prison" stood out in her mind.

"It would be terrible. I am so sorry…"

Her voice trailed away as he smiled across the table at her.

"It wouldn't be so bad for me only my dear. But you—your name is so well known."

"I see." She said again slowly: "I see."

"I'm very proud of you as my daughter. My name—father of the famous night-club star—would be splashed across every newspaper. It would indeed be terrible for you."

She could not look at him.

"How much money do you want?"

She felt as if she was living in a dream. Some horrible nightmare.

"About five hundred pounds perhaps. That would clear me for a time anyway."

She threw a startled look.

"Five hundred pounds! I haven't got it. Nowhere near that amount."

Her face was white with shocked dismay.

"Nothing else will help. It must be that or nothing at all."

She looked at him again. His eyes now were cold and hard.

"Perhaps you know some friends who would lend it to you?" he insinuated.

"I cannot borrow money from friends for you."

Suddenly his whole attitude changed. He leant across to her. His voice was low, menacing. His face seemed distorted.

"Why not? They know you'll be able to pay 'em back. Anyway, you're not trying to tell me you haven't put by five hundred pounds—and more—all the time you've been in London? You can't bluff me, my girl."

He leant back, eyeing her.

She gazed at him steadily.

"I have no money to give you…"

He answered her firmly.

"You've got to help me, my dear. It's a fair bargain. Listen. All my life I've done nothing to be proud of—more the reverse. But help me now, and I'll fade out completely—never bother you again."

Suddenly she saw Larry striding across the restaurant.

Her father looked scared when he came over. Mitsi felt her only hope now was Larry. He could deal with the situation.

"Mr. Linden?" Larry said, giving the man a dubious glance.

"That's right." Then added: "Father of the Marvellous Mitsi."

"Extraordinary. Who would have thought it?"

Linden glanced sharply at him, but seeing Larry smile, smiled back.

"Shall we have coffee in my sitting-room?" Mitsi suggested.

"Good idea," agreed Larry.

They went up to her sitting-room where they were served with coffee. Presently Linden rose.

"I must go. Perhaps I shall see you at the Gardenia tonight, Mitsi. I shall be going there with my friends again."

She rose too.

"I am glad that you have realized it is no good," she murmured to him as she saw him out.

She told Larry the story of the lunch.

"Demanding money with menaces, eh?" He rolled the phrase richly on his tongue. "Quite a melodramatic old bird!"

"Are you going to tell the police?"

He looked at her in amazement.

"My dear girl—has it sent your mind wandering—this meeting with your father?"

"What do you mean?"

"I mean he's right when he says it'll ruin you to be mixed up with him!" He shook his head grimly. "There are better ways of dealing with him. Leave it to me. Ask him round to your dressing-room tonight after your show and I'll put up a cosy little proposition to him then."

She glanced gratefully at him.

"You are so good. You help me so much."

"That's all right," he replied roughly. "Being a newspaperman has many consolations—especially when you want to get something on someone."

That evening at the club, she saw her father was drunk. The party he was with appeared to be toasting him, and Mitsi wondered for a moment whether he had told them about her.

After her show, she hurried to her dressing-room and dismissed Hattie. Then she sent a message to her father.

She sat down and lit a cigarette.

He arrived shortly afterwards. He was unsteady on his feet. His voice was thick.

Almost simultaneously Larry came in. He was smiling with deceptive geniality.

"Good evening!"

Linden blinked owlishly at him.

Larry threw a glance at Mitsi.

"He's a little sozzled," he said, with distinctness.

"I know."

Larry suddenly turned on the man.

"Trying a little gentle blackmail, aren't you?"

The other sat up and looked uncomprehendingly at him.

"That's your little idea, isn't it?" Larry insisted.

"Yesh."

Larry turned to the dressing-table and extracted a cigarette from the box. He lit it deliberately, puffing the first smoke out in a cloud.

"You may know I'm a newspaperman. I get around a bit. Have various ways of finding out things about people."

He was staring steadily at Linden.

The man sat up slightly. He appeared to be sober enough to take in what was being inferred. His eyes lost their drunken film and for a moment looked almost afraid.

"What of it?"

"Just that you know perfectly well you can't afford to blackmail anybody," Larry told him easily. "There are several things in your own life which, if they were followed up, might possibly be of interest to Scotland Yard."

Mitsi gave a horrified gasp and looked appealingly at Larry.

He said to her:

"Bob'll be in soon. He'll wonder what I'm doing in your dressing-room talking to a strange man. When he arrives, go and dance with him—at least keep him away from here."

She nodded.

Larry once more addressed his attention to his cigarette, and examining the glowing tip thoughtfully, said:

"You understand what I mean—do you Linden?"

"I'm afraid I don't."

Linden appeared to be growing more sober.

"I'm afraid I don't see what you're driving at," he said. He passed a hand across his brow. "Why don't you leave it to the morning? I'll be able to understand the conversation a bit better then."

"Do you think I'm letting you go before I make certain that when you do, you'll go for good?"

A step was heard along the passage. Bob's head appeared round the door. He grinned when he saw the three of them.

"Conference?"

"Just a friendly chat," Larry smiled at him.

"Come on down all of you and have a drink or something."

Bob tendered his invitation giving Linden a slightly puzzled frown. He glanced from Mitsi to Linden and back to Larry.

Larry eyed Mitsi and she crossed to the door.

"Come down with me. Larry and Mr.—er—Mr."—she mumbled a name—"probably want to continue their chat. It's all right—you can stay here Larry," she said turning. Then she led Bob firmly away.

"Who's the human wreck?" he queried.

"Somebody Larry's trying to do something with."

"I noticed him in the club this evening. He's been here once or twice lately with a pretty rowdy crowd. Seems a little under the bottle doesn't he?"

"Yes." She glanced at him, and suddenly smiled. "Let's dance. I was getting bored with the conversation in there."

He slipped his arm round her waist. "Darling, you're quite adorable and should not have been subjected to the company of the gentleman with the soup-stained front!"

Back in the dressing-room Larry was wearing down the other's insobriety.

Once he got him sufficiently sober he could get him out of Mitsi's life once and for all.

"What do you want to do anyway? I wasn't asked here for fun I suppose?" Linden at length inquired.

"You wouldn't be my idea of fun."

"For goodness" sake come to the point, then. I'm just about ready for something more to drink."

"You'll go when I've finished with you. There are certain little matters of gambling debts, and there's a forged cheque, too—quite a lot of things a man wouldn't want the world to know."

"Digging up my past, eh?"

"Exactly."

"That's what I'm trying to get away from now."

Larry eyed him coldly.

"Well—suppose we come to some arrangement?"

Linden looked keenly at Larry.

"What exactly is your interest in my daughter?"

"As the father you might have been you've a right to ask that. But as the sort of father you turned out to be, you've no right at all. The only thing I *will* tell you is I'm managing her affairs for her and I'm determined she won't have her career ruined by you. You're going to clear out *now*—d'you understand?"

"Suppose I won't?"

"I'm afraid I'll have to put the matter into the hands of the police."

"I've got nothing to lose and all to gain by staying. Supposing I blow this whole story to a lot of extremely interested pals of yours? They probably won't be quite so unselfish about hurting Mitsi—for the sake of a story on their front pages."

He leered at Larry, who asked:

"How about money so you can clear out of the country and get free of it all?"

Linden leant forward eagerly.

"Now you're talking. If I'd known you meant that in the first place, I'd have agreed long before this."

"How much?"

"A couple of thousand? I don't want to be hard on my daughter."

Larry grinned at him amiably. "She hasn't got it. I can perhaps manage a couple of hundred."

Linden laughed immoderately.

"Where'll that get me to? Make it five hundred, and I can do something."

"Five hundred then."

Larry continued to conceal his satisfaction. He thought the price steep enough and it would be a drain on Mitsi's resources, but it had to be done.

He produced from his pocket a legal-appearing form carefully typed. He laid one copy in front of Linden together with a fountain pen.

"You might just sign this if you don't mind. Then we all know where we are."

Linden peered at it with the over-carefulness of a drunkard and without understanding a word. He signed his copy and handed it back.

Larry made him out a cheque.

"Here you are. Look after it well. I'll come down and see you on the boat tomorrow at Southampton. Send me a card from South America when you arrive. It's all written down in your copy of the agreement you signed. So if your memory fails you, you can refer to that from time to time to see what's expected of you."

The other blinked at the paper he was clutching, then he nodded, folded it and pocketed it carefully.

"Now," said Larry. "Let's go down and have one."

They went downstairs.

Linden laid his arm fondly round Larry's shoulders.

"You know I trust you somehow. Look after my little girl for me," he said brokenly.

"Forget you've got a little girl from now on," Larry told him grimly, "or you'll come up against a typhoon!"

After Linden had gone, Larry joined Mitsi and Bob.

Presently, when Bob left them for a few moments, she turned to him eagerly.

"What happened?"

"It's all right my dear. Everything's quite settled and you won't be worried. He sails for South America on a boat which leaves tomorrow. I'll see him off."

She looked at him.

"I shall not see him again?"

He caught the expression in her eyes. He said gently: "It's best that way."

Mitsi nodded, her eyes fixed somewhere past him.

"Yes, of course."

She was quiet for a moment then:

"You're so good to me."

He looked down at her.

"I'm glad to help you," he said.

He never told her it was her father who had saved her from disaster the night of her first appearance at the club. The grey-haired man who had stood up and started singing "*J'attendrai*," beating time with a fork till Mitsi had got going.

He wondered why Linden hadn't mentioned it himself. Drunk at the time, Larry concluded, probably hadn't even remembered a thing about it the morning after.

31

Levinsky put the idea into Mitsi's head of getting a car.

She arrived one morning to see him and having paid her taxi, found she had not enough money to get back to the hotel.

"I guess you're about the most extravagant young woman I've known. Why the heck don't you get yourself an automobile instead of spending all your dough on cabs?"

"I will get a car!" she said then and there. She telephoned Larry when she got back to the hotel.

"I want a car."

"A what?"

"An automobile."

"Why don't you use words you can pronounce properly?"

"I mean a car—C-A-R!"

"Oh, a car. We'll get one for you. I'll come round and see you at the club tonight about it."

That night he expounded to her his idea she should have an enormous pale blue saloon car which everyone would know as belonging to Mitsi Linden.

"I wish to drive it myself though."

"You can drive it yourself. If you'll learn how. I can't teach you, too darned busy."

"Perhaps Bob will give me lessons."

"No doubt he will," he remarked acidly.

"He is a very clever driver. He can even get round buses in Regent Street."

"Well, you just tell him you don't particularly want to learn how to get round buses in Regent Street. You just want to learn how to drive straight and careful."

They finally decided on a big rakish-looking sports job.

"I wish to learn to drive before Julia leaves for Paris again," she told Bob. "How long do you think it will take me?"

"Do you think she'll pick it up easily?" Larry asked Bob.

"She doesn't look as though she had the intelligence to ride a bicycle—far less drive a car."

"Anyhow, don't teach her any funny tricks. Just enough to drive sensibly and keep out of trouble, no more. See?"

"As you were. I'd hate to see that lovely neck broken."

"What a ghastly mind you've got."

Her car, when it arrived, looked even more enormous and spectacular than when she had first seen it. Bob took one look at it and shuddered.

"I'll lose my good name if I'm seen driving that thing around town!"

"Why? I think it is very beautiful."

"It'll be more beautiful with you at the wheel. Somehow, I think powder blue isn't quite my colour."

"You're laughing at me! Don't laugh at my car, please! There is nothing really wrong with it surely?"

He chuckled and opened the door for her. She got into the beautifully upholstered car.

"It is much more comfortable than your car," she remarked.

He let in the clutch and drove gingerly off.

"They need a tremendous lot of handling, these monsters!"

As the great car swept down towards Piccadilly, many people turned and stared.

"I expect they think it's some Hollywood film star doing a spot of showing off."

"Oh, please do not be so unkind about it."

"I'm only teasing. I like the darned thing myself a hell of a lot. It's a great car to drive."

They were approaching the turning that led from Marylebone Road into Regent's Park.

"This is where we'll have our first lesson."

They swept into the Park and found the quieter road. He began to teach her the intricacies of driving, of how to start, releasing the brake, putting in the clutch, steering, and then changing gear.

She was rather stupid at first, and he stopped to mop his brow in mock despair more than once. But he managed to remain marvellously patient with her.

I've never stood this from anyone else before, he thought. My God, she's completely dim-witted! Doesn't seem to have the slightest bit of intelligence about it. But she's so sweet when she tries so hard to understand what I'm telling her. I suppose I'm really enjoying myself.

Then he suddenly smiled to himself:

Gosh, I *must* be in love to cope with this!

32

Like a child with a new toy Mitsi practically ate, lived and slept in her new car.

Photographs were taken of her in it and the weekly press did her a good show on it. It became quite a familiar sight around London.

Mitsi had quite captured the imagination of the public. Her fair, fragile exquisite beauty, her shyness, gave her a mysterious allure to those who knew her, and to those who merely read of her and saw her, as it were, from a distance.

Bob and she appeared in public so much together that the newspaper and magazine gossips hinted at a romance.

Photographs of them at the theatre, at cocktail parties, at the Ritz or the Mayfair, excited the usual comment.

'You realize, darling, we're causing quite a lot of talk?'

Bob asked her the question one afternoon as a passing cameraman snapped them walking in the park.

"Does that matter?"

"Of course it doesn't. Except that they'll be listening for wedding bells soon."

She smiled up at him.

"And you I suppose do not like that sound?"

He laughed easily.

"It depends who I hear them with."

"It is good publicity Larry says, for me to be photographed with you."

"Good old Larry! So glad I'm doing him a good turn."

"I think it is good publicity too."

"Darling, I'm tremendously flattered! I had no idea that's why you go out with me such a lot."

"Well—it is," she said, laughing up at him again.

"Like me to introduce a couple of duchesses and three or four earls into the party just to make the position stronger?"

He was smiling, but all the same she thought she detected a slightly resentful note in his voice.

She laughed secretly.

"If you can—it would be much better."

He tucked her arm under his and led her firmly towards her car which had been parked by the Serpentine.

"I wish to go to Paris with Julia. She is going on Sunday morning. I could go with her and return on Monday afternoon," she said as they sat in the car and watched the water.

"It would be a bit of a rush for you. Unless, of course, you fly. What's the attraction of Paris anyway?"

He glanced cautiously at her over the cigarette he was lighting.

"There is no attraction except seeing Leo and Max Cooper. I can get him some work perhaps, because of this song he wrote for me. And I like Paris—I like the studio. And I must get some new clothes."

"Shall I come over with you?"

"That would be lovely! I am sure Julia would be able to give you a bed just for the one night."

She looked at him delightedly.

He said slowly:

"I thought perhaps we could stay somewhere together—the Crillon? Good place, you know."

He gave her a half-smiling glance.

She turned to him astonished.

"I think that is perhaps—how you say?—unconventional?"

"Does that matter?"

"But do not only married people stay together at hotels?"

"Oh, I'm not trying to put improper suggestions to you!"

He laughed suddenly at her shocked expression. It sat strangely on her sophisticated face.

She looked at him puzzled. Not quite sure what he was thinking.

"Why cannot we stay with Julia?"

"Staying with friends you never get the same service you get in hotels. Besides when you go away it's a darned sight more fun to stay at an hotel."

"I have so much hotel life now—I think of Julia's studio as home."

Conversation lagged. Presently she turned the car towards her hotel.

Bob sat silently puffing at his cigarette. He wondered how she had taken his suggestion. He had not realized she was such a darned prudish child.

Mitsi's thoughts were a confused whirl. He wishes me to stay with him in Paris. That's what everyone does I suppose, she thought. Perhaps it would not be so bad for me to do it—and yet… I expect he thinks I am like that although he has never suggested it before.

Somehow it was not only his suggestion that worried her. There was her feeling that he could not be trusted. That he would not be faithful to her—even if he gave her all of himself both mentally and physically. Even if they were married. He would still spare time to flirt with others while he yet believed himself in love.

They arrived at the hotel. She turned to him with a shy smile.

"You are having dinner with me tonight?"

"Thank you darling. I haven't changed so we'll have to go into the grill."

"We can dine in my sitting-room if you would like."

"No—let's go down into the grill. Always masses of people one knows down there. Much more amusing."

He smiled mockingly at her.

"All right. I do not mind at all."

She minded terribly because she thought he might have wanted to be alone with her.

"I'll have a cocktail down here while I wait for you. Like them to send anything up to you?"

She refused and hurried away to her bedroom. She entered the little sitting-room, switched the light on and looked round as if for the first time.

Here she had lived the exciting days that had changed her life. Here she had slept and dreamt. Wept and laughed for what seemed to her to be a little lifetime.

Here had grown her love for Bob, and here now was being planted her distrust of him.

He was obviously so much in love with her, and yet he could be unfaithful to her. That she felt sure of somehow. She realized she was being a fool.

In that moment she grew up, years of experience were added to her life.

She sat down in front of the glass, renovated her make-up, and combed out the pale gold hair. She brushed it right back from her forehead. It made her look years older and tremendously sophisticated. She leant her chin on her hands and gazing at herself in the mirror said aloud:

"Mitsi Linden. Don't take it all so seriously."

She suddenly laughed at the serious expression on her face and thus found that armour which she realized she had needed ever since Larry had launched her into this new life.

33

Bob took her down to the grill-room.

Over dinner, she succeeded in making him laugh at some particularly amusing remarks she passed. Before he had never laughed with her, but rather at her.

"You haven't taken to drugs have you, darling? All this feverish humour."

"I am just feeling rather happy."

"Mitsi—I'm sorry about—about this afternoon. I didn't mean anything by it, really. I hope you haven't taken it to heart?"

His face looked anxious and rather like a small boy's who has been caught stealing jam and wants to apologize for it.

"Of course I do not mind. You thought that perhaps I would do a thing like that—and now you know I will not. So we forget it."

"I'll still come across with you though. There are one or two people I'd like to look up over there."

"Shall I ask Julia to put you up?"

"Thanks, my dear—I'll stay at my usual place."

She looked up at him, guessing that he was trying to disassociate himself from her because he was ashamed of his proposal. He looked back at her, and then away. He was uneasy. It amused her tremendously. Her face broke out into a broad smile—a smile she couldn't control. He looked back to her and saw it. He reddened slightly—a thing she had never seen him do before.

It was strange, her sudden, new feeling of superiority towards him. He whom she had adored, admired, and been half-frightened of.

Presently he left her to go and change, and she telephoned Larry's flat. Julia came to the phone.

"I'm coming to Paris with you on Sunday, Julia, if I may."

"Good, darling. We're flying you know. Won't upset you, will it?"

"I wish to try it again. It will not be so long a journey this time anyway."

"Larry's coming, too."

"Larry?"

She was surprised.

"A few days away from work will do him good."

She had a feeling of jealousy as she realized he was going with Julia to Paris and he had not mentioned it to her. She felt unwanted, quite absurdly—but she did. She felt lonely, and to her annoyance and surprise, two large tears rolled down her cheeks.

She couldn't trust herself to speak for a moment and Julia called across the wire.

"Hello? Hello? Oh, you're still there. I thought we'd got cut off."

"I'm still here," she managed to find her voice. "I would like you to come to the club tonight, Julia. Will you come?"

"Going to a sort of party with Larry and some newspaper pals later on this evening, I'm afraid, so can't make it. I'd love to've done, too. You're not worried are you?"

"No," she said. Then heard herself saying: "I think that I will not come to Paris after all."

Her voice sounded petulant, Julia thought quickly at the other end of the wire. Strangest thing has happened, she thought, the kid's jealous. Of me?

"All right, darling. You know you're welcome, if you want to come."

"I should be in the way I think."

She attempted a hard little laugh. Everything was going wrong. She felt all alone in the world. She commiserated with herself, and knew all the time she was merely being idiotic.

"Aren't you being slightly stupid!" Julia said sharply. "I'll come and lunch with you tomorrow—or would you like to come over here and spend the day quietly with me?"

"All right. Perhaps I will. I do not know yet what arrangements I will make."

"Please yourself. And now I must really run and get changed."

Julia rang off.

Mitsi slowly replaced the receiver, and burst into tears.

What's the matter with me these days? she asked herself. Everything seems to be so stupidly important. I am too open to being hurt. I'm a fool. Perhaps I'm going to be ill?

She pulled herself together and went and bathed her face, angry with herself and at the knowledge that she would have to completely make up once more.

Arrived at the club, Mitsi found Bob sitting with a party including Louise and Carol Lewis. They didn't notice Mitsi.

Bob was leaning towards Carol Lewis telling her something. When he finished speaking, she looked up into his face and burst into laughter. They looked so happy together that Mitsi felt her world had completely collapsed.

She went to her own room. In a few minutes Bob came in and she turned to him a tear-stained, miserable face.

"I can't sing tonight. I must go away," she said urgently.

He came towards her and put his arms round her comfortingly. He looked at her puzzled by this sudden change of mood.

"Darling—don't be so crazy. What's the matter, anyway?"

"Everything has gone wrong today," she sobbed.

"Take it easy. Things often go wrong, but we can't suddenly throw down our jobs and go away to get over it."

"I want to. I cannot go on. Look at my face."

"I've been looking at it. It's in a dreadful mess."

He smiled kindly at her, and she buried her face in his shoulder and sobbed.

"Come on, pull yourself together. I hate to see you cry. Please!"

"Do you love me?" she choked.

"Of course I do. I wouldn't be here if I didn't."

He preferred to give the information when he felt like it. He had always thought Mitsi would take everything he gave her and then when the time came for their ways to part, she would take that also. He had hoped she was one of those exceptional women who just took things on the chin—and forgot about them quickly.

Apparently she wasn't. She was very much in love with him obviously. He always began to get afraid when he saw a woman becoming too devoted and spilling tears for him.

He supposed he was in love with her. He adored her lovely face, her quaint foreign accent, and her strange, childlike ways. They had got under his skin. He would hate to think of another man loving her... But somehow, things seemed to be getting difficult. He wanted his women to be gay and always happy. He hated tears and serious discussions.

"Darling. I adore you. Powder your little nose and come along. Sing for me."

Then Hattie bustled in, and Mitsi pulled herself together.

That night she sang the love song Levinsky had composed for her so that it brought tears to other eyes as well as her own.

Especially when she looked across the restaurant to where Bob usually stood at the back, and found he was not there, but sitting at a table deeply occupied with Carol Lewis.

34

Beneath them the Channel swam blue and placid. The sun shone. In a little while it seemed the great plane was flying over the green fields of France.

Then the hangars of Le Bourget lay ahead and the plane began to descend slowly.

Driving from the airport to Paris in the omnibus Larry sat beside her. He was very solicitous towards her for though she had not been so terrified this time, air-sickness had racked her. Now she felt weak and faint, her head throbbed painfully. She was grateful to Larry for his sympathy and attention.

She opened her eyes wondering what had happened to Bob. He was sitting beside Julia giving her his secret charming smile which she thought was for her only. I am a fool to be in love with him she told herself. She closed her eyes wearily again. Larry comforted her with some smelling-salts which he had managed miraculously to procure.

John Foster, who had suddenly decided to accompany them to Paris, did not go on with them to Julia's apartment. He'd call them up later, he said. But Bob, at Julia's invitation, went with them.

Leo was not at the apartment. Instead there was a note, hastily scrawled, explaining he had gone to Aries. (Leo was an ardent Van Gogh "fan"). So they could have more room to kick around in, as Leo put it. Max Cooper had gone with him.

Larry was disappointed at missing his two friends. Mitsi, too, was depressed.

"I expect neither Leon or Max wished to see me looking all glamorized and—how is it?—commercial!" Then she added ruefully:

"I do not feel so very glamorous at this moment!"

"I think you ought to rest," advised Julia. "Just for an hour. It'll do you any amount of good."

"Why should I rest? I am all right now."

"Just look at yourself in the mirror. Lie down and try and sleep. You'll feel much better for it."

Mitsi stared at her reflection and saw a white, pinched face, with great dark shadows under the eyes, hair all disarrayed.

"I look terrible."

"That's why I want you to rest."

"I have come here for a holiday—not to sleep. I could sleep in my hotel in London if I wished to."

"It's not much good trying to do anything in the state you're in. It's only common sense my dear. We shan't go anywhere this morning. Perhaps we'll lunch somewhere, and you'll be quite fit for that if you rest now."

Julia spoke kindly, but she was becoming annoyed. Mitsi was difficult to understand these days. She put it down to the reaction to her sudden change in circumstances and life, and to her emotional adventure with Bob Raymond.

"If you'd rather I rested, I will. You and Larry and Bob can go out. I do not mind being left."

Julia ignored her.

"You think I am being stupid, I know Julia. I am not blind. But I wish that people would leave me alone."

She spoke slowly and evenly, although her fingers were nervously picking at the counterpane on Julia's bed.

"Aren't you being rather silly?"

"Silly?" Her voice rose. "I am tired of being called that. You all think I am a silly child. I am not. I am grown up now."

Red spots rose on her cheekbones, her eyes grew dark with anger. She ran a hand through her hair and left it more disorderly than before.

Julia couldn't help reflecting how rebelliously lovely she looked.

"All right my dear. I'll leave you to think things over, and you can please yourself what you want to do this morning. You'll find me in the studio when you're ready."

Just as she was closing the door, she turned back.

"But remember, I'm a good ten years older than you are, and I've been through it all myself."

She closed the door quietly.

Mitsi sat on the bed forlornly. She felt too weak to weep.

Julia had an unfortunate way of making her feel in the wrong, and yet she felt somewhere deep down that somehow she was right. She wished suddenly she could get away from everyone—Larry, Bob, Julia—all of them, and go away somewhere and start over again. These people had given her everything—they had also made her more unhappy than she had ever been in her life before.

She had loved the beginning of it all. The excitement, the glamour, the admiration, the unexpectedness of everything. The thrill in meeting new people, making new friends. Being admired and loved.

Now, all had gone stale, and even her love had become a doubting, unstable thing—a desperate thing these days. She felt herself clinging on to it—hoping it would last and knowing it wouldn't. She had become jealous and unhappy. She no longer felt complete trust in anyone, it seemed.

She stared out of the window at the trees across the road, bare and glinting in the sunlight of the autumn day. Christmas would soon be here, she thought suddenly. She remembered her last Christmas spent with her mother in Zurich. Even then, the easy tears wouldn't come. She laid her head down on the soft pillows and within a moment, had sunk into a troubled sleep.

The door softly opened and Larry came in. He leant over the bed and seeing her asleep, smiled down at her. Looking up his eye chanced to catch his reflection in the mirror by the bed.

Hastily he drew up, pulled his tie straight, and muttering: "Sentimental mush," stalked with dignity towards the door.

She turned in her sleep and heard his heavy determined step on the polished boards. She opened her eyes and seeing him murmured:

"Larry."

He came back, his expression firm and business-like once more.

She stretched up a hand, and he clasped it in his own.

"Feeling better?" he asked brusquely.

"Julia said you were feeling rotten, so I came in to take a look at you."

"Julia is a nice person."

"She's all right," he replied nonchalantly. But she knew all the while that he meant a whole world in those few off-hand words.

"Where's Bob?"

"Making omelettes with Julia. Hope you can eat one. He's going to a tremendous amount of trouble over them, but they look quite impossible to me—at the moment anyway. They might rise some day of course. You can never tell with omelettes, can you?"

She drew her long, slim legs up and sat up in bed.

"Give me a comb. I will get up now."

She ran the comb through her hair and, ignoring a shiny nose, went with Larry into the studio.

The familiar room helped still further to restore her confidence in herself. The large earthenware jar on the hearth was filled with enormous double hothouse chrysanthemums. Another jar of them stood on the piano. The lid was covered with dust. Running her finger over it she said:

"Leo just lets the housekeeper do nothing when Julia's away. I expect he pays her just to admire his paintings instead of working!"

She picked up an old paint-duster of Leo's, found a clean spot and rubbed it over the piano. The tawny flowers gleamed in reflection on the dark wood.

Larry smiled at her.

"You're a silly kid, aren't you?"

"Everyone calls me silly."

And this time she laughed.

Julia came in.

She looked untidy from her exertions in the kitchen.

"It's really too bad having to cook on a Sunday morning, isn't it? Leo's very conveniently the complete artist when there's any preparing to be done in the house."

"Let's go out for lunch, Julia," Larry suggested.

"Yes, darling. But we've got to have breakfast yet, don't forget! Bob's being completely stoical as far as cooking goes. He's making the most amazing omelettes—simply bunging everything we've got in the larder into them." Bob's sleek head appeared in the doorway.

"Better darling?" he queried of Mitsi.

"Yes thank you."

They ate Bob's omelettes amid a babble of facetious remarks from Larry and Julia. Mitsi prepared to enjoy her second visit to Paris.

Julia decided after all that she could put Bob up if he didn't mind sleeping in the studio on the divan.

He readily agreed.

35

Just before lunch, Julia telephoned Sadie Harris.

Sadie was entertaining some people from the States, however. They decided not to break in on her. She offered them her car for the week-end and they decided to motor out to Fontainebleu that afternoon.

Mitsi joyfully suggested lunching at the small restaurant she and Julia had visited when she had first tasted Sauterne.

"Cold to lunch outside, isn't it?" Bob commented.

"It is beautifully sunny and warm," she argued.

"All right. Let's sit out on the pavement and freeze! It'll be a new experience for us all, and ought to be very amusing!"

They found the little restaurant.

To Bob's surprise, there were other people also enjoying the sunshine at the cheery looking tables.

"Human nature's beyond me," he remarked. "My soup'll be frozen by the time it reaches me, and it's not exactly the time of year to have it iced!"

Julia and Mitsi recalled their last visit, and Mitsi begged for Sauterne again, and by the end of lunch was in a gay mood.

They drove out to Fontainebleu. The woods were gaunt-looking now, the branches of the trees almost leafless, clothed only in the autumn sunlight.

They wandered about there till dusk was falling. Then Sadie's car purred back to Paris with them.

"After tea, we'll drift over to Sadie's," said Julia.

"Are you sure she won't mind me appearing on the scene?" asked Bob.

He was at the wheel.

"She'll probably mind very much after she's met you, but she's too well brought up to show it!"

Bob flashed her an over-elaborately charming smile.

"Thanks, pal! Matter of fact, I wouldn't be surprised if she's heard of me anyway, I know plenty of people who know her."

Mitsi was looking forward to seeing Sadie again. She hoped she would sing to them.

"John'll be there I expect," she said.

It happened to be John Foster himself who opened the door to them when Mitsi, Bob, Larry and Julia arrived at Sadie's that evening.

He beamed on them and ushered them into the large room which Mitsi remembered from her last visit.

"The visitors have departed," John grinned at them. "There's only Sadie and me left. Others will be arriving bit by bit during the evening. I've got a new cocktail for you all… 'Mitsi's Mixture' it's called! Come right on in ladies and gentlemen!"

Sadie was reclining on a divan when they entered and she rose and came to them with arms outstretched. She hugged Julia affectionately.

"Darling—it's grand to see you back. I had an idea I'd go away this week-end with the Jacksons—they've just left, and then when I got your wire, I decided to stay."

Bob Raymond was introduced.

"Raymond? I've heard someone—let me think—we've got someone in common I'm sure?"

She wrinkled her surprising nose at him.

Then she exclaimed: "Of course! Carol Lewis and Louise what's-her-name! All that crowd."

Bob shook hands with her decorously.

Sadie wore vividly jade green pyjamas, and her amazing hair was even redder than ever. Bob wondered what people could see to make a fuss about in this vastly common-looking woman.

He recalled Carol speaking about her many times. She had stayed with her in Paris. He supposed people made use of her money. Most certainly Carol would, although she had enough and to spare herself.

"Let me see, aren't you engaged to Carol Lewis?" suddenly broke in Sadie, her memory returning as she scrutinized him frankly.

"I was. I'm not now."

He went hot and cold all over, wondering what next she would un- earth in front of Mitsi.

"When she was last over here I got the notion you were all set for wedding bells!" Sadie laughed. "But ain't that women all over! You'd better do something about it."

Mitsi looked at Bob, and he smiled uncomfortably at her. She gave him a funny, twisted sort of smile back.

Sadie rattled on.

"Well, after all that digging up the back garden, what about a cock- tail? John's inventive genius has been at work again. He's dedicated one to Mitsi! I say, my dear, I'm so glad you went over big in London. But then, you've got the goods!"

And Sadie put an arm round Mitsi's shoulders and led her to the bar where John was vigorously manhandling a cocktail-shaker.

Mitsi was amazed to learn Sadie knew so much about her adventures in London. She seemed to have followed her career right from the beginning. She knew her various programmes at the Gardenia. What songs she sang. That Levinsky was writing for her. Everything.

"How did you know all this?"

"How would I know all of it, except by a scout?" Sadie teased her. "Matter of fact, John Foster has been following things about you pretty closely. Larry, too, has kept me well-informed. Now I've retired, I feel a kind of interest in you, for I guess you're about the nearest to my kind of act as anybody yet. But my dear—I hope you get better breaks than I did—"

Her face clouded over.

"But you were a great success," Mitsi protested. "People speak of you even now. Al, my pianist at the club has all your records, and always talks about you as being the greatest singer ever."

"Bless him!"

Sadie smiled wryly. Then she eyed Mitsi intently.

"The one thing you want to be careful about in this job my dear, is—scandal." There was a bitterness in her tone. "It just dogs the footsteps of anyone in the limelight."

"Why?"

"People still have the notion stage and film folk live right up to the hilt. That they have little or no morals, therefore, they're news! Everything you do is watched, and if there's the slightest breath of gossip, you bet your boots you'll suffer before they're through with you!"

Sadie drew a deep breath.

"Believe me, kid—I *know!...* "

Mitsi saw that her mouth was drawn in a bitter line. Her eyes were pools of suffering. Sadie patted her arm with an almost maternal touch.

"So don't forget—watch out—or they'll get you!"

And she turned away to call out a joke to someone who passed.

Mitsi looked round the pleasant room, restful and peaceful. The big windows with their long green curtains. Everything seemed so light, so gay, so happy. Laughing people round the cocktail bar. Sadie in her green pyjamas and flaming hair, her lustrous black eyes shining like jewels out of a dead white face. The radiogram beating out dance music.

Who would guess that tragedy had stepped into the lives of any person there?

Who would guess, to look at Sadie now, laughing and waving to someone, that her life had finished five years ago. And the years between and years ahead were dead, years to be lived through the best she could.

That behind the white mask of her face was tragedy she had only hinted at?

Mitsi could not prevent a shudder passing through her.

"Come on Mitsi, stop day-dreaming!"

It was Larry's voice and she felt his hand, cool and friendly, slip into hers. Her life, she sought to comfort her own apprehension, was real and ordered anyway. Nothing like that could happen to her.

He swept her into a dance, and John Foster danced with Julia. Bob turned to Sadie by the cocktail-bar.

"Do you know Carol Lewis very well?"

"I got to know her through Louise—known *her* years. Louise brought her over to Paris once for a week-end when I was feeling kind of flat and I wired her to bring some of her friends. I think she's very lovely to look at."

She paused and sipped her cocktail.

She looked up at Bob as if to measure exactly what sort of person he was, and what his ideas on Carol Lewis were. She was certain Carol had mentioned she was still engaged to this Bob Raymond. She was also certain she wore a ring all the time she'd been over during her last visit.

"Yes. But we're *not* going to be married, you know."

"She was wearing a lovely sapphire ring on the right finger about three weeks back anyway! She and Louise were stopping at the Hotel Meurice and I saw them every day."

Bob's face grew set.

Sadie went on mercilessly: "Big square sapphire it was. I remember remarking on the stone. Still, maybe it's someone else. Maybe I oughtn't to have mentioned it just now. Didn't realize I was being tactless!"

She gave him an ingenuous smile.

"That ring was one of my mother's I had re-set and gave to her before we were engaged. She wore it as an engagement ring too, until I bought her another one. We broke off our engagement just before she went to the States. She thought I liked women in general too much to be particularly faithful to any one!"

He laughed.

She didn't smile back at him this time.

He added more seriously:

"I don't like her going around, saying we're engaged. But can't very well tell her myself."

"To be honest, I'd say Carol Lewis is just a bit treacherous. I'd watch my step if I were you."

He lowered his eyes and fingered his glass thoughtfully for a moment.

"Carol's all right, really… As a matter of fact we get on amazingly well. But the idea of being tied to each other didn't work out."

"Maybe I oughtn't to talk like this. But then I'm just a rather outspoken Yank!" Sadie chuckled. "And I guess when it comes to knowing people, I know my onions!"

"I'm sure you do."

He looked across the room at Mitsi dancing with Larry.

How beautiful, cool, and attractive she was. He tried to imagine her as his wife. He felt suddenly tender as he thought of it. But it was damned silly for him to think of marriage—especially with little Mitsi.

He turned to Sadie.

"Let's dance."

36

The door-bell pealed loudly and Sadie dived towards it.

Amid a babel of voices, she ushered into the room about half a dozen young people. Mitsi dancing with Larry recognized some of the party who had been present when she had first visited Sadie. She dragged Larry towards them.

Larry sighed and looked appealingly at the ceiling. Unwillingly, he accompanied her and joined the noisy newcomers. As he eyed them with a jaundiced eye he was thinking: I don't even get a thrill after writing a good column, or getting a good scoop. He decided he needed a holiday—right away from everyone and everything. And there and then determined Christmas would find him miles away from anywhere, in peace and quiet.

Mitsi was swept up in the noise and talk. Most of the people who had burst in were Americans and had been away from Paris during the time since she had last seen them. It amazed her, as they babbled on, that people lived the sort of lives they did.

Restless. Always going to the right places at the right time. Doing something different every week. Spending an infinite amount of money on the feverish, endless pursuit of pleasure.

"You know, there's always something going on somewhere that one has to rush off to... There isn't a dull moment in this world!"

It was a small peroxide blonde with startling artificial eyelashes who made this announcement energetically.

Bob seemed to suddenly appear at Mitsi's side. He nudged her elbow.

"Don't gape darling," he whispered.

"Gape? What is it?"

"Stare in a lunatic fashion!... I know you hardly believe they're real!" He laughed.

"They are extraordinary people!" she said.

He handed her a drink. She refused, but he pressed it into her hand.

"Must get the convivial atmosphere!"

She sipped it.

It was John's concoction, the "Mitsi Mixture," as he called it. In a moment it seemed she was seeing as though through a mirror.

The room, the people, the colours seemed to be conveyed to her brain through other eyes than her own. She felt immensely distant, cut off from it all, and a golden glow surrounded her. She turned and found herself speaking to people—saying things which she felt were correct, but was hardly conscious of saying. It was as if another identity had taken possession of herself.

The sound of the chatter and laughter, the clink of ice, the crackling of the fire, Bob's voice in her ear, were distinct, but seemed far away—unrelated to her.

She found herself immersed in a conversation with the peroxide blonde.

"I guess you get the best undies in the whole world from Chambrun on 56th—don't you?" said the blonde.

"Yes, I think so."

"I got some of the nattiest pairs of step-ins there. They look swell on. I always think it takes a super-humanly good figure to look good in panties, but these just are the last word. My husband—that's him over there, the fat one making animal noises—he thinks they're great."

Mitsi nodded.

"It is so important he should, isn't it?"

"I guess he wouldn't notice anything anyway unless I told him. He just takes me for granted these days, but we get along. I guess I wouldn't get along with anybody else but Jack. He understands my moods, and I understand his."

Bob appeared again and led her away.

"Sadie's making food in the kitchen. Let's go and help her."

They went down the broad staircase towards the kitchen.

"Funnily arranged house this, isn't it? Rather fascinating though," he remarked as he steered her downwards. Then with a shrewd sideways glance at her:

"Just the tiniest bit tight aren't you?"

"I have a strange feeling," she admitted. "I do not like drinking this."

They found Sadie whipping some cream in a bowl.

"Hello, chicks," she said as they entered. "Guests are never allowed in the kitchen. Go on—beat it upstairs. I told you to keep people out, Bob!"

She smiled a brilliant smile at them, and they left her.

Halfway up the stairs, Bob stopped and took her in his arms.

"There's something about you I can't get out of my system."

She clung to him fiercely. His arms tightened round her.

"Let's go—let's leave them. They won't notice we've gone."

"Yes—let's go."

She found her fur cape and joined him in the hall. He opened the door, and a rush of cold air blew in on them. He closed it quietly and they went down to Sadie's car.

It was dark except for the light shed from the head lamps of the cars parked outside. He held her close to him. She was trembling.

"Let's take it and drive to the stars."

And he opened the door of the great car for her.

Then they both stood transfixed.

"Party all over?" asked Larry, rousing himself from the sleep he had been taking in the front seat. He was staring up at them enquiringly.

37

"No—er—going more strongly than ever," said Bob.

He tried to hide the annoyance in his voice.

"What are you leaving for then?"

Larry was wide awake by now.

"Mitsi's got a headache and I thought we'd go for a run in the Bois just to get rid of it."

"I know a better thing for a headache than a run in the Bois." He smiled up at Mitsi slowly. "Come right back with me, and I'll put you right."

She looked at Bob. He shook his head slightly.

"I wish to go for a run in the park," she said.

Larry stared at her levelly. He saw the flushed cheeks, the bright eyes, the disordered hair as she stood in the glow of the head lamps.

She's popping off with him he told himself with certainty. And she's a bit tiddly. So's he. They neither of them know what they're doing.

He got out of the car. Took Mitsi by the arm, and turning to Bob said quietly:

"Sorry, old boy. She's not used to Sadie's odd drinks. Nice of you to suggest taking her for a run to cool the old fevered brow, but that wouldn't do a bit of good. She needs a pick-me-up, and Sadie's got the finest in Paris."

He led her firmly towards the door and rang the bell.

Bob followed. He was angry, but he wasn't quite sure whether Larry himself was sober or not. Whether he really meant what he said, or whether he had guessed their game and was deliberately and politely trying to stop it.

Somebody answered the door and they went in.

Bob watched Larry hurry Mitsi off, then with a scowl he made straight for the bar, found himself another drink, and attached himself to a red-haired girl who was standing near.

"Loose?" he queried.

"In what sense?"

She smiled provocatively at him. "My husband's disappeared to show a girl called Peggy Sadie's Chinese lamp. Wherever that may be."

He smiled back into her eyes.

Mitsi, still held firmly by the arm, was led into Sadie's magnificent green and white bathroom. Larry sat her down on the edge of the bath and opened the medicine chest.

She suddenly felt flat, and cold and miserable. She remembered how she had clung to Bob on the stairs, and blushed at the memory. She watched Larry bending over several bottles, trying to find the right one.

He finally filled a medicine-glass with something and told her to drink it. She gulped it down, hardly tasting anything, and then collapsed, head in her hands.

He regarded her with a set jaw.

He hadn't believed it was in her to make herself cheap with Bob. She leant against him, and he thought for a moment she would either be sick or burst into tears. He drew her up.

"How do you feel?"

"Very bad."

"You'll feel all right in a minute. Sadie's having some food sent up and you must try and eat some. Then you'll be quite all right."

He began to feel sorry for her.

"I'm so glad you were in the car," she said.

"I seem to have butted in."

"You didn't. I was feeling—" she broke off. "Oh, I don't know. I'm glad you were there, anyway! I don't feel like that any longer."

"That's all right. Better?"

Her head began to clear. She heard his voice close and real once more. The bath, the medicine chest, the bath-stool, the green rug on the floor, adjusted themselves.

"I'm all right now."

Suddenly she threw her arms round his neck. Taken by surprise, he stood limply leaning against the white tiled wall. Her head rested on his shoulder. She looked up at him, a golden curl tickling his nose.

"I do like you so much—so very much," she said, her eyes shining into his.

"Good!"

He thought: I'd better not kiss her. She's had enough of that already this evening I expect. He patted her shoulder paternally.

Once again she realized the depths of his strength, as she had done the first time she had met him. Rock-like, that was what he was, she thought. Sure and certain.

"Let's get back and nose out some food, shall we?"

She nodded and clung to his arm.

Perhaps that'll just about cure her of Bob, he hoped. She looks a bit sick about it all. Funny how she seems to think I'm a sort of big brother! Never guesses I might feel exactly the same as Bob does.

When they got back to the room, Bob Raymond was not to be found anywhere. Mitsi was surprised by her sigh of relief when she found he wasn't there.

"You're a prize chump, you know," Larry said presently. "Getting yourself tight like that. You should never drink more than you can take."

"I don't think Bob thought I was anywhere near being tight," she said.

"Blast Bob!" Larry told her cheerfully.

38

Christmas Day would fall on the Saturday.

Bob invited Mitsi and Larry down to the house-party he was giving at an aunt's house at Leamarket, which he'd borrowed for the celebrations. They were to come down together early on the Thursday.

Bob realized the club would do "gala" business that night and on Christmas Eve, so it was arranged he and Mitsi should drive up to the Gardenia Thursday and Friday evening, returning after the show.

Mitsi drove Larry down to Leamarket in her blue car. They passed through the little village and approached the house through a large park.

Larry had told her something about the place but she was quite amazed at the sight of the magnificent old building which stood at the end of a long drive.

The drive was lined with great trees, their branches bare and brittle-looking against the hard blue of the winter sky. The house was built of old grey stone, creeper-clad, and weathered with age.

Smooth green lawns stretched out in front of it. The windows were mostly latticed. As they drew nearer, Mitsi saw a great stained glass window which caught and held the rays from the sun like jewels. This window was above a mighty oak door which was the main entrance.

Not a soul was to be seen. It was quiet, and the old house stood an almost living, quiescent mass. Involuntarily, she shivered.

"What's wrong? Don't you like the place?"

"I do not know. It looks so cold and grim. It is very beautiful, of course. But I do not feel I could be happy here."

"Bosh!"

She smiled at him, but she could not dispel the feeling the place gave her.

It was as grim and chilling as the castles she had seen perched high up among the fir-covered hills and mountains of the Tyrol. Always, those dark buildings had awed and frightened her. In the towns and villages she lost that fear. But she felt as if in the ancient stones antiquity spoke, the dry rot of Age laid a disapproving finger on the present.

"I feel almost ashamed to bring my car here!" she said. "It is so new, so modern, and here everything is so old. I feel it must frown on us!"

He laughed outright.

"Much too impressionable, my child—that's what you are."

She swung the car up to the great door, heavy oak and massive iron hinges.

Larry hopped out and pulled a great bell, which echoed and re-echoed throughout the house beyond.

Over the portals of the door a coat of arms had been cut out of the stone. She stood beside him and stared up at it. Beneath the shield she made out some worn words. She read them out haltingly:

"Deus—nobis—haec...ot—what is that?—otia—fecit..." she read.

"Latin."

"What does it mean?"

He translated for her.

"It means: 'God has given us this place of peace'."

Lips apart, she stared up at the impressive Latin legend which had been cut there centuries ago. She drew a little sigh, and repeated the words to herself, as if deriving some comfort from them.

"God has given us this place of peace."

At that moment the door swung open and Bob himself was greeting them. Behind him Mitsi saw the figure of an old butler shuffling in answer to the bell.

"Did it in good time," cried Bob. "Lunch is almost ready."

He smiled expansively at Mitsi.

"Hope you'll like it here. A real old-fashioned English Christmas!" He laughed at Larry. "Eh, old boy?"

"Oh, very hearty!"

He turned to the sedate and rather broken-down butler at his elbow.

"I'll get your things taken up. Expect you'd like a wash and brush up."

The butler took the suit-cases, assisted by Larry, and they followed him up the immensely wide highly-polished and uncarpeted staircase.

"Nobody else is arriving until tomorrow. Couldn't cope with them today," Bob explained.

"I put you both on the first floor. The rooms aren't quite so damp and musty—they smell a bit more lived-in. Besides, it's more convenient in case of fire!"

The butler threw open a door.

She found herself in a vast room, furnished with old, heavy, but what must have been extremely valuable furniture. The room seemed to her to be like a cathedral, and she wondered how on earth she would ever get to sleep in the midst of all that space. It will feel rather like sleeping in a bed in the middle of Waterloo Station, very exposed and faintly indecent, she thought.

"Hope you'll be comfortable, my dear," said Bob and he proceeded with Larry—who carried his own suit-case—along the corridor.

Mitsi's suit-cases were placed on the floor beside the bed by the old butler, who appeared to suffer from asthma.

"I'll send someone up to help Madame unpack," he said, and wheezed his way back to the door.

She gazed round her. Amid the heavy furniture, the several water-colour prints of fox-hunting scenes struck a flippant note.

She walked across to the windows and then sighed deeply at the perfect view which lay before her.

Miles of unbroken field and park land. In the distance the smoke curling up from the chimneys of the cottages in the village. It was a bitterly cold, frosty December day. There was no wind, and the window panes felt faintly warm from the sun as she leant her forehead against them. A discreet tap on the door drew her away.

"Come in."

A small, neat maidservant entered. She swung the door of the great wardrobe open and hung Mitsi's dresses and suits on little padded and lavender-scented hangers. Mitsi watched her silently.

Presently Bob appeared at the door.

"Coming down to have a look round before lunch?"

Since the episode at Sadie's party, she had felt almost embarrassed by his evident longing for her. What scared her most was the knowledge that despite what she felt about him in her saner moments, he had even more power now to stir her. She knew she could so easily make a fool of herself over him. She knew she still could love him.

They went downstairs. In the spacious hall a large log fire burned on the hearth.

"You'll meet my favourite aunt at lunch," he said. "Don't mind her, though. She's a very abrupt way some people take for sheer rudeness. But she doesn't mean it a bit."

Larry came in.

"It's simply grand here, Bob! Gosh! The timeless ages this old house must've been standing."

Bob nodded.

"It's quite a place."

"Nice of you to ask us along before the gang break up the peaceful atmosphere," said Larry. Then he turned to Mitsi.

"Wonderful old lady—Bob's aunt. Always has her own way—even against her obstinate—not to say pig-headed—nephew!"

"Not so far as the night-club went. However, she's reconciled to that now, because the money's coming in!"

They entered the long, sunny dining-room, and Mitsi decided it was quite the most pleasant room in the house. Long french windows opened into the garden. They were closed now, and the garden outside was barren of flowers, but the sun shone into the room and made a golden pathway across the old polished boards of the floor to the elaborately carved and highly-polished legs of the long dining-table.

"Aunt's not here yet. Likes to make an entrance when everyone else is here and waiting for her. Would you care for anything to drink? Somehow or other, we always have our pre-lunch sherry in here."

Both Mitsi and Larry refused.

"If I lived down here, I'd go completely off drink," said Larry. "It's so solidly healthy!"

Mitsi privately thought the atmosphere of the house, apart from the dining-room, was too depressing and sombre.

"Makes me drink all the more!" said Bob. "Feel I must keep up all the old traditions. And drinking has remained a Raymond tradition since they started a few hundred years ago!"

He poured out a sherry for himself. As he laid the glass down, his aunt came in.

She was a tall and handsome old woman. Her hair was completely white and gathered softly back from her face into a large bun at the nape of her neck.

The contrast of the soft white hair framing the white, hard, arrogant face was startling. She wore black, a dress of nondescript material and style. Mitsi felt inferior and small as she watched her cross the room towards them.

She'll hate me, she thought. She'll hate me first because I'm foreign. Then she'll hate me because I'm a night-club entertainer.

Bob introduced her. The old lady's hand was cold and Mitsi felt her long nails claw into her hand as she gripped it.

"You're helping my nephew with this club idea are you?"

Mitsi muttered a reply, feeling foolishly tongue-tied.

The old lady crossed over to the head of the table and sat down. The others followed suit, and the butler entered ready to serve.

Mitsi was glad the old lady ignored her. She seemed to like Larry. He amused her, and flattered her. Nobody could help liking Larry though.

There was a lull in the conversation for a few moments. Then the old lady turned suddenly to Mitsi.

"You're French, aren't you?"

"Yes."

"What part?"

"Paris."

"Very nice too... I found the Parisians very gay and quite unreliable."

"Mitsi doesn't take after them" Bob broke in. "She's very quiet and *extremely* reliable. Never let us down yet, has she Larry?"

Larry shook his head.

The old lady gazed at Mitsi. Took in her golden hair, her beautiful expressive eyes, her fine features, her clothes and beautifully manicured hands.

"Surely Linden is an English name?"

"My father was English. I am really half-English, but as I was born and brought up in France I consider myself French."

"Don't cross-examine the child, aunt!" Bob grinned.

His aunt held up her eating operations to glance at her nephew in annoyance.

"I don't cross-examine people. You don't understand the value of direct statement nowadays. That's what's wrong with young people. They don't look facts in the face. Fritter their lives away doing nothing, wasting a lot of energy in enjoying themselves!"

Bob laughed outright.

"Tell that to the Y.M.C.A.!" he said.

"No respect for their elders either!" was the snapped response. "I wouldn't dare to have answered *my* aunt like that."

"Thank God my aunt isn't as bad as yours was!"

She looked up at him and smiled. Then she said sweetly:

"By the way—I've asked Carol down. I knew you'd really like her to come. Although you do keep on pretending you're not friends."

Bob gaped at her, surprised and angry.

"I thought this was to be my house-party," he muttered.

He looked as if he'd been struck by a thunderbolt.

"I was only trying to help," she replied mildly, buttering a biscuit.

Bob started to say something. Instead, his voice trailed away into dumb fury.

Larry began talking animatedly.

Mitsi didn't hear what he said. She suddenly felt if she ate any more she would choke. Bob looked miserable, unhappy and furiously annoyed all at once. She felt angry, rebellious. Why should Carol Lewis always intrude on her happiness?

Larry thought: Going to be a storm!

Presently lunch was over. The old lady tactfully indicated Larry to take Mitsi round and show her the place. She wanted to talk to her nephew.

Larry took Mitsi round the garden, down the orchard, over the house. Showing her the antiques, the cameos, the pricelessly valuable chairs with the *petit point* upholstery. The piano made like a spinet in gilt-covered wood.

By the time they had finished and made their way back to the hall, she was quite weary, but still she had not mentioned Carol Lewis or Bob.

He felt he must say something to reassure her, to try to make her holiday happy.

"You know, she's a tactless old devil," he said. "You must try and make this easier for Bob, by not showing anything. He didn't want the Lewis woman down, of course. Try and let him see it doesn't bother you."

39

Mitsi did not see Bob again until they met in the hall for tea. His aunt didn't join them, for which fact she was grateful.

He looked almost himself as he came downstairs to the tea-table laid invitingly in front of the great fire, and Larry looked up sympathetically at him. Bob smiled ruefully back.

Larry sensed that whatever the other's feeling on the matter, and he doubted even those, he would never be allowed to marry Mitsi. Auntie would put her foot down. He saw the end of Bob's and Mitsi's relationship in view.

As this realization hit him a sudden thought followed, and with it some feeling of alarm: Did Mitsi also realize that? Did she believe so implicitly in Bob? Did she think they *would* one day be married?

Mentally, Larry heaved a mighty sigh.

Said Bob, helping himself to buttered toast:

"What time do you think we ought to start up for town Mitsi?"

"We came down in about two hours… Perhaps we should leave about nine o'clock?"

Bob turned to Larry.

"What about you, old man? Will you come up too? Or would you prefer to stay down here and entertain Aunt?"

Larry smiled grimly.

"I'll be the brave boy and stay down here."

"Right. I can ask one or two people in after dinner if you like just to help entertain you."

"No thanks. Your Aunt and I will be quite happy, I'm sure."

"Stout fellah!"

"I should feel very lonely if I stayed down here too long," Mitsi said.

"Why?" asked Larry.

"It's so large. It seems so quiet—so—secret."

She glanced round the hall, lit by great old bracket lamps in the walls. Admittedly, it looked cheerful enough now with its long red curtains drawn against the black night outside. The fire was crackling merrily enough. The tea-table looked human—with Bob and Larry on either side of the fire. But the place seemed to cast a spell on her.

"You're too imaginative."

"There's nothing much wrong with the house, actually."

Bob took another piece of toast and added, his mouth full:

"Of course during the Reformation one or two bloody deeds were carried out here. Otherwise we haven't any sort of a ghost or anything to create any creepy atmosphere. Perhaps we might perpetrate one or two bloody deeds over the week-end. Just to give Mitsi something substantial to worry about!"

"Feeling homicidal old man?" Larry queried.

"Pretty near it!"

He switched on the radio. They were rewarded with a dance band playing one of Mitsi's tunes.

"That's better!"

And Bob gave her the little, secret smile that stirred her so.

As they played, she hummed the words softly.

Larry said nothing, but after giving them quizzical looks puffed contentedly at his pipe and gazed into the fire. Bob looked up across the hearth at her.

The firelight played over her face and her softly curving lips as she half-sang to herself. The flames made a golden halo of her hair. Her long slim legs were crossed under her and the tightened skirt showed the lovely line from hip to knee. Her fascinatingly husky voice softly singing seemed to change her personality—from that of a young girl to a woman of mystery and allure.

He thought with pleasure of driving her up to town tonight. And coming back through the quiet night, away from the noisy city to the peace of the country.

The warmth of the fire made Mitsi drowsy. Presently her head nodded and she fell asleep.

"Poor girl's tired," murmured Bob.

"Let her snooze, then."

And Larry relaxed again in his chair and closed his eyes.

"Have I been asleep?" Bob mocked her presently in time with her wakening remark.

She smiled sleepily at him.

"I'm so sorry. It is the fire—it is so warm and soothing."

Mitsi decided to wear a black long-sleeved dress. It was correct to wear semi-evening dress for dinner in private houses wasn't it? She mused as she took it out of the great wardrobe.

A discreet rap sounded at the door and the maidservant came in.

"I didn't put anything out for Madame, because I wasn't sure what you would like to wear."

"Thank you. Oh, what is your name?"

"Ellen. Your bath is ready, Madame."

Her voice had a slight burr which Mitsi found attractive.

"Is there anything I can do for Madame?" she asked.

"I don't think so Ellen."

The maid smiled at her and went out. Before closing the door, she popped her head round and said:

"If you want me Madame, there's a bell by the bed, and I'll be up in a second when it rings."

Mitsi put on a dressing-gown of heavy quilted satin and ventured out into the corridor towards the bathroom. Along the passage two doors were open. She could hear Larry and Bob calling to each other. She hurried into the bathroom, a vast room like all the others, fitted, however, in modern chromium, and it had a shower.

By the time she got back to her room, she had decided in a panic that she would return to her London hotel tonight and never come back to the old house. She frankly dreaded the thought of tomorrow and Carol Lewis.

She slipped into the dress—long and slimly fitting black velvet with long tight sleeves.

She went downstairs.

She found a cigarette in a box on the mantelpiece in the hall and lit it. When Bob and Larry came down they found her smoking nervously.

She answered their comments with an excuse. She did not tell them what was in her mind.

"I'll get you a nice mellowing sherry," smiled Larry. "That'll comfort you."

He went out of the hall towards the dining-room.

Bob came close to her.

"Darling…" he murmured. "You make me forget all the things that trouble and bother me. All the things I've done and don't want to remember. All that I am and hate being… Your skin's so soft—like the velvet of your dress."

She looked up at him. She loved him when he was like this. She could understand him. But when he was with others, he went so far from her. He seemed a stranger.

She kissed his dark head lightly.

40

They heard Larry returning.

Bob turned away and leaned against the mantelpiece.

"Here you are—three light sherries I think."

He raised his glass. "A toast!"

"To…?" queried Bob.

Larry was looking at him seriously.

"To a lot of things you hope for, and fight for against other things. And to those things you fight against which turn out to be the proper *and* the best things in the end!"

Bob smiled a crooked smile at him.

"Good old philosopher, Larry."

They drank.

At about nine o'clock Mitsi got into Bob's car and they roared off through the night towards London.

It was dark, almost pitch black. No stars or moon lighted the way for them. Only the big headlamps which cut a brilliant pathway through the night.

She was snuggled comfortably into her seat beside Bob.

"I'd like to be tearing off down to Southampton now and hop a boat. Get away from all this damned business doing what other people expect of you and tell you."

His face was grim, as he steered the great car expertly through narrow roads towards the big main road to London.

She was silent. There seemed nothing for her to say.

At length they arrived at the Gardenia and she hurried to her room to change.

The club was full of revellers celebrating Christmas early, and her show got a wonderful reception. Her spirits rose, as they always did when she felt she had helped people to enjoy themselves.

"No dancing tonight. As soon as you've finished, change and meet me out by the car," Bob told her.

She hurried out of the club where the car was parked in a quiet street.

She saw the red glow of his cigarette as he sat by the driver's seat, already waiting for her. She got in beside him and he started off.

Neither of them had much in the way of conversation.

Lulled to sleep by the movement of the great car, she presently found herself nodding.

"Lean on my shoulder and go to sleep."

He put an arm round her and she slept for the rest of the way back on his shoulder. She was still asleep when they drew up outside the great house.

He lifted her gently out of the car and carried her indoors and upstairs. He laid her down on the bed in her room, still half-asleep.

"I am too lazy," she said, looking up at him and smiled drowsily. "But I loved the way you carried me in. It made me feel quite small and completely in your power!"

"Big strong man!" he mocked, looking down at her slim length on the enormous bed.

He bent over and took her in his arms.

"You're so sweet," he said.

Then he closed the door quietly behind him and went along to his own room.

The following day dawned brightly, and promised another day of brilliant frosty sunshine.

Downstairs Bob found Larry and Mitsi finishing their breakfast. Mitsi was standing by the window with a cup of coffee in her hand gazing out at the frost-covered lawn.

Bob helped himself to breakfast and sat down. She watched him from the window. Ever since she had woken up, she had looked forward to meeting him at breakfast.

Every time she was away from him, she looked forward to seeing him again.

"When are you expecting your other guests, Bob?" enquired Larry.

"Most of them are arriving for tea—some of them won't be down until dinner-time."

"Who's coming?"

"You know most of them... Louise Dalvanya's bringing her husband—he seems to be about these days, so I've heard!"

Larry nodded. Looking out of the window, said:

"If I had some breeches I'd go riding if I had a horse, if I could ride!"

"There's some good walking if you like."

"Thanks! I'll go and leave you in peace."

Larry gave Mitsi an expansive smile and went out of the dining-room.

"You must excuse Aunt," Bob apologized to Mitsi. "She always has breakfast upstairs in her sitting-room."

He looked at her approvingly. In her bright yellow woollen suit she looked charming. He put out his hand and as she took it, drew her towards him.

"I've made up my mind this week-end's going to be hell!" he said unhappily. "So whatever happens, don't take any notice, and we'll try and make the best of it ourselves."

She put on some strong brogues and they set off for a walk together. It was a wonderful morning; the ground firm and frosty. The air was biting and invigorating.

They returned to lunch, with Mitsi in high spirits.

Even Bob's aunt did not seem quite so terrifying.

The first of the guests to arrive was Louise Dalvanya and her husband.

In the Count, charming, middle-aged and slim, Mitsi felt she had found an ally. They chattered away in French to each other and Mitsi experienced a comforting sense of happiness in talking her own language once more. Louise herself was as inevitably charming as ever and tea was very gay.

After tea, the great door-bell rang to announce Carol Lewis. Almost before the butler had closed it again, a clamour of voices outside told of yet other arrivals.

Six people came in to be introduced by Bob. To Mitsi they all seemed somewhat cheery and red-faced. Carol Lewis only just condescended to notice her.

At length the guests dispersed to dress for dinner. Mitsi decided to wear the same dress she had worn the previous evening.

Carol contrived to keep everyone waiting. But when she came down, dressed in green, with a tight bolero coat, even Mitsi had to admit she made a picture worth waiting for.

After dinner Carol Lewis strolled up to Bob.

"Didn't want me to come did you Bob?"

"I didn't I'm afraid."

"Too bad I should spoil your nice week-end."

"You haven't—yet!"

"Charming person!"

He sighed, then said slowly:

"I'm afraid I'm getting like that nowadays. I find it easier for me to say what I mean."

"I see. But you're lying! You don't tell yourself the truth."

He didn't answer.

Larry was whispering to Mitsi:

"What've you got Bob for Christmas?"

"A silver mascot for the bonnet of his car. He admired it in Bond Street the other day. I know he will like it."

"He'd better!"

Presently Bob came along to remind her it was time to leave for the club.

Mitsi hurried to her room to change. She paused to take out the beautifully modelled silver greyhound she had bought for Bob. It was perfect in every detail. She longed to see his pleasure at her gift.

She unfolded another parcel and examined two beautiful old prints she had bought for Larry. Julia had once told her he was a keen collector.

She replaced them carefully, and with a little smile on her lips continued with her dressing.

41

Christmas day was crisp and frosty with a brilliant blue sky. A bright sun awoke Mitsi.

She knelt on her bed looking out of the window at the clear fresh view.

Larry knocked on her door just as she was ready to go down to breakfast.

"Merry Christmas!"

"Merry Christmas!"

She came out of her room and they went down together.

In the morning light, the house looked wonderfully cheerful with holly and mistletoe all over the place.

Mitsi was astonished at the way in which everybody seemed to become young again as the day progressed and the festive spirit became more pronounced. She loved every moment of it. Especially she loved the pleasure her gifts gave to Larry and Bob.

She had a long gold cigarette case engraved with her own name from Bob, and a delicate ivory powder-box and lipstick case combined—straight from Paris, she guessed—from Larry. She wondered if he had got Julia to buy it.

And so her first English Christmas Day passed—the spirit of kindliness and happiness enveloping her in a golden haze. She adored every moment of it. Sunday was spent in a more somnolent, but equally enjoyable style.

On Monday evening, before dinner, Bob led her into the little drawing-room which led off the picture gallery.

"I've got something I want to give you," he said seriously. "Something for you to remember me by—always."

She stared at him, puzzled, vaguely afraid of his seriousness.

"You mean you are going to leave me?"

He laughed.

"Darling, haven't you seen these last two or three days how much you mean to me? How happy we can be together?"

She smiled back.

Somehow, through all her happiness, she had sensed it wasn't to last. There was some undercurrent of unreality about everything. About Bob especially.

He was drawing a small box out of his pocket and opened it.

She saw inside, on a velvet rest, an old antique ring. He held it out to her.

"It's not in the least valuable, but it's old and rather quaint. You may not be able to wear it."

She took it out of the box.

It was a dull amber stone set in a strange lace-work pattern of old gold. The gold was tarnished slightly, but it only added to its charm.

She slipped it on the third finger of her right hand. It was too large. She slipped it on the middle finger.

"It's beautiful," she breathed.

"Don't tell anyone who gave it you. Let it be just something between ourselves."

He led her downstairs to dinner.

They had to go up to town that night. There was money to be made at the Gardenia on Boxing Night.

The club was crowded. A gay throng threw streamers and burst balloons all over the restaurant. Everyone was having a good time.

When Mitsi's show was over Bob suggested they should stay for a little while and join in the fun.

They danced. At every step they were greeted by people they knew. As well as people they didn't. Just after midnight, John Foster, back from Paris, arrived with Sam Levinsky and two men friends.

They joined them in a bottle of champagne and John thanked Mitsi for the present she had sent him.

"I guess you haven't got yours yet. I sent it to your hotel."

"What is it?" she asked.

"Guess it's a silly kind of present, really. But I sort of knew you'd everything, and I tried to be original. You'd better wait till you see it. It's a cute kind of thing. The head-waiter's looking after it for you till you get back."

Then Sam was dancing with her.

"Thanks for the present, Mitsi. Guess it's appropriate! I always look as if I need a shave, don't I? That's the blue blood though—grows blue hair on my chin!"

She screamed a reply above the noise of shouting that filled the ballroom. But he didn't hear—just beamed at her with his expansive smile.

He led her back to her table. Bob murmured to her:

"Let's go back now."

In the car, she said:

"I think Larry wants to leave tomorrow. I feel I ought to as well. Will that seem very rude?"

"No darling. Most people will go then."

"I'll be staying down for a day or two longer. I'll miss you—badly. It's been grand."

"It's been lovely. But surely, we can have other times like this?"

"Of course. I hope so anyway darling. But you know, you can never repeat this sort of thing. The first time's always the best."

It was almost four o'clock as they drove up the drive to the house.

He looked up at the sky which was an angry sea of clouds, before he went in. She had a strange feeling that this would be the last time she would stand on that doorstep with him. This would be the last time they would look up at the old Latin inscription over the door, side by side.

He swung back the massive door and they went in.

To their astonishment, they found two figures sitting by the hearth talking in low voices. The man turned, and in the dim light of the hall, they saw it was Larry.

"Thank heaven, you've got back at last," was all he said.

A cool voice beside them spoke.

"Why didn't you phone you were going to be so late, darling? I thought perhaps something had happened to you so we waited up for you. Wonderful for you to come in and find a woman waiting on the doorstep for you—isn't it?"

Carol Lewis's voice sharpened on the last words. Then she laughed a little, as if to take the edge off them.

42

"Carol was worried. She asked me to stay up with her," Larry said.

"Ridiculous—but very nice of you both, I'm sure!" said Bob drily. "We are still very sober and even when not, we can still drive a car tolerably safely."

He left them abruptly and went upstairs alone.

Mitsi looked from Carol to Larry and back to Carol.

Carol's face was white. Her hair was untidy and her eyes made large dark smudges in her face. Mitsi felt a sudden rush of pity for her.

"Don't wait any longer, Larry," Carol said.

"Righto. Good night. You'll follow us up?"

He took Mitsi by the arm.

"I'll come up as soon as I've finished this."

Carol indicated a drink which was standing on the arm of her chair.

Larry led Mitsi upstairs.

"Whatever was the matter with you both?" she asked him.

"She got worried and all het-up about you both. Bob had apparently promised dear auntie he'd be back by two. Carol's been clock-watching for over an hour. Everyone else shoved off to bed, so I stayed with her. She thought perhaps Bob'd had an accident or done something silly. We tried to phone you but couldn't get through. Local breakdown, or something."

"But surely you guessed we had stayed to see people at the club and dance a bit?"

"I knew, but she got worried stiff. So what could I do but sit with her? Couldn't leave her waiting down in that mausoleum of a hall all by herself at this time of night."

They reached her door.

"Well, you'd better try to get some sleep."

He left her and strode down the passage towards his own room.

She undressed, listening all the time for the sound of Carol's footsteps as she returned to her room. After half an hour, when there had been no sound, she began to get alarmed. Throwing a dressing-gown round her, she crept downstairs.

There was only one light left in the hall now and crouched by the fire, was the figure of Carol. She was smoking a cigarette. Mitsi stood on the stairs and watched her for a moment. Then she called softly, "Carol."

Carol started and turned her head.

"Oh, it's you."

"Aren't you tired of sitting alone down here among the shadows? I'd—I'd be afraid!"

"I'm not afraid of anything here hurting me."

Mitsi came to the bottom of the stairs and stood hesitantly.

"Do come to bed."

"I don't want to yet. I've got to think. I shouldn't go to sleep even if I came now."

Mitsi moved quietly towards her.

Carol looked up at her without saying anything. Mitsi saw she had been crying.

She could hardly believe it.

She turned her head away, embarrassed by this revelation of the other's weakness.

Carol spoke to her profile:

"Why—you're young... You're almost a child." She looked at her wonderingly.

It was as if they were meeting for the first time.

"You look so much more sophisticated in the daytime," the other went on. "Such a woman of the world."

Mitsi gave a little laugh.

"I am not really."

Carol suddenly bent her head in her hands.

Mitsi looked at her, without knowing what to say or do to comfort her. What can be wrong? It cannot be Bob. Of what can she be afraid?

As she watched her, the bent shoulders shook. A broken sob fell upon the silence of the great hall. She moved closer. But she felt so utterly helpless. She had never expected such a thing would happen.

Carol, woman of ice, of calm poise, crying!

What could she do? Should she leave her? Quietly creep away? Should she bring Bob down? Louise?

She suddenly bent down and kneeling beside the girl, took the cigarette that was burning down to her fingers, and threw it into the fire.

"I'm so sorry."

"There's nothing for you to be sorry about," Carol choked without looking up.

"I wish I could help."

She sat silent listening to the hard dry sobs. All she could say, was:

"Shall I bring Bob?"

"No please don't—not him."

Her sobs gradually subsided, and she looked up, her face ravaged and stained with tears. Mitsi saw now her expression was softened, had lost its usual arrogance. She wanted to put her arms round her shoulders and say something sympathetic. But she felt the girl did not want her sympathy. I will stay a little longer until she feels better, she thought.

Suddenly Carol turned to her.

"You think I'm a fool. You can't imagine me ever crying can you? I'm such a hard proud piece! But I've got an attack of regret now. I'm simply sorry for myself. Sorry for things of years ago."

"You mean Bob?"

"I know him so well. These moods of his. When he gets desperate and fed-up and revolts against things. I know what he's capable of doing. I thought perhaps he'd—"

She broke off and dabbed her eyes.

"It didn't matter," she went on. "He's all right, and he hates me because I know him so well—because I understand him. Because I live every minute of his day—"

She broke off again.

Then she rose and smoothed her dress. She stood tall and slender and very beautiful against the dying embers of the great log on the hearth.

Mitsi could not help remembering how she had been at Louise's party, when she had so triumphantly carried Bob off and left her lonely and bewildered.

Suddenly, taking Mitsi's hand she said:

"It's nearly daylight. I shouldn't have allowed you to stay." She gave her a tremulous smile. "But it was nice of you—and all very ironic!"

They went upstairs together, and Mitsi watched her go to her own room.

It was all extraordinarily puzzling. Carol and Bob had been engaged at one time, but she had broken it off to go to America. She had returned and was apparently still in love with Bob. But now he wasn't in love with her.

Mitsi thought of her words just now:

"I know Bob. These moods of his. I know what he's capable of doing."

Wondering about them, she realized with tremendous force that she didn't know Bob at all.

She drew back the curtains and the faint light of dawn streamed in through the windows. She threw off her dressing-gown and crept into bed.

For some minutes she lay and shivered, wondering whether the events of the evening would make Carol any more friendly towards her.

She thought not. Even while she was explaining herself, it it had been as if there was always some impenetrable barrier between them.

The door opened just as she was at last dropping off to sleep.

Carol stood in the door.

"Please try and forget all this. Don't mention it—especially to Bob."

Mitsi smiled understandingly. Said "No," drowsily, and the door closed quietly.

43

Mitsi came down very late for breakfast, and she found the dining-room empty.

When her breakfast appeared, Larry appeared with it.

"What happened to you last night?"

"I told you."

His voice was hard, challenging:

"I mean after I'd left you."

She glanced at him sharply.

"How did you know?"

He said with elaborate casualness:

"I happened to look in on you a little time after I left you. I wanted to ask you something rather important. I found your bed turned down, your clothes strewn all over the place, and you gone. Where were you?"

His attitude angered her.

"Do I have to answer that?"

He eyed her levelly.

"It's my job to look after you."

He was getting angry now, because he knew he was sounding pompous. Besides he had no real right to cross-question her. What she did with life was her own affair.

She told him as much. And seeing his anger, laughed at him.

Then she said:

"If you really want to know—if your curiosity cannot bear to go un-satisfied, I was having a little talk with Carol Lewis."

She smiled as she spoke.

He looked at her with frank disbelief.

"I see."

To her surprise he walked abruptly out of the room. She realized he suspected her and Bob. She was filled with righteous and angry indignation.

She finished her breakfast alone. When she went back to the hall she found Louise and her husband sitting by the fire, dressed for walking.

"Say—know what's happened?" Louise shot at her.

"What?"

"Carol's had a wire—you know what I mean—and caught the early train back to town."

Mitsi looked up at her in surprise. She didn't understand Louise's implication.

"Anything serious?"

"A ruse of course! She left a message—only the butler saw her off. Nobody else was up. What I can't imagine is why Carol should want to get away from here. It's peculiar."

Mitsi shook her head.

"I cannot think. I am afraid I never knew her very well."

"You didn't hit it off did you?"

Louise was looking curiously at her. "Oh, well, I guess it's like that the world over! You never get two people feeling the same way about another."

Her husband changed the conversation by intimating they were going out walking, and they both set off into the crisp morning.

Mitsi watched them go. Then wandered up to her room where she rang for Ellen to help her with her packing.

Just before lunch-time, she came down to find Bob in the hall before the huge fire. He looked up as she entered, and she saw he was troubled about something.

"What's the matter?" she asked quietly.

"Nothing. Nothing at all."

Mitsi bit her lip in annoyance.

"All right. If everybody's in a funny mood this morning, I will be too."

"Don't be a fool. After all, it is rather worrying when one of your guests leaves suddenly at break of day without any warning—and after sitting up half the night, too!"

"I know—but still—"

He interrupted her.

"Everybody's talking about it. It's not like Carol to let me in for this kind of thing."

She turned away and kicked the edge of the carpet thoughtfully. She said:

"I am leaving directly after lunch."

"Larry going with you?"

"I don't know. I shouldn't think he'll come with me. Why should he?"

He stared at her.

"What's wrong with you? Why be bitter about Larry? What's he done?"

"Nothing. Nothing at all," she mocked him.

Bob groaned, completely perplexed.

Lunch was a doleful meal. Larry was not present. He had already left.

Mitsi's last remembrance of the old house was the old Latin inscription over Bob's head as he stood by the door waving good-bye to her as her car disappeared down the drive.

She repeated it to herself as she drove away:

"God has given us this place of peace."

* * * *

When she arrived at her hotel she found a number of Christmas gifts awaiting her.

She ordered tea in her sitting-room and prepared to see who the presents were from. The gifts only served to make her feel more miserable than ever.

Bob was so far away, Larry believed that she had lied to him. Had believed that she and Bob—oh, it was all beyond her!

Life was so complex. Even the day had turned cold and miserable, and a misty rain had begun to fall. She shivered and drew closer to the bright fire.

There was a sudden knock on the door and the page-boy came in with a small Aberdeen on a tartan lead, and wearing a large tartan bow on his neck.

"This is for you, Madame! From Mr. John Foster. The head waiter's been lookin' after it for you."

The puppy leapt at her and wagged its small tail deliriously. She lifted it in her arms and it licked her chin in a frenzy of affection. Clutching it to her and with two large tears unaccountably trickling down her cheeks, she lifted the telephone receiver and asked for John Foster's number.

44

New Year's Eve.

She woke with a feeling of elation. It was deceptively bright and sunny and she looked at the telephone waiting for it to come to life and break the silence with its noisy clatter.

Yesterday she had received a note from Bob saying he would be coming up from Leamarket to help her celebrate New Year's Eve. He expected to be in town early and would telephone her on his arrival.

But there was no call that morning. Mystified and troubled she put a personal call through to him, but was told he was not there. She decided to stay in until lunch, in the hope he would telephone.

It was about midday when the instrument shrilled impatiently. She hurried to it eagerly, and lifted the receiver in excited anticipation.

"Hello, darling?"

It was Sam Levinsky who answered.

"How did you guess it was me!" he chuckled. "Developin' second sight or something?"

She could not keep the disappointment out of her voice.

"I thought—"

Levinsky laughed loudly.

"I guess I know what you thought—that I was your boyfriend, huh?"

"I am sorry, Sam," she apologized. "But I did think it was someone else."

"You're telling me!"

She did not answer him. He went on:

"Well, I just called you to wish you a happy New Year, that's all."

"That's sweet of you—but won't I be seeing you tonight at the Club?"

"I guess not, I'm hopping to Paris this afternoon. Guess I'll see the New Year in at one of these dumps where the blondes only wear smiles and accents!"

He laughed uproariously at his own joke.

She tried to join in but her effort was feeble. There was a dull, sickening ache in her heart.

Levinsky caught her dejection.

"What's on your mind? You sound blue as hell!"

Her reply was evasive and he went on:

"Guess if love don't make you happy it's a thing you oughta drop. What d'you do with friends you ain't pleased to see? You drop 'em quick! Misery ain't no good to anybody but song writers—then it's a nice sentiment to put over sometimes!"

"It is all very well talking like that," she said. "But love does not *always* make one happy. And when it does not it is difficult to stop being miserable."

"Gee, *I* can stop or start myself doing anything or feeling anything! Guess that's why I'm such a good song writer. I just switch on the love current and I write like I'm crazy in love. Or switch on the sob stuff and I write like I'm heartbroken!"

He chuckled again.

"I guess that's how *you* oughta regulate your life… It'd make things easier and a sight less complicated for you."

He added some further words of wisdom and then rang off.

The only effect his advice had upon her was to make her feel more depressed than ever. As if it is possible to talk about being in love like that, she thought. Besides Levinsky knew, no more than anyone else, the complicated emotions she felt for Bob.

Everything was identified with him. Without him nothing was the same. Her days were made up of the times when she was with him. When she was not they were spent in mere living for the moment when she would see him again.

By lunch-time he had still not telephoned.

Then when the telephone did ring she fought the wild beating of her heart. It *cannot* be him, she told herself.

For a long moment she eyed the jangling instrument without making a move towards it. She had almost made up her mind not to answer it when a stronger impulse forced her to lift the receiver.

"Hello?"

Her voice was empty of any hope that it would be him.

It was Larry.

It was the first time he had spoken to her since he had walked out of the breakfast-room at the old house and left her. Since then she had not seen him at the Club nor had he made any attempt to get in touch with her.

She herself had no intention of seeking him out. For she had still been angry and indignant over his accusation against her.

But now she heard his voice again all those feelings vanished. She felt a great gladness that he, the one man, whom deep down she knew she could count on, had not deserted her.

His warm friendly tones drove some of the misery out of her. Momentarily her bitter disappointment over Bob was forgotten.

"I thought you were angry with me for always," she said.

His laugh was a little embarrassed.

"How could I be—with you?"

"You thought I lied to you about—that night. Do you still think I lied?"

There was a pause.

Then hesitantly he replied: "I'm not sure. I'd like you to have lunch with me so we could talk, and I *could* be sure."

"Where are you?"

"Downstairs waiting for you."

They did not talk very much over lunch. Neither of them mentioned Bob. She was not sure whether he was being discreet, or whether he sensed her unhappiness over him. She guessed it was the latter reason for his silence and she felt grateful to him.

Presently he asked her:

"Did you really spend very nearly an hour with Carol after I'd left you that night?"

"Yes."

He shook his head slowly.

"It seems funny. A woman you disliked. Who had always been particularly unpleasant to you. A woman who's—"

He hesitated, looked at her levelly, then went on:

"I was going to say a woman who's your rival, and now I've said it I don't quite understand it."

He leant across and took her hand.

"You must forgive a suspicious old newspaper reporter like myself."

She laughed.

"There is nothing to forgive. I was hurt that you did not believe me—that is all."

"I'm sorry about that—but as I say, I'm suspicious by profession. What you told me just didn't seem to fit."

"It was this," she explained. "I had still not heard Carol come to bed. So after a little I became worried. She was so upset I knew when we came in. I wondered what had happened to her. And I went down to see."

She gave him a look.

"That was only a most human and natural thing to do?"

He nodded.

"I found her in the hall where we left her."

She paused. Drew a pattern on the table-cloth with her fork. Then she said:

"We talked for a little. Then we came upstairs."

There was silence for a moment. The waiter came up and served them with their sweet. After he had gone Larry eyed her curiously.

"What did you talk about?"

She poised a spoonful of her hot soufflé before she replied.

"I cannot tell you that," she said. "It is very private."

He smiled at her obvious determination to shield Carol. The realization of his misguided suspicion made him feel very humble. Now it was an open book what had taken place between Mitsi and the other woman that night.

His keen sense of perception saw well beneath the hard and sophisticated exterior which was Carol Lewis's armour against life. Shrewdly he guessed her cold beauty could melt into softness and tears.

"You believe me now?"

Her eyes were calm and level as they looked into his.

He nodded.

"Afraid I was a little hasty. And unkind. Unfair, too—all those things which you shouldn't be!"

He smiled ruefully at her.

"I am glad you do believe me," she answered simply. Then added: "I should hate it for you, of all my friends, to think I could not be trusted."

He held her gaze with his.

In that moment there was so much he wanted to say to her, longed to blurt out.

But he said nothing. Merely gave her a crooked smile.

She caught something of the sudden tension that had arisen between them. She felt the electric current which had been switched on, and which was now flickering out.

Animatedly she began to tell him about the puppy which had been John Foster's Christmas gift.

45

They did not linger over lunch, Larry had to hurry back to Fleet Street.

He wished he could have stayed on and talked to her. She seemed desolate and unhappy and he longed to comfort her.

Not that he could have done as he knew full well, he told himself as he hunched himself back in his taxi. He wondered where it would all end. When the dangerous game Mitsi and Bob were playing would blow up. Wryly he told himself that anyway he'd be around to pick up the pieces that had been Mitsi Linden and put them together again. I started the whole damn thing, he mused, so it's only right I should be there at the finish.

Mitsi drove to Regents Park. There was still no news of Bob. She had telephoned his aunt's home again but she knew nothing about him or his movements. He was not there, that was all.

She parked the car in the Outer Circle and started for a brisk walk. She felt numbed and cold. All her emotions seemed frozen up

She drew her furs close around her. People turned to look at this beautiful girl who walked along so quickly, so oblivious to everyone and everything.

She turned back to the car. It was no good thinking, worrying herself almost frantic with the same fear. Always the same thoughts chasing themselves through her brain. She felt sick and ill with misery.

She got into the car and drove off without knowing what she was doing.

"Oh God, oh God," she whispered aloud, "don't let me lose him! Make me happy again, let me keep his love just for a little longer."

She found a small teashop in Baker Street and decided some tea might warm her, help pull her together. As she went in she discovered she'd been here before with him. One or two people stared at her as she halted with the door half opened. Although she wanted to rush away she forced herself to sit at a table.

She gave her order mechanically to the little waitress, mechanically she poured out her tea and somehow managed to drink it. She experienced no taste, all she knew was it was hot and burnt her throat.

Quickly she paid her bill and hurried out.

She drove back to her hotel. In her sitting-room some magnificent orchids greeted her. And there was a note from Bob. He would be along that evening at eight o'clock to take her to the Club.

He signed it: "Love, Bob."

She stared at the orchids and at his note unbelievingly.

Suddenly she was crying.

She could not stop the tears. A great elation flooded her being. Through her tears she saw the time was five o'clock.

In three hours she would see him again!

She looked again at his note, read and re-read the few words he had scribbled there. On the middle finger of her right hand gleamed the dull yellow stone of his ring. She pressed it to her lips.

She went into her bedroom and laid down and tried to sleep but could not. For an hour and a half she tried to forget everything in the oblivion of sleep. But her thoughts kept going round and round, wondering what had happened to him, where he was, longing for his arrival.

Would eight o'clock never come?

She awoke from a restless doze and found it was half-past six. She chose a white gown which reminded her of the one she wore for her first appearance at the Gardenia.

She dressed herself with nervous care and found by half-past seven she was ready. She stared back at her reflection in the mirror, her hair was burnished like living gold, her eyes looked like damp violets.

She lit a cigarette and tried to relax. Then she rang for some drinks. With a sudden shock she realized it was the last night of the old year. New Year's Eve. Everybody at the club would be gay. There would be balloons and streamers and silly caps.

Just after eight o'clock Bob walked into her room. Without speaking he took her in his arms.

She stared at him as if she could not believe that he was there. With a little embarrassed laugh he put his hand over her eyes.

"I'm not a ghost my pet! Don't look at me like that."

She clung to him desperately. He found it very affecting. It was as if she would never let him go. When he was able to break free from her embrace he poured himself a stiff brandy and soda.

"Where shall we have dinner?"

He was laughing. But he seemed to avoid her eyes. "Shall we have it here or at the club?"

"Oh, let us have it here, please. It is quieter."

"Where have you been?" she asked him, as a waiter led them to a table.

"Been in town since ten o'clock this morning," he said.

She stared up at him. "Why didn't you let me know?"

"I've been so frightfully busy, my dear...couldn't have seen you anyway."

She remembered her lonely panic-stricken day.

"But you could have telephoned me... I tried to speak to you at Leamarket twice."

They were seated at their table and he leant across, patted her hand sympathetically.

"So sorry darling, but really I haven't had a moment."

"Were you so very busy?"

He gave her a smiling look.

"Very busy."

"I love you so very much," she whispered. "I know it now. I have always loved you."

He didn't reply.

His eyes wandered over her shoulder, then he picked up the wine-list. At that moment a page-boy hurried over to them.

"You're wanted on the telephone, sir."

"Who is it?"

"It's the Gardenia Club, sir."

Bob hesitated a moment.

"All right, tell them to hang on."

The boy hurried off. Bob apologized to Mitsi and followed him.

When he returned he made no reference to the phone call, but over their glasses said to her:

"New Year's Eve, darling! A New Year ahead of us with all sorts of lovely possibilities. Doesn't that make you happy?"

She looked at him as if to remember him for ever.

"You make me happy, whether it is this year or next year."

He gave a little laugh.

"Here's to you, my sweet."

He did not talk very much during dinner. But she did not care. She was so tremendously happy to be with him and to know she had not lost him.

He drove her to the club in her car. As they purred along Piccadilly she thought: He has driven this car so often. He knows it almost as well as I do. We have had so much happiness with this car. It seems to have brought happiness with it. I wonder what it will bring tomorrow? And the day after, and the day after that?

On their arrival he excused himself, explaining he had to see one or two people about arrangements for the special celebrations that night. She went to her dressing-room where Hattie was awaiting her.

She was about to sit at her brightly-lit mirror to put on her make-up when she suddenly remembered he had not said he would see her before she went on for her show. Perhaps he will be too busy to do so, she thought. She wanted him to be standing there at the back of the Club when she sang that night. The last night of the old year... He *must* be standing there. She would sing for him, and him alone. She wanted him to know that.

Singing softly to herself the song she always associated with him she hurried out of her room:

> *"J'attendrai,*
> *Le jour et la nuit,*
> *J'attendrai toujours."*

She saw a light showing beneath the door of his room. Quickly she went to it. She knocked quietly. There was no answer. She started to move away. Then she thought she heard his voice.

She turned the handle and opened the door a little. She heard him speaking to someone in the room.

"I'll make everything up to you now. You know I've always been mad about you. It's marvellous to have you back again."

She opened the door a little wider. She saw him reflected in the mirror with Carol Lewis. His arms were about her.

They did not see her because they were so close together, his head bent to hers.

46

For Mitsi the world stood still.

She stood there, frozen, a great pain tearing at her heart. Then automatically pulled the door close, to shut out the two figures clasped tightly in their embrace.

As she closed the door silently, something died inside her. Then as the shock of the revelation subsided a little, she sought wildly for some action to take.

What could she do?

As she moved blindly away she knew there was only one thing she *could* do—escape. Escape from the dream that was crashing about her ears like a tower uprooted by an earthquake.

Escape, anywhere…escape, quickly. ESCAPE!

The word seared her brain.

She closed her eyes, closed them upon those two who had made a picture there, in that room she would never forget. She seemed to be moving as if in a dream.

Only the sick feeling in her stomach, the horrible iciness at her heart were real. She hurried to the door which was a fire-exit and which opened into the street.

The chill night caught at her, but she never noticed it. She moved like an automaton. Moved to her car, which was drawn up to the kerb, a little way along the street.

One or two people brushed past her, turned to eye her curiously. But Mitsi never knew. A man hurrying past, and knocking her arm, apologized. But she never heard.

She had completely forgotten that in a very short while the crowd who packed the Gardenia would be waiting for her to sing. Would be awaiting her appearance in the glare of the spotlight as a signal for their applause.

> *"J'attendrai,*
> *Le jour et la nuit,*
> *J'attendrai, toujours."*

She found herself still half-singing to herself. She broke off with an agonized gasp.

She got into the car.

As she did so, another car drew up to the kerb some several yards behind her. A man jumped out and hurried towards the blue car just as it drove off.

The man called out: "Mitsi!"

But his voice was lost in the roar of the exhaust as Mitsi swung at a dangerous speed into Piccadilly.

For a second Larry stood watching the tail-light till it had gone, his hat pushed back on his head in perplexity. What the devil did it mean?

Mitsi was due for her show in about twenty minutes—and there she went dashing off in her car like a lunatic!

Pushing his hat even further back on his head, he turned back to the club. At that moment, the door through which Mitsi had come banged open, and Bob came out. Behind him was Carol.

Bob made a grab at him.

"Where's Mitsi?" he gasped.

His fingers dug deep into the other's shoulder.

Larry saw the agitation in his face. Saw, too, Carol's eyes, wide with apprehension.

Saw her link her arm in Bob's and move close to him.

"Don't worry so, darling!" she said.

And Larry knew. Knew, just as if they had told him with their own lips, just as if he had seen them as Mitsi had seen them. He knew, too, Mitsi *had* seen them together. And that was why she was tearing off in her car.

She was running away!

Bob gripped him harder.

"Have you seen her? Where is she?"

Larry pulled his hand away. He eyed him with contempt.

"She's gone."

His voice was cold, his jaw set. He added in words that were a whip-lash:

"You rat!"

And he turned on his heel, got into his car and was swinging into Piccadilly after the blue car.

* * * *

Her eyes fixed on the road, Mitsi drove automatically.

She obeyed traffic-lights, applied brakes, accelerated and threaded through the traffic without being in any way aware of what she was do-ing, where she was going.

All she could see was the picture of two people locked in an embrace. Bob's dark, handsome head bent to those other lips. And the only thing she could hear—which drove out all other sounds of traffic, hooting and screeching of brakes—were the words:

"I'll make everything up to you. You know I've always been mad about you. It's marvellous to have you back again."

Every nerve of her being urged her to escape. Faster! Faster! Away from that picture, away from those words.

Away from the smashed dream!

The car was roaring through Hyde Park towards Marble Arch. She wondered how she—the living she that was guiding the steering-wheel, that was breathing and thinking—was alive, while her heart felt so dead.

Her life was over.

She swerved up through St. John's Wood Road. Swung into Finchley Road, and headed north. Now the roads were clearer.

Faster! Faster!

Escape! ESCAPE!

Cold, a graven image, she sat at the wheel, her face the colour of chalk. Her hair blown back by the wind that rushed to meet her. Her hands gripped the wheel so hard her knuckles showed white through the skin.

Faster! Faster!

Now she was on the Barnet by-pass. A great stretch of road that was almost empty and ribboning away into the darkness ahead.

The needle of the speedometer rose.

The roar of the car and the rush of the wind sang a mad song. Her eyes never moved from the road ahead. Never strayed to the dashboard and the quivering needle which climbed higher and higher.

Sub-consciously she noticed the illuminated face of a clock on some building as she tore past. It was nearly twelve o'clock. Nearly midnight.

Nearly the New Year!

Bob's face rose before her eyes, strained, fixed on the road being eaten up before her.

He was smiling across at her.

"New Year's Eve darling. A New Year ahead of us. With all sorts of lovely possibilities. Doesn't that make you happy?"

She gave a little moan. Shook her head to drive the taunting, mocking vision away.

The needle crept higher.

The mad song of roaring engine and tearing wind sang louder. The blue car tore northwards into the night that was cut only by her headlamps. Houses and buildings rose out of the darkness, stood for an instant in the glare of the lamps, then fell away.

Suddenly there was the hooting of a car ahead. Mitsi's lights held a small car as it came out of a turning into the road. The driver, dazzled by the blinding lights, tried to brake, but failed. His brakes were faulty.

His car was right in Mitsi's path.

She applied her brakes. And as they screamed, swung her wheel over. There was a whine of tires trying to grip the road, a wild yell from the occupants in the small car, and the blue car slewed violently round and smashed into a wall.

It was as if a giant suddenly wrenched the steering wheel from Mitsi's hands. The world turned upside down. Something crashed against her head. Somewhere, miles away, a voice was saying.

"New Year's Eve, darling. I'll make everything up to you. A New Year ahead of us. ALL SORTS OF POSSIBILITIES. IT'S MARVEL-LOUS TO HAVE YOU BACK AGAIN. NEW YEAR'S EVE. D-A-R-L-I-N-G... D—A—R—L—I—N—G..."

Then a great searing pain tore into her head.

Blackness.

47

Larry pulled up just as the two men from the small car had managed to get Mitsi out of the wreck and lie her on the grass footpath.

More by luck—or instinct—than judgment he had managed to hang on to the blue car's trail. His own car, though not so fast, could move. And he had kept his foot jammed hard on the accelerator as much as he could.

Even so, he had been too late.

One of the men had taken off his scarf and with it was trying to staunch the frightful gash across Mitsi's head.

"Drivin' like a mad woman, she was," said the other man, as Larry came into the circle of light from the small car's head-lamps, where Mitsi lay, the men crouched over her.

"Where's the nearest doctor?"

The man with the scarf answered him.

"A long way. We might get to my mother's house first—that's where we've just come from. Telephone him from there."

"Right."

"Think we oughter move her?" asked the other man.

"We'll have to risk that," replied Larry decisively. "The three of us lift her as carefully as we can into my car."

"Okay."

They bent to lift the inert figure—then paused. There came the distant pealing of bells. Church bells carried on the night.

Larry glanced at his watch.

It was midnight.

The bells were bidding farewell to the Old Year and greeting the New Year.

The three men looked at each other. Then at the still form on the grass. Larry knew what they were thinking.

Happy New Year! Happy New Year for her, all right!

Without a word they bent and with extreme care lifted Mitsi, keeping her as level as possible. They carried her to Larry's car, and laid her gently across the seat, supported by their rolled up overcoats.

Larry managed to drive the car, while the two men hung on to the running-board. He drove slowly and cautiously along the dark country lane towards the house.

And the joyous clanging of the distant bells was a dirge for their funereal progress along the lane.

Every detail of that nightmarish night was to remain in Larry's memory and haunt him for long afterwards.

The slow, torturing journey in the car. The limp figure, crumpled like a poor, pathetic doll on the bundled overcoats.

Then the agonizing minutes of waiting which seemed so many years while they waited at the house for the doctor to arrive. The doctor's grave face as he examined Mitsi's head, from which blood still oozed through the improvised bandage.

"Concussion. Bad," was his verdict. "We'll have to get her to hospital immediately."

And he reached for the telephone.

There followed the waiting for the ambulance to arrive. The man's mother, whose house it was, got some tea for them all. Larry gulped it down without knowing what he was doing. He felt he must wake up from this hideous nightmare.

The faces of the old woman, in her shabby dressing-gown, handing him tea; of her son, his companion and the doctor seemed unreal.

Presently, after what seemed another age of waiting, the ambulance arrived and took Mitsi away.

He stared down at her chalky face, the colour of the bandages which swathed her head, as she lay on the stretcher. She seemed hardly to breathe. She made no move whatsoever. The brown blankets might have covered a dummy.

He followed the ambulance in his car, alone.

At the small cottage-hospital to which she was taken, he waited while they operated. He paced up and down the small hall. He hunched in a chair and even dozed a little, waking out of it, his face and hands wet with sweat as he awoke out of confused and hideous dreams.

Then the doctor came out to him, his face wearing a false mask of cheerfulness.

"There's no more we can do, now. She's in a pretty bad way, I'm afraid. But—well—we'll pull her through all right."

He patted his elbow sympathetically.

"She's had a nasty crack on the head. No bones broken anywhere else, fortunately, but that head's in a bad way. Pretty severe concussion, I'm afraid."

He searched the doctor's face, as if to read behind the words he was speaking. Were they words which were simply to prepare him for the inevitable?

The other's eyes told him nothing.

Larry asked in a cracked, harsh whisper:

"Is there—hope? At all?"

The doctor answered him with simulated heartiness.

"Of course, of course! Going to be a stiff fight—but we'll win, don't fear! She's young and strong. Now, don't you worry. Get along and try and grab some sleep."

Larry shook his head impatiently.

The doctor took his arm gently.

"Nothing you can do here. Leave me your phone number, and I'll promise you we'll ring you as soon as there's any news."

He urged him towards the door.

"Be a good fellow. You look all in yourself—" He brought some more joviality into his voice. "Don't want you on the sick list, too! That wouldn't help anyone!"

On the steps outside Larry paused.

"I can't just see her before I go?"

"You won't be able to see her for a few days, yet. But don't *worry*! She'll be quite all right here. Good night. Good night."

Larry lit another cigarette. He had smoked so many that tasted of nothing, but merely burnt his mouth. He got into his car and drove back to London.

The grey fingers of the dawn were beginning to draw back the curtains of the night as his car sped away from the little hospital. He shivered at the wheel in the chill of the new day.

The new day of a new year...

And back there was the girl he'd made into a thing of tinsel and artificiality because it suited his humour and he had the power to do it.

Yes! It had blown up all right, his bright, clever little stunt! With a vengeance!

There she lay, back in that hospital. Broken in heart, trampled in spirit. Crushed in body.

A groan forced itself to his lips.

The girl he'd found. And loved. And lost, perhaps for ever.

As he drove into London, he saw a newspaper van rush up to a man waiting at a corner. The man grabbed the parcel of newspapers thrown at him. As he unrolled them he saw a headline which flared out:

"FAMOUS NIGHT-CLUB STAR IN CAR SMASH"

He looked at the legend as he drove past, curiously, wondering. Then he realized it referred to Mitsi.

Arrived at his flat he poured himself a stiff whisky and soda.

It was eight o'clock when he heard the housekeeper stirring. She was startled to find him slumped in the chair in his sitting-room. He still had his overcoat on.

She gaped at his bloodshot eyes, his grey face.

"Why, it's home wi' the milk ye've brought yeself this morning!"

He cut her short and ordered strong coffee. She hurried out to prepare it for him.

He reached for the telephone.

* * * *

He practically lived on the telephone for days...

At first it was:

"No, Miss Linden is still unconscious. Everything is being done that is humanly possible. Please don't worry. We will inform you the moment there is any news. No, we can't say when she will regain consciousness. Miss Linden is still on the danger list. But please don't worry."

It so happened that a tremendous pressure of work engulfed Larry which made it almost impossible for him to get out to the hospital. He managed to do so three times, however. And though his questions and their answers were the same as on the telephone, he found some comfort in being near to Mitsi.

Actually, though he never realized it at the time, the work that he was forced to handle helped him to bear the waiting. It kept him from thinking of that white-faced, bandaged and helpless figure lying there.

Bob telephoned him once. And once only.

Larry told him with almost savage harshness to keep out of it—from now on.

"It'll be the straightest thing you'll ever do for her! If you'll do just that—*keep out of this*. Understand? Keep away from her. Never try to see her again—unless she asks for you, which pray God she never will!"

Bob's injured tones of protest he cut short with:

"Stick to Carol Lewis, my son. You *can't* hurt her! And, believe me, you've hurt Mitsi. I don't blame you alone. I'm in it, too. But from now I'm taking care of her, which means you're *not* wanted."

Again he cut short the other's protestations of remorse and sorrow— and injured dignity, by slamming down the receiver on him.

On the fourth day, they told him over the telephone Mitsi had regained consciousness, and was "as well as could be expected."

"No—you cannot possibly be allowed to see her yet. No visitors for two or three days at least. But don't worry, we'll keep you informed as to her progress. Yes, we will let you know when you will be able to see her."

And so he had to be satisfied.

During all this time there was a multitude of enquiries from Mitsi's friends. John Foster called every day from Paris, as did Sam Levinsky. Julia and Leo both made frequent and anxious telephone calls to London. Louise rang him up frequently, and came to see him. She also pestered the hospital with well-intentioned suggestions and enquiries.

Every evening, too, Sadie Harris's drawl came over the wire from Paris. Al Young, almost crying with anxiety, telephoned continually.

These were only a few of the many friends, admirers, and acquaintances who set Larry's phone continually ringing—at his flat and at his office—with their sympathetic enquiries.

Carol Lewis was not among those who telephoned.

The newspapers played up the story in a big way.

"GLAMOROUS FRENCH STAR LIES IN COTTAGE HOSPITAL"

was a favourite headline, with variations.

"FAVOURITE NIGHT-CLUB SINGER INJURED
IN NEW YEAR'S EVE CAR SMASH"

was another caption underneath various photographs of Mitsi looking her most alluring. This caption, too, was used with variations and embellishments.

Larry glanced at them, as they leapt from the pages of the newspapers, with a grim smile. Poor kid! She'd made the front page all right—and how!

If only he could have foreseen all this.

If only he could have known that the little girl of the pinched face, mousey hair and drab clothes, whom he had transformed into a glamorous creature, was to have been caught in such a tangled web of drama and tragedy. If only he could have foreseen she was to hold his heart in her little, unknowing hands.

One afternoon, on the seventh day following the accident, they told him he could see her.

48

The surgeon who had performed the operation wished to have a word with him before Larry could talk to Mitsi.

They shook hands. The doctor eyed him through horn-rimmed spectacles. Then he said crisply:

"Now about Miss Linden. I—er—I must ask you to prepare yourself for a little shock—oh, nothing serious, I assure you—"

Larry had stepped closer in alarm.

"Nothing whatever to worry about," the other went on smoothly. "Only you must understand the young woman has had a bad time. She's pulling through marvellously well—but, you can't get a bang on the head as she's had without it upsetting you!"

"What's the matter, Doctor?"

Larry's throat was dry, his voice a rasp.

What was this man trying to tell him? What was the shock he was preparing him for? *What was wrong with her?*

The surgeon cleared his throat.

"Simply this. Her brain is not—at the moment, understand that—functioning normally. You might find it difficult to understand what she is talking about—"

"You mean—?"

The other man calmed him with a gesture.

"I mean there's absolutely no cause for alarm—none whatever. But the patient is suffering from the effects of the smash. Her reactions are a little—unusual. I have met many similar cases. As a matter of fact, you may be able to throw a little light on her reactions."

"Anything I can do to help—"

The surgeon took off his spectacles and held them up to the light. He produced a handkerchief and began to polish them with absent-minded thoroughness.

"Quite, quite. Well, can you recall any other shock which Miss Linden has suffered in the past? Within the last year or so? Not such a severe shock, perhaps. But anything which you feel might have upset her mental equilibrium?"

As Larry pondered, the other surveyed him expectantly, polishing his glasses the while.

"Anything which may have knocked her out," he suggested. "An unexpected tragedy. Something which might have caused her to faint, collapse—umph?"

Larry started.

"There was something—some months ago."

"Yes?"

"She heard—very suddenly and in a very startling way—of the suicide of someone."

Larry told him of his first real meeting with Mitsi, at Le Bourget, when he caught her in his arms as she fainted dead away on learning of Henri Tallier's tragic end.

The surgeon listened intently. At the end he replaced his spectacles on his nose with a gesture of satisfaction.

"I see—I see!" he exclaimed.

He took Larry by the arm, and led him towards the little private ward in which Mitsi lay.

"Well, all you've got to do is this: just humour her; don't be disturbed by what she says. Talk to her as if she was perfectly normal. *Don't* try and explain anything to her—Understand?"

Larry nodded.

"That's the idea. Just let her babble on as she likes, and everything will be all right."

He gave Larry a reassuring pat on the shoulder. They reached a door at which the surgeon stopped, and knocked gently. A nurse opened it, and smiled at them.

"Ten minutes you can have, and that's all—this time," she said.

She came out of the room. Larry stood hesitantly for a moment.

His heart was thudding painfully. His throat was tight. He was trembling a little. The surgeon gave him a little push.

"Go on."

Larry licked his lips, gave the nurse a faint smile, and entered the ward. The door closed behind him.

He moved over to where a little white figure lay propped up among the pillows.

It seemed impossible that it could be her.

Her head was still bandaged. Little was to be seen of the blonde glory of her hair. Most of it had been cut away to enable the operation to be performed.

Her face, pale and thin beneath the bandages, looked strangely boyish and childish. Larry stared at her. He realized suddenly what it was about her that gave him such a profound sense of shock.

She looked like the Mitsi he had first known!

The hiding of her blonde hair, and its part removal, accounted largely for this, he saw. But it was her pathetic little face, the wondering, almost frightened expression in her eyes which recalled her appearance, as it had once been.

A great rush of feeling swept through him. He longed to hold her tight in his arms. Comfort her and protect her.

She lifted a thin hand from the counterpane.

"Larry."

Her voice was a low whisper. Filled with that quaint huskiness that had been so alluring—but which now seemed to hold deep echoes of the pain she had suffered.

He crossed to her bedside quickly and pulled a chair close. He sat down without speaking. He held the wan hand in his.

The room was bright and sunny. There were flowers in profusion. Lovely, expensive-looking blooms which he knew had come from Julia, Sadie, Louise and others of her friends.

She followed his gaze.

"Are they not beautiful?" she smiled.

"Mitsi—my dear. I'm so glad you're better."

Her eyes were wide, still shadowed with pain. She looked at him with that childish trust which made his heart melt. She gripped his hand tightly.

She said:

"It was strange of me to faint like that. I have never done that before."

He stared at her, his brow wrinkled in puzzlement.

What on earth was she saying? Then he remembered his instructions. He replaced his expression of utter bewilderment with a smile of sympathetic understanding.

"Of course."

"Poor M'sieur Tallier," she whispered.

"Tal—?" he began, then stopped. She was talking of something that had happened *many months* ago! What on earth—?

Suddenly, he knew.

That's what the doctor had meant. The car-smash had knocked a chunk clean out of her memory. Through the shock and the concussion she had been carried back in her mind to several months before. *Right back to the moment she had fainted on hearing of Tallier's suicide.*

A deep breath escaped him.

She was talking. In that whisper, her hand still holding tightly on to his.

"I have had such strange dreams. Wonderful dreams, they were. You were in them. And so many other people—men and women. There was one man. He was tall—very good-looking, and dark. I used to sing to him. To other people, too. In a place where there was music and dancing. Everybody was happy there. I was different. I wore wonderful dresses. My hair was a glorious golden colour. The dark man told me I was beautiful."

She gave a little laugh, and looked at him.

"That was so funny, I think! Oh, everything was so strange. I was so gay, so happy. And yet—I was not really happy. I think I was frightened of something. The handsome man I think. Oh, yes—and there was a tall woman, too. Very beautiful. But with a cold heart."

She held his hand more tightly. Smiled at him.

"I was not frightened of *you*. You were kind to me. You helped me."

He held her hand tightly in both of his.

She talked on. Backwards and forwards, her mind wandered. Reliving the past months of excitement in the dazzling world into which he had thrown her. Of which now only echoes of the songs and music came back to her. Only the dim ghost of Bob Raymond reached out to her.

Only a muddled procession of phantoms: Al Young, Julia and Leo, John Foster, Sam Levinsky, Sadie Harris, the frightening wraith of Carol Lewis, and the others walked, danced and laughed and grimaced across her mind.

Against the shimmering backcloth she paraded in her dream array of glamour and beauty. To the music of tin bugles, saxophones and the fanfares of moaning trumpets she had sung.

All this she babbled to him as a child re-telling a dream.

"It is strange I think," she said, "that only you seemed real and steady throughout all this dream. All the others got mixed up. They seemed to become other people. But always you were you—with me, guiding me."

She turned to him, her eyes dark pools of wonderment.

"And yet I hardly know you," she murmured, smiling gently. "You spoke to me in the air-liner."

She laughed softly at a sudden recollection.

"You told me—do you remember?—you told me I was quite safe. 'As safe as houses,' you said."

She smiled again.

Then added with pathetic seriousness which clutched at his heart:

"You were kind to me, when I felt so frightened and ill in that awful aeroplane—just as you were kind to me in my dream."

He said little. Just listened to her as she talked.

"I like your name," she said to him shyly. "I called you 'Larry' often in my dream. Can I always call you that?"

The anxiety in her face brought a lump to his throat.

"If you want to," he assured her. She smiled with the happy contentment of a child who has been promised something for which it has always longed.

"What will happen to me now?" she asked. "There is only you that I know—now that Henri Tallier is dead…"

"You mustn't worry about anything—ever again. I—I'll take care of you—"

"Like you did in my dream?"

"Like I did in your dream."

"Look at me, Larry," she said. He turned and gave her a feeble attempt at a smile.

She stared into his face searchingly.

"You *want* to take care of me?"

Again that pathetically anxious note.

How he longed to tell her he would never leave her, now. That so long as she wanted him he would watch over her.

He said:

"I will take care of you always, if *you* want me."

"Always," she whispered. "Always."

Such tenderness was in her smile as he had never hoped to see.

"Some of my dream—the best part—is coming true."

The nurse entered quietly.

"Time's up," she said. "You must go to sleep, Miss Linden." She spoke to him.

"Afraid you must say *au revoir*—Too much excitement's bad for folk with banged heads!"

The nurse smiled cheerfully at Mitsi.

"I'm going."

Mitsi had relaxed among her pillows. Now she lifted her head. She had not let go his hand, though he stood up. Now she clutched him tightly.

"It is not *au revoir*," she whispered, "but *j'attendrai.*"

He nodded.

"*J'attendrai,*" she repeated, smiling. Then relaxed again, closed her eyes. She was smiling gently to herself.

She began to sing to herself so softly he could only just catch the words.

> *"Le jour et la nuit,*
> *J'attendrai toujours."*

Her voice died away.

He bent down to the thin, pale hand in his and kissed it. Then placed it carefully and tenderly inside the bedclothes.

She lay quietly, the sweet, gentle smile on her lips.

"J'attendrai," he said to himself.

The nurse was looking at him. He smiled at her a crooked sort of smile, gulped and walked to the door. She accompanied him.

"She's talked about you so much," she said.

He nodded. He could say nothing.

They stood outside and she closed the door upon Mitsi, asleep now.

The nurse watched him as he walked slowly along the white corridor to the glass doors which led to the hall, and the sunshine was streaming through the windows.

www.ingramcontent.com/pod-product-compliance
Lightning Source LLC
Chambersburg PA
CBHW031427250626
47155CB00004B/1653